A BATTLE WORTH FIGHTING

By Sarah Hanks

Praise for
A Battle Worth Fighting

Generations apart, two women follow unique paths to win back their husbands in this expertly-woven tale by award-winning author Sarah Hanks. I was in awe of the author's storytelling ability, dynamic history, and sterling prose as I turned pages, invested in the journeys of Bernie and Sahara. The lessons each woman learned along the way were poignant and perfectly executed, resulting in a satisfying and edifying read.

Heather Wood,
author of *Until We All Find Home*

Hanks weaves together the stories of these two godly women to form a beautiful tapestry of faith, hope, and love. I was especially drawn to the determination of the female soldier determined to find her husband somewhere in the midst of the American Civil War."

Rachel Kovaciny,
author of the Once Upon a Western series

Sarah Hanks weaves a tale of two lives, fashioned together in an intricate balance of human frailty and emotions placing the reader in the midst of a constant flurry of raw sentiment and heartache. Both women's stories begin with the recognition of their deep love for the men God has placed in their lives and continues with their passionate pursuit to keep the relationships intact. Hanks expertly pulls the reader from one time era to another as she captures the emotions and heart of her audience.

Jen Cassidy,
author of *Waiting at the Finish*

In *A Battle Worth Fighting*, Sarah Hanks has presented lovers of historical fiction a dual timeline adventure that I didn't want to put down until I had read it all the way through. This book is full of emotion, nail-biting drama, and deep theological and moral questions. Hanks doesn't shy away from tough issues yet doesn't drown the reader in them either. This story of two women fighting for their future as they also fight for their husbands is relevant and poignant in any timeline. No matter the genre you regularly read in, this is a book that will capture your attention and keep you reading until you learn the ending to each character's story.

Lisa R. Howeler,
author of *The Farmer's Daughter*

A gripping and compelling story of two women, separated by time, who find themselves not only struggling to save their marriages, but in a battle to discover what true love is.

Jamie Ogle,
Minnesota N.I.C.E Writing Excellence Award Winner 2020 & 2021, Genesis Award Winner 2021, First Impressions Award Winner 2020 & 2021

Sahara and Jaxon captured my heart from the beginning. They love each other, but the divide between the perfectionist Sahara who never steps out of her comfort-zone, and the free-spirited, adventuresome Jaxon is deeper than the Grand Canyon. Hanks does an excellent job of taking the reader into Sahara's battle to save her marriage. Theirs is a love worth fighting for, and I kept turning the pages eager to see the final victory, of a withered love rekindled into a flame that melts all walls and melds two hearts into one.

In *A Battle Worth Fighting*, Hanks shows us that when you love someone, you fight for them.

Sherry Shindelar,
First Impressions Winner 2020, Genesis Semi-Finalist 2021, Maggie Finalist 2021, Crown Finalist 2022

Sarah Hanks is a master of dual time line novels. Drawing the reader into two journeys that inform each other and build a unified emotional narrative. A Battle Worth Fighting explores the challenging lengths a wife will go through to the save her marriage, while discovering why she's worth the fight.

Kristine Delano,
Genesis Finalist 2022

Being determined and unwavering in the fight for one's marriage doesn't always look the same for everyone, but the proof of a battle will surely be evident. With her compelling, side by side style of modern and historical storylines, Sarah Hanks beautifully captures the grit and determination it takes to never give up on love and marriage.

Abraham and Sara Washington,
marriage ministry leaders, Gateway Family Church

This novel brilliantly uses fictional characters to depict the powerful transformation that happens in real people's lives every day when they receive Jesus' love in order to love. Dance Again Ministries has seen countless relationships brought back to life, just like the ones in these stories, as individuals receive God's love on a daily basis. This story will resonate with anyone who has ever made a mess trying to love in their own strength, and introduce the power of learning to receive.

Brittany Roach,
Dance Again Ministries Leadership Team

Sarah Hanks beautifully intertwines two love stories to eloquently bridge the gap of time. Her attention to the details will immerse you into the lives of Sahara and Bernie and cause you to be emotionally connected to them. As you embark on this amazing journey with them, you will feel the healing power of choosing Jesus as your Source of truth and how God's agape love can transform lives.

Tricia Horton,
Dance Again Ministries Leadership Team

LOVERS, FORGET YOUR LOVE,

AND LIST TO THE LOVE OF THESE.

SHE A WINDOW FLOWER,

AND HE A WINTER BREEZE.

WHEN THE FROSTY WINDOW VEIL

WAS MELTED DOWN AT NOON,

AND THE CAGÈD YELLOW BIRD

HUNG OVER HER IN TUNE,

HE MARKED HER THROUGH THE PANE

HE COULD NOT HELP BUT MARK,

AND ONLY PASSED HER BY,

TO COME AGAIN AT DARK.

HE WAS A WINTER WIND,

CONCERNED WITH ICE AND SNOW.

DEAD WEEDS AND UNMATED BIRDS,

AND LITTLE OF LOVE COULD KNOW.

BUT HE SIGHED UPON THE SILL,

HE GAVE THE SASH A SHAKE,

AS WITNESS ALL WITHIN

WHO LAY THAT NIGHT AWAKE.

PERCHANCE HE HALF PREVAILED

TO WIN HER FOR THE FLIGHT

FROM THE FIRELIT LOOKING-GLASS

AND WARM STOVE-WINDOW LIGHT.

BUT THE FLOWER LEANED ASIDE

AND THOUGHT OF NAUGHT TO SAY,

AND MORNING FOUND THE BREEZE

A HUNDRED MILES AWAY.

"WIND AND WINDOW FLOWER" BY ROBERT FROST

Chapter 1

Sahara
Present Day
Georgetown, South Carolina

Enough stalling. She needed to call him. There was nothing left to clean, rearrange, or organize. Well, she could alphabetize her old recipe cards. Currently, she'd organized them by date added, but it would make more sense to— No. No more procrastination.

Sahara took several deep breaths before she picked up the phone to dial Jaxon's number. He was in Utah this time. A world away. But soon he'd finish that job and head home. To her. Finally. He'd hardly even gotten to enjoy their new house. She'd wanted to buy a home downtown ever since she was a little girl, but they were so expensive. He'd given her dream to her … and then disappeared. Whatever. He'd be back soon.

She picked up the phone. She could do this. Just a phone call to her husband. No big deal. The air filter hummed quietly in the background, the only sound other than an occasional passing car. How different would it be if they'd had children? Much noisier, for sure. And messier. Of course, they still could add children to their family. Jaxon only needed to find consistent employment, then he'd fulfill his end of the bargain. Good money was only adequate security if you could count on it to come in year-round. Not when you hopped around from job to job and place to place, taking months off when the weather didn't cooperate. Surely, he could find something more consistent in the construction field. Or as an architect. Or wait, what did he call himself? An artist?

Once he got his act together, they could have children. Maybe then he'd want to stick closer to home.

Sahara plopped onto the couch and pushed two on speed dial. She forced the edges of her mouth to turn up. If you made yourself smile, you sounded friendlier. She'd read about that somewhere. Or had she heard it on a podcast? No matter. She tried it.

"Hey." Oh, good. He picked up.

"Hey, Jax." Nope. Still awkward. "So." She ran her toes through the plush carpet. "You coming home next week?"

A sigh. As if she'd pestered him with the question. "No."

"No?" Her spine straightened.

"This other rich guy saw my work on the Swanson Estate and was impressed. He wants me to build him a mountain getaway. It's good money."

Her stomach dropped like lead. "You're staying in Utah."

"Yes." The sound of saws filtered in behind his words.

"For how long?"

"However long it takes."

She rubbed her temples. "Is it just me, or are you looking for a reason not to come home?"

"Give me a break."

"No, really. Tell me. Are you avoiding me?"

A beat of silence. "It doesn't seem like there's much to come back for."

Pain sliced her heart like a paring knife, cutting off the outer layers. If she kept pushing, would he carve up more of it? "You're kidding me right now." What about her? Since when was she not enough for him?

Silence. And … more silence. So help her, she would not be the first to—

"Well, I hope you're happy there." The words slipped out from between her tight jaw before she hung up the phone.

Her breath came out in fiery bursts. Chocolate. She needed chocolate. No. She needed to throw something. Storming to her closet, she held tears at bay.

"If you're not going to live here, get your stupid stuff out of my closet!" She hurled hangers laden with khakis and dress slacks into a pile outside the closet door. Shirts. Suit jackets. That ridiculous shabby brown hoodie she told him to get rid of a decade ago. Good. Now she had her nicely organized space back. Nothing cluttering it up.

Her gaze fell on worn work boots. There. A perfect outlet. With a yowl that rivaled the main character in *Braveheart*, she hurled them out the closet door, then snatched another pair. This time, she stumbled with the throw and caught herself on the doorframe, clenching it with white knuckles.

Tears stung her eyelids as she studied the limp, lifeless piles in front of her.

"He doesn't want me." She doubled over and clutched her stomach. "Why doesn't he want me?"

Falling to her knees, she grabbed the brown sweatshirt and slid it over her head. All she had were shadows of a love that had once been wonderful.

~

Jaxon shoved his cell in his back pocket. Well, that had gone great. If a person could shoot daggers through the phone, he'd be dead. He'd meant to break the news for two weeks now, but there was no good way to say it. She'd never understand.

"Hey, Boss Man," Miguel called out, startling him out of his mental fog. "Delivery truck's here. He needs you to sign off."

"Sure thing." He strode to where a man with a clipboard leaned against his truck, fresh paint waiting. *Boss Man.* Sure sounded nice. After years—decades really—of others passing him over and counting him out, people finally treated him with respect. And after putting in his time, he finally got to do what he loved. Not just build houses but build dreams. Create functional pieces of art that would stand the test of time. Poetry. He created poetry. Not with words—he'd never been great at that—but with wood and mortar and stone. With gabled ceilings, arched doorways, and slanted walls. His senses tingled with purpose. He was doing what he'd always dreamed of.

Too bad he couldn't do it with the woman he'd dreamed of sharing his life with.

He signed for the delivery, then helped his men unload.

Sahara. The thought of her name made his heart ache. The sound of her voice a reminder of his biggest failure of all. Because after over a decade of trying, he had to admit defeat. He'd failed to win her heart.

How foolish and naive he'd been as a young groom, thinking he could convince her of his love, his sincerity. What had he believed? That if he kissed her with enough passion, she'd eventually melt? That if he showed her his affection through enough acts of kindness, the thick walls she'd erected around her heart would magically tumble down? What a fool.

Instead, she'd spent twelve years holding him at arm's length, never truly letting him in. At times, he thought she'd been close to opening the door of her heart, but then she'd slam it in his face. And the criticism. As if he hadn't gotten enough of that growing up, his wife treated him like a child, berating him for every little thing she perceived he did wrong. Every. Little. Thing. Her constant judgment basically shoved him out the door and halfway across the country.

His throat tightened. He took a swig of Gatorade, but it did little to alleviate the tension. He'd tried so hard for so long. He loved that woman with every fiber of his being. Loved her from the moment she first tore into those sugar packets. He lifted a sad smile. If only his love was enough. But what good was his love when she continually pushed it away? Year after year after year. Heaven help him, he was tired of offering the same dish only to have her refuse to take one bite. He was done failing.

A black BMW pulled onto the property. Trescott? Why was the owner here? He ran a hand through his hair, threw on a smile, and walked out to meet the gentleman in his three-piece suit despite the summer heat.

"Mr. Trescott, to what do I owe the pleasure?" Jaxon extended his, hopefully not too sweaty, hand.

"Please, call me Mike. Just peeking in on the progress."

Jaxon breathed a sigh of relief. If that was all the man came for, no need to worry. They were ahead of schedule. "What do you think?" He waved a hand in the direction of the house.

"Excellent work, Frost. It's everything I imagined."

The man continued to mistake Jaxon's company's name for his last name. Jaxon didn't correct him. It would be flattering to have the same last name as his favorite poet.

"Glad to hear it, sir."

"I've recommended your company to several of my coworkers and a few members of my country club."

Jaxon grinned. What would that mean for business? "How kind of you."

"It's not kind, son. It's deserved. You've got a knack for this." Trescott slid his hands into his pockets and beamed at his new home.

"I appreciate it."

After a few minutes of updates and chitchat, Trescott drove off the property. Jaxon could almost float back to where the crew nailed shingles on the roof. This house was almost under roof. Time for subcontractors to take over and for him to slip into supervisor mode. And nearly time to start a brand-new project—a millionaire's breathtaking mountain getaway. Was he living the life or what?

But an unsettled feeling oozed over his elation. This success, as thrilling as it was, equated to a silver medal, a second-place trophy. He'd settle for it and be happy because he could never have a first-place one. He could never win Sahara's golden heart.

~

Pins and needles jabbed at Sahara's legs as she awoke on her bedroom floor. She swiped at her eyes. She'd fallen asleep in Jaxon's hoodie huddled among strewn clothing. Pathetic. She closed her eyes and grasped at fragments of a dream. Slowly, vague colors materialized into mental images. Hot air balloons everywhere, just like on the night Jaxon proposed. Only in her dream, unlike in reality, they were floating in one, high above the crowds and chaos. He'd kissed her in the dream. She touched her lips, trying to hold on to the fragment of tenderness.

Maybe if she'd jumped with both feet into his spontaneity that day, things would be different now. Was that where she went wrong? Right from the beginning? She could still picture him sliding that flyer across the booth to her.

"I just found out there's a hot-air balloon race tonight on the beach. I was thinking maybe you'd go with me."

She'd said sure, then focused on adding three sugar packets to her unsweetened tea, as always. Just the right ratio. The memory of the look on his face as he watched her still made her breath hitch. Then he'd fashioned those empty packets into a makeshift paper ring as only a construction worker could. And then he'd slipped it on and changed her life forever.

"Maybe when we go watch the balloons, we could get married and sail away in a balloon into the sunset?"

What if she'd said yes? Not just to marrying him in a respectable amount of time in a respectable way, but to all of it? Would she be here now with carpet marks on her cheek and a stiff neck pining for the man thousands of miles away? The man who wooed her with poetry and put his foot down with her boundaryless mother when Sahara—for the life of her—couldn't say no. Oh heavens, she loved that man and hated him and wanted to throw a boot at his head and kiss him until they both couldn't breathe.

She picked up her phone from the floor.

Her notifications indicated another text from her mother. A groan crawled up her throat. She couldn't deal with this right now. Not without Jaxon.

Ignoring the text, her thumb hovered over Jax's number. If she could say something to make things better, she would. But it was too late for that. She dropped the phone, pulled the hoodie off, and let it crumple to the floor.

~

Later that day Sahara was startled as her friend Myra burst through the front door, springy black hair bouncing.

"Oh no," Myra said. "It's that bad?"

Sahara paused with her hand inside the bag of Doritos. The crunching sound was a dead giveaway of her misery. "Come on in."

Myra threw her designer handbag onto the love seat as if it were a clearance item from a bargain bin and planted her hands on her hips. "You look like a Muppet."

"Huh?"

She made an exaggerated gesture around her umber-brown face. "You're orange."

"Oh." Sahara swiped at her mouth with her sleeves, leaving orange streaks all over her pajama shirt. Great. As if she needed another reminder that she was a mess.

Myra slid onto the couch beside her and snatched the bag of Doritos from her lap. Sahara's fingers grasped a lonely chip. She shoved it into her mouth and chomped as Myra rolled the top of the bag down and set it aside on the end table. "Enough of that."

Sahara stuck out her lip.

Myra cast a glance at the TV where the home shopping channel played at low volume. "What have you been doing with yourself?"

Sahara's eyes threatened to well up, but she swallowed the burning in her throat and pushed the tide of emotion back. "Looking at pictures."

Myra scanned the area, clearly devoid of any photo albums.

"On my phone." She pulled her phone from her lap. "I was going to watch TV but got distracted."

"Don't know how that's possible with such riveting viewing material."

Sahara almost smiled.

"Pictures of what?"

"Shoes."

"Shoes? Jaxon's shoes?" Myra's eyebrows shot up.

She bit her lip.

"Please tell me you haven't resorted to that again."

She shrugged.

"You're a psychopath."

"It's all I have of him now." How could she explain? "Look." She hit the button and brought up her gallery. Holding out her phone, she swiped right. "His work boots were right there a foot from the front mat." She pointed to the spot where they'd been. A tear leaked out. She brushed it away with the back of her hand and swiped again. "His tennis shoes right in front of the bathroom door. How could you not trip over those?" A laugh and a sob tussled together in an escape from her mouth. She pressed a fist to her lips. Took a shuddering breath. Swiped again. "A sandal in the middle of the living room floor. Just one. I have the picture of the other one somewhere …" She searched through half a dozen pictures until she found it. "There. In the kitchen. How does that happen?" Another tear. Shoot. A stream of them. What was wrong with her? Crying over pictures of shoes.

Myra slid her arm around Sahara's shoulder. "You should get these printed."

Sahara's breath caught. Printed? She grabbed Myra's hand. "You're a genius."

"I was kidding."

"No. Let's go find frames."

"Sahara, calm down. It was a joke."

"No." She jumped up and headed toward her bedroom. "Let's go right now. I'll change."

Myra called to her as she ducked inside the bedroom door. "Girl, you better be glad I love you."

"I am."

Myra had always loved her, despite her quirks. Sahara squirmed out of her pajamas and kicked the pile of Jaxon's clothes aside. His stuff was always in the way. It was why she'd started snapping those pictures to begin with. She was forever tripping over his shoes. And his clothes, but mostly his shoes. The man could not figure out how to put them on the strategically placed shoe racks. How hard was that? Apparently, nearly impossible for her husband, no matter how many different options she gave him or how much help she provided. She'd even special-ordered a mat that read, "Shoes Go Here." Was he blind? Or out to drive her crazy?

So, after tripping over his shoes for the umpteenth time, she'd taken a picture of them. The next time, she took another. And so on.

Myra thought it ridiculous. She looked at Sahara as if she'd grown horns. Of course. Yeah. She was the bad guy here for trying to instill a little order in life.

The way Myra had jutted out her hip and crossed her arms was etched in her memory. "You're building a case against him? Petty."

"No." Sahara had crossed her arms too, ready to square off. "I've got to prove to myself and to him—but mostly myself—that I'm not crazy. He'll say, 'I threw my clothes in the hamper' or 'I didn't leave my shoes in the middle of the walkway.'" She held her phone up. Self-righteous indignation brewed hot in her chest. "Evidence. I need evidence, or I'll go insane."

"As if you aren't already."

"Oh stop."

"How many pictures?"

Sahara shrugged as if she didn't know.

Myra's eyes bored into her. "How many?"

"One hundred and twelve."

"Petty."

"You don't understand."

"You're right. I don't. Because if I had a man who loved me as much as Jaxon loves you, I wouldn't be so darn concerned with where he put his shoes. It's as if you're looking for a reason to …"

"To what?"

"Forget it."

But Sahara hadn't forgotten. Even though Myra and she had been besties since middle school, it seemed her friend always sided with Jaxon. As if he needed another ally. Didn't everyone take his side? He was the sweet one, and she was the neurotic, demanding wife. Well, someone needed to maintain order. They couldn't all flitter around through life doing whatever fit their fancy for however long they wished before moving on to something more appealing. There had to be structure. Someone had to pay the bills. Someone had to make the budget and ensure they stuck to it. Someone had to be responsible. How dare he shove her back into the role she'd played her entire childhood while he floated through life obliviously?

Where was his boot again? There, on top of that stupid hoodie. She picked it up and hurled it toward the wedding picture that hung above their dresser. She missed, and it smacked against the wall and landed with a thud. Of course she'd missed the mark. No, he did. Maybe they both did. Nope. She could not be wrong in this.

"Is everything okay in there?" Myra's voice called.

"Fine." Sahara blew a wisp of hair from her face and snatched her jeans from the dresser.

Everything would be fine. She'd find a way to fix this, fix all of it. She could do that. She'd always been able to do that. Because she did not give up. And if her free-flowing poet boy thought he could float away from this marriage, he'd better think again.

A few hours later they returned with thirty eight-by-twelves of her favorite shoe pictures and the same number of black and gilded frames. Thirty pictures. Where was she going to put thirty pictures? But she'd had such a hard time narrowing it down that far. Oh well. She'd been meaning to decorate the place anyway.

Myra set a handful of bags on the dining room table and then said, "It's been fun, but I've got to go."

"Thank you." Sahara set down her own bags and embraced her friend.

"Of course. Whatever you need. Anytime."

Sahara pulled away and studied her wall. She could fit at least five pictures there, maybe six.

"Oh, before I forget." Myra put a hand on her shoulder.

Sahara turned. Myra handed her an eight-by-eleven photo envelope.

"While you were getting ready, I grabbed the picture of your great-grandmother Bernie from your photo album. At the photo printer, I asked them to enlarge it."

Sahara's breath hitched as she slid the picture out of the envelope. The woman who stared back at her was a relative born in 1840. Her great-great-great-great-grandmother Bernice. Steely eyes. Stern expression. Wearing a Confederate uniform.

"I remember you telling me about her, about how she signed up to fight in the Civil War because she couldn't stand to be away from her husband. She fought for her marriage. Literally fought." Myra's expression prodded. "I thought you could use the inspiration."

Sahara's mouth parted. "You did this for me." Her beautiful, Black friend willingly enlarged a picture of a Confederate soldier. Her throat tightened.

"There's not much I wouldn't do for you."

"But—"

"Hang it up, will you? I got a frame for it."

Sahara nodded, unable to say more. She wrapped her arms around Myra's neck again.

"Love you." Myra rubbed her back, solid and sure.

"Love you, too," Sahara eked out.

As the front door clicked closed, Sahara stood and stared at Bernie's picture. When morning came, only one picture hung on the wall. That of a soldier.

Chapter 2

Bernie
April 12, 1861
Shulerville, South Carolina

Something was wrong. Bernice Reisenfeld heard it in the panicked bleating of her sheep, in the incessant padding of their hooves, in the rustle of the grass. A peek out the window didn't tell her what it was, so she dried damp hands on a towel and stepped onto their farmhouse porch. The door creaked closed behind her. She shaded her eyes against the glaring South Carolinian sun and studied the south pasture. There. A flash of gray among the white dotting the slight hill. A coyote?

The sheep cowered, herding together as the prairie wolf made a slow circle around them. Bernie's pulse rocketed in her throat. No, siree. That rascal would not make a lunch of her babies. She scanned the horizon for Hermann. That's right. He said he'd be in the north pasture with the cows. Too far. Looked like it was up to her.

Spinning on her heels, she barged into the parlor and headed straight for the rifle mounted above the mantle. With no time to waste, she loaded it, slung it over her shoulder, lifted her skirt, and ran. How close did she need to get? Hermann had taught her to shoot using tin cans lined up on the fence post. She'd never had a moving target before, and never did a steady hand and clean shot matter like it did right now.

The coyote had one sheep cornered, separated from the fold. It paced back and forth, eyeing its prey. Was that Cecil? Oh no. Not Cecil, the sweet, scrawny scrap of a thing they weren't sure would make it through his first night. Bernie had slept in the barn next to his little copper-faced, red-legged self for near his first full week, giving him attaboy speeches and bottles of milk 'til he grew strong enough to nurse. After all her boy had been through, there was no way she'd let some haughty coyote take him down now.

This had to be close enough. That coyote looked ready to lunge. She couldn't waste another minute. Steadying herself, she slung the rifle off her shoulder, cocked it, and aimed at the splotch of gray. She took a deep breath, held it, and fired. The blast caused her teeth to chatter and sent her rocking a half step back. Sheep bleated and ran this way and that in confusion, but there in the field, the gray form swayed then fell. She'd gotten him! Her breath rushed out in blessed relief. After slinging the gun behind her again, she spanned the distance between her and her babies.

They flocked to her, their beige heads and coal noses upturned in question as if asking if they were safe now, if all was well.

"It's all right, Lillybell. You're fine. You'll be fine now." She scratched the ewe behind the ears and underneath her chin before moving on to Francis. "You're okay, Frannie." One by one, she comforted her sheep until Cecil nudged her skirt. She bent down and grabbed the wooly sides of his face. "You were so brave." A raise of his head and flick of the tongue seemed almost like a thank you. "You're welcome, Cecil."

Now, if her heartbeat would only slow. The danger had passed. She cast another glance at the lifeless coyote on the ground. It wasn't moving. She'd gotten it good. It wouldn't come back to harm them anymore. See? No sense in her heart hammering in her ears any longer. She straightened, smoothed her skirt, and squared her shoulders.

Time to get back to her task of cleaning dishes, then washing and mending clothes. But she'd only taken a few steps toward the house when she spotted Hermann running from the north field straight to the house, arms pumping. Her stomach sank. What now? Hadn't they had enough excitement for one day? Or perhaps he'd only heard the gunshot and had come to check on her.

"Bernie!" he shouted.

She waved a hand overhead. "Over here."

His gaze swiveled in her direction. He changed course and barreled toward her. He stopped a few feet away and bent over, planting his hands on his knees as he heaved in deep breaths. Clearly he could see she was fine. Why was he rattled?

"Whatever is going on?" How rare to see her docile husband in such a state. Unease twisted her insides.

"Fort Sumter."

Her gut clenched. "This is it, then? We're at war?" She'd heard that Davis ordered Beauregard to take Sumter. Still, she'd held out hope the two sides could strike a truce, that something could be done to avoid the bloody, bitter path of war.

Hermann's nods came vigorous as he straightened. "We struck early this morning."

She bit the inside of her cheek. *We.* As if she'd had a say in seceding from the Union, in declaring war on fellow Americans ... in any of this. War was about to rip the land she loved in two, and she wanted no part in it.

Her husband removed his hat and ran a hand through his short hair. Uncertainty was written on his face.

She kept her voice even. Calm. "What are you going to do?"

He fiddled with the hat in his hands. His gaze fell to his shifting feet. "I don't know. The men in town will expect me to enlist."

She crossed her arms over her chest. "That doesn't mean you must."

"No."

Mary Sue stepped between them and nudged Bernie's hand with the top of her nose. She petted the sheep without taking her eyes off Hermann's vacillating expression. He was clearly torn. How could she make it obvious the best course of action was to stay out of the conflict between the states?

His countenance brightened. "Maybe it'll blow over. We'll win Sumter and the North will let us be."

She flashed an ingenuine smile. "Maybe." Sweet, naive man. Her quiet husband always believed the best, against all odds.

"Yes." He settled his hat back on top of his head and straightened his suspenders. "That's it. The North will see what we're made of and let us be. Let us govern ourselves. We'll live peaceably side by side. No need for war."

She could hold her smile no longer but managed to push out words of agreement, "No need."

With a satisfied nod, he turned and headed back to the north pasture, back to the cattle he loved. What a tender heart her husband had, talking to his animals as she did to hers. How he hated to see any living thing suffer. What would cold-blooded war do to a man like that? Would it wring him out and leave him a shell of the idealistic, compassionate man she'd grown to love? He'd taught her to shoot at cans because he couldn't bear to even shoot a rabbit. How could he stop the lifeblood of a man?

No. She couldn't let that happen. Couldn't let this wretched conflict rip his sensitive soul apart. Surely, her wit and charisma could persuade him to stay settled on their farm, far away from bullets and cannon blasts, blood and gore.

Because if he went to war, the thing most in danger was her very heart.

Chapter 3

Sahara
Present Day
Outside of Jamestown, South Carolina

Sahara's Honda Civic crested the hill and hit the 200,000-mile mark. She patted the dashboard. "Good job, old buddy."

At least some things in her life were reliable. Like the silver Honda Jaxon had nicknamed *Dreamboat* and the sheep farm located around the next bend. If only she could count on her husband like she did these constants. Then again, that was why she was here.

She'd spent the past week staring at Great-grandma Bernie's picture. She'd taken the smaller snapshot to work and tucked it in front of a framed photo of Jax and her on their fifth anniversary. Whether she was on the job or at home, her gaze gravitated toward that soldier woman's eyes. So full of resolve.

Aunt Trish always said stubbornness ran in the family. Perhaps she'd have wise words to help Sahara figure out how to direct her own. What good was being thick-skinned and determined when her husband was across the country? How could she convince him to return? Make him see she was worth coming back to?

She slowed as she hung a left onto the dirt road. The sign that boasted Summer Hill Sheep Farm needed sanding and a fresh coat of paint. She could tell Trish, but her aunt wouldn't listen. She never did.

Sahara pulled up to the gate and pushed the button on the post. The gate creaked open, and she inched the car forward until she cleared the sloth of a monstrosity. Then she sped up to fifteen miles an hour, passed the fields to her right, and winded around the pond to her left. Shetland sheep ambled through the grass, taking a few steps here and there before they stopped to munch more. She slowed and stopped as a few crossed the path in front of her. Was that Paiton? Sahara hadn't been out to the farm since shearing, and they looked so different without their coats. The oatmeal-colored sheep stilled and stared back at her, bleating. Yeah. It was Paiton, for sure. She rolled down her window.

"Nice to see you again too, Pait."

The sheep gave a flick of her head and then continued along. When the other two followed, Sahara applied light pressure to the gas. She kept the window rolled down and breathed in the fresh farm scent that made her stomach swirl with an emotion she couldn't quite pin down. Something in between homesickness and coming home. In between longing for what was just out of her grasp and finding contentment. It smelled like hay and manure, fresh air and sunshine. And a home that wasn't home.

Gravel crunched under her tires as she rounded the last bend and pulled up in front of the pale yellow two-story farmhouse. Trish appeared on the porch before Sahara had even switched off the ignition. She'd pulled her shoulder-length copper-red hair back with a dark gray woolen headband. Though there was no way to tell which sheep it was from since their wool looked completely different once it was off and spun, it was fun to guess.

As she exited her car, she pointed to her aunt's head. "Brenna?"

"Close. Brayley."

Shoot. That was close. Brenna and Brayley were twins. Even Trish couldn't tell them apart until she got her hands on them at shearing time. Then their personalities shined through. Brayley had a bit of an attitude.

Her aunt wrapped her in a hug. "Oh, Dawn. It's been too long."

Should she remind the woman she went by Sahara now? She'd given up going by her middle name twelve years ago when Jaxon looked deep into her eyes and said he thought her first name was exotic. Never mind her mother named her after a desert. Never mind Sahara means Dawn, so she was named *Dawn Dawn*. Talk about redundant. Never mind she'd hated her first name all her life until that point. When Jaxon's mouth dripped her name like poetry, she acquiesced. She went from being Dawn to being Sahara in an instant. The only ones who didn't follow Jaxon's lead were family. But why bother correcting them? Maybe she needed a minute where Jaxon's expectations didn't define her.

"Where's Uncle Jeb?"

"With the cows. We can go out and see him in a bit. You want to say hi to your babies?"

Sahara laughed. "They're not babies anymore."

"That's the truth. Ten of them will turn fourteen this year. *Ten.*"

A wistful smile danced across Sahara's lips. "I remember that year. When they were born." Little six-pound lambs birthed one after another, all spindly legs. The twins were two pounds. Proud mama ewes nudged them forth into the new day. Everything seemed full of possibility back then. "How are they now? Everyone healthy?"

"Mostly. The vet was out here yesterday to check in on Leslie."

Sahara grimaced. "Not Leslie."

"She's old. Sixteen. Not much we can do. I hope she'll go on her own terms, and we won't have to put her down."

A stinging sensation bombarded the back of her eyes. How stupid. No use crying over an old sheep. It was part of life. Part of the business. She swallowed the rising emotion. "Let me see my babies."

Trish whistled and ears perked up from all directions. Then small hooves padded toward them. Sheep in a variety of colors. Warm gray and light gray, black and brown, oatmeal and cream. Several she recognized. Some she didn't.

"How many do you have now?"

"Forty-one."

A cool-gray sheep nudged her hand. "Is this Nessa?"

Trish nodded.

She rubbed the animal under her chin. She'd missed the soft, soothing feel of wool. Even with hay and grass stuck in her coat, the neck wool was as soft as a cloud. Trish preferred the longer rump wool because it worked best for spinning yarn, but to Sahara, nothing could beat the downy soft wool near the neck. And if she could rub the right spot … there. Nessa wagged her tail. How satisfying to know exactly what to do to please someone. If only every relationship were that easy.

"Here." Trish handed her some treats. "Remember—"

"Only one or two at a time. I know. Do you think I'd forget?"

Trish gave a sheepish smile. "I guess not."

Sahara dumped the stash in her pocket and then placed two treats in her open palm and held it out to Nessa, who promptly ate them. The lick of her rough tongue sent a shiver down Sahara's spine. That was a texture she wasn't crazy about, but she'd bear it for her babies. She pulled out another couple and held them out to an oatmeal-colored ram.

"That's Connor. He's new. Bought him last month."

"I wish you still bred them."

Trish scoffed. "Too much work. I've gotten too old for that."

Sahara rolled her eyes. "You have not."

From behind the house, a rooster crowed.

"Heard from your mom lately?" Trish's voice softened as if that could lessen the sting.

"Sure. Got a text just yesterday asking for money." Her words tasted as bitter as they sounded.

Trish nodded, lips pressed tightly together as if mulling over what to say next. Only Sahara didn't need a lecture on loving her family, or her enemies. She did love her mom, despite the woman's neediness. Sahara had practically raised the woman. Her teenage mother was not prepared to parent, so who was the one who made sure Mom got to work on time, packed a lunch for herself, paid the bills, and went grocery shopping? Sahara did. No wonder she had such a hard time setting boundaries now. If Jaxon hadn't stepped in to be her backbone, her mother might have sapped her dry. Sahara studied the aunt who had been there for her when her own mother couldn't. Wouldn't? Those lines blurred with an ache she couldn't define. Her mother had dumped her on this farm more times than she could count. Her unsafe safe place. Crows feet creased the corners of Trish's eyes. Maybe she was getting old.

Her aunt shook her head, as if shrugging off an unpleasant thought. "Enough of that. Tell me what's going on with you. How's your job? How's Jaxon? How's the new house?"

"Work is fine. I've seen a thirty-five percent increase in business this year, which has been great. The house is lovely. You should come out and see it. Built in 1899. Beautiful brass doorknobs. Four fireplaces. Bay windows. Right down the street from my favorite shops."

A sheep flicked its tongue at her, and she offered her last treat.

"And Jaxon?"

Shoot. She wasn't going to let that slide?

"He's fine." She pressed her lips together and avoided Trish's gaze.

"So that's why you're here, huh? Problems with Jaxon?"

Sahara bent to rub another sheep—was it Iyla?—under the chin. "Jaxon is perfectly happy. In Utah. Without me." She bit her lip.

"Oh, Dawn."

She straightened and glanced at her aunt's concerned face. "I need to figure out how to get him to come home to me. I thought …" She toed the gravel. "I thought you might have a bright idea or two."

Sad lines creased Trish's forehead. "Let's go inside."

"Okay."

Sahara petted a few more sheep still gathered around her, then followed her aunt up the stone walkway to the worn porch steps, which could also use a fresh coat of paint. Old things were great, as long as they were also clean, functional, and in good order. This farm needed updating. Last time she mentioned it, however, Trish met her with silence and a hard stare.

"You want iced tea?" Trish called over her shoulder.

"Sure."

Sahara followed her aunt into the house, past the den-turned-workstation, and into the kitchen. Trish poured two glasses of iced tea, scooted over a container of sugar packets, then pulled out a box of Nutri-Grain bars from the pantry and tossed one to Sahara.

"There. Snack on that. Then we can spin while we talk."

The edge of Sahara's mouth curved upward as she tore open three sugars. "Putting me to work again?"

"Why not?"

Trish ripped open her own bar and finished it off in four bites. After tossing the wrapper in the trash, she grabbed her glass and headed back down the hall. "Come on."

Sahara had barely begun to nibble at her own bar. She huffed.

"Bring it with you."

When Sahara reached the den, Trish was already sifting through large brown bags of wool. "Who do you want to spin today? Paiton? Iyla?"

"I'll spin Iyla."

Trish took a heap of fluffy black wool from the bag marked with Iyla's name and set it beside one of the spinning wheels.

"I've been working on Hailey." She nodded to the other wheel, where a spool of heather-gray yarn was already in process.

"She's a beauty." They all were, each distinct and unique with subtle variations in color. She sat, took the soft wool from the bag, and drew a piece out to lay it on the lead. When her feet got pumping on the double treadle and her fingers pulled, loosened, and pulled again, the tension eased from her shoulders. How grounding, this monotonous task. Making something useful from a pile of discarded covering. Spinning purpose into being. She'd forgotten how it relaxed her.

"Now tell me what you did to scare Jaxon away."

And here came the tension, creeping right back in.

"I didn't scare him away." She kept her gaze zeroed in on the spinning wheel in front of her.

"Why do you think he doesn't want to come back?"

Did she attract this kind of harshness in people? Couldn't she have one person in her life, just one, that would say "poor baby" and douse her in sympathy? Sure, she appreciated a straight shooter, but brutality wasn't always a necessity. Her teeth ground together as her feet pedaled faster.

"I don't know. Maybe I nag too much. I'm too particular. Too stubborn. Too exasperating. Too … too me." She choked on a sob. That was it, wasn't it? She was altogether too much. Of course, he'd figure it out eventually. Stupid tears pushed their way out of her eyes as she clenched her jaw, spinning faster and faster, trusting her hands to work by memory. Her eyes couldn't guide her through the watery shimmer.

Trish's hands gripped her shoulders. Her aunt hushed next to her ear. "Stop, child. Settle down."

Sahara's feet stilled on the pedals.

"It's going to be okay." Trish rubbed the tops of Sahara's arms, massaging her biceps. Reminding her of the muscles there. The strength. "You might not be able to convince him to come back to you, but it's okay. You go to him."

"What?" She balked. "He's in Utah."

"So?" Trish came around and knelt in front of her.

"Do you know how far away that is?"

"Do I need to belt out 'Ain't No Mountain High Enough'?"

Sahara's lip trembled. "Please, no." A weak chuckle. She wiped her cheeks with the backs of her hands. Had she really broken down in her aunt's den? How embarrassing.

"Do what you need to do." Trish's eyes held steely determination.

"I've never left the state."

Her aunt raised her eyebrows. Okay, it did seem like a lame excuse.

"The bigger issue is"—Sahara blinked long and hard—"no matter where I go, I can't outrun this. Can't outrun me. I'll be the same person in Utah as I am here. And he'll have the same reasons to avoid me." She shook her head. "I can't change."

Trish scoffed. "I've known you from the day you were born, and I have never known the word *can't* to be in your vocabulary. Whatever you've set your mind to do, you've done. Don't you try to sell me on your inability now, sweetheart. I ain't buyin' it."

Sahara frowned. "You really think I can do this? Fly across the country and win my husband back?"

"It isn't what I think that counts." Trish patted her knee, then rose, went back to the wheel, and continued to spin.

~

After an hour of spinning, Sahara couldn't take it anymore. She had to move more than her feet and hands, had to stop her mind from racing out of control. "I'm going for a walk."

Her abrupt announcement didn't elicit as much as a raised eyebrow from Trish, who kept pedaling away. "Let the chickens out while you're at it. There are saltines on the counter."

"Sure."

She snatched a sleeve of crackers and slid open the back patio door. Humidity smacked her in the face.

"Temperature's climbing," she mumbled.

The hens squawked from behind their wire enclosure. Robby threw his head back and crowed, his ridiculous white feathers splaying in all directions. Silly rooster. Sahara unlatched the gate and opened it wide, and the chickens filed out, clucking their greetings.

"Hi, Betty." Sahara nodded to a golden-brown hen, the biggest of the bunch.

Was it her, or did the chicken cluck hello back? Perhaps she was losing it. Sahara took a couple crackers and crumbled them into small bits, then threw them on the ground. The chickens scrambled for their treat in a mix of black, white, yellow, gold, and brown feathers.

"Look at you all. *You* fight for what you want." She threw out another handful. If they could do it, she could too. Couldn't she? Peck and prod and scramble until she got her prize. Her Jaxon.

A squawk rang out on her left. Robby again. "What's with you? Why aren't you going after the crackers, huh?"

He cocked his head and fluffed his feathers. Because he was a rescue, that was why. No telling what kind of environment he'd been in prior to Trish and Jeb bringing him here, but judging from his behavior, it wasn't pretty. He did things … differently. And needed a little extra TLC.

Was there a reason Jaxon wasn't fighting for their marriage right now? A reason that fit better with his character than her assumption that he didn't care? Because apathy was hard to reconcile with the man she knew him to be— passionate to a fault. He'd practically begged her to marry him. When had his feelings toward her changed? What if his obnoxious behavior was born out of hurt instead of pure jerkiness? If she thought of Jaxon more like Robby the rescued rooster, her frustration faltered like dying embers and her heart welled with compassion for him.

She broke up a cracker for Robby and threw it in his direction. "There you go, buddy. Eat up." She blocked a few other chickens from sneaking in to steal his portion. "Go get your own," she said, scattering more near the crowd.

She finished distributing the crackers, then left through the gate and wandered toward the front of the house. Where were her babies? She needed to dig her fingers through wool again. Normally, at least a few gathered along the side of the house and another few in front, but none were there. She shielded her eyes from the sun and scanned the fields. No sheep in the far-right pasture? Odd. What about—

The sound of hooves pounding and sheep bleating came at her in waves as a flood of sheep crested the hill. What in the world? She stood open-mouthed as they ran past her, eyes radiating panic, their bleats fast and loud. They raced toward the sheering barn, the place Trish always took them when they were sick or needed help. Something was wrong.

Sahara took off in a jog in the direction the animals had come from. When she got closer, her stomach dropped. A coyote. At the edge of the field. Alone with two sheep.

She spun around and raced to the house. Banging the door open, she yelled, "Trish, come! Now!"

Within seconds, Trish was at her side, and they ran back to the field together. Sahara braced her hands on her knees, hunching over but never taking her eyes off the scene before them. One sheep knelt, in all probability hurt. The other sheep paced back and forth at the fence line, as if guarding the property. The coyote stood directly beyond, as if seeking the opportunity to attack again.

"Who are they?" Sahara asked.

"I can't tell from here. It's a ram. Maybe Connor? The other one … I'm not sure." She cast a glance over her shoulder. "I'm going to get my gun."

The space beside her gaped with Trish's absence. *Hurry!* The coyote took a step forward, and Sahara's pulse jumped. Heavens, no. No, no, no. She could not stand here and watch this ferocious animal tear a precious sheep apart. What could she do? How could she stop it? Make a loud noise? Shout?

The pacing sheep stopped as if staring the coyote down, then stomped its feet.

Woah. Brave little thing. Who did she think she was?

Just then a group of sheep brushed past Sahara and headed down into the field, toward danger.

"No! Stop!" What were they doing? She took a few steps toward them to … what? Haul the sixty-pound sheep back up the hill to the sheering barn? She stopped. Crossed her arms. Bit her lip.

Seconds later, Trish was by her side again, rifle in hand. "What's going on?"

"No clue. Those five up and decided to go back into the danger zone."

Trish watched on, brow furrowed, as the sheep made their way to the bottom of the hill.

"Go on. Shoot the thing."

"Wait. I want to see what they do."

Yeah. Great plan. They could watch them die.

But as Sahara looked on, the five sheep surrounded the hurt ram, pushing close. A minute later, the ram stood, albeit on shaky legs. Sahara's hand flew to Trish's arm as she gasped. And then they walked together up the hill. All save the guard ewe who held the enemy off with a few stomps of her feet.

"They're bringing the hurt ram to safety." Trish shook her head, awe radiating from her face.

"I didn't know sheep did that."

"They don't. At least, most sheep don't. Other breeds, not a chance. I've been telling you since you were little that Shetlands are special."

"No kidding."

Trish raised her rifle and released a warning shot. The noise sent the coyote scurrying.

Sahara rolled her eyes. "Why didn't you do that earlier?"

"We would have missed seeing that." She pointed to the procession of sheep on their way to their safe place, together. "Isn't it a miracle? The way God made us to care for each other?"

Of course, Trish would see God in anything.

"I think that's the miracle." Sahara nodded toward the ewe who had singlehandedly stood down the Big Bad Wolf, saving her man without a hint of fear in her demeanor. That ewe now trailed the others. Was that smug satisfaction all over her sheep face? Hard to tell.

Trish laughed. "Same thing. But someday, you'll need to acknowledge a source outside of yourself."

Sahara groaned. "I'm not doing this with you." God. Whatever. Let Trish do her thing. And leave Sahara to hers.

Trish hooked an arm around Sahara's shoulder. "I know." She kissed the top of her head. The warrior ewe drew closer, baaing a hello as she did. "Oh, it's Iyla. Same one you spun earlier."

Sahara's breath caught. Was it a sign? Or was she being ridiculous? Still, out of the forty sheep's fleeces that she could have spun yarn from today, she'd chosen this tenacious, take-no-prisoners, stare-down-the-enemy, baa-in-the-face-of-danger fighter. She might not give much credence to Trish's God, but neither did she plant her faith in coincidences. The world was much too orderly for those. Or it should be. Perhaps the universe was trying to tell her something, trying to push her forward into the terrifying unknown. She reached out and ran a hand along the mighty female's back.

"If you can be brave, I can too," she whispered to the animal.

Iyla flicked her tongue. An agreement?

She jutted out her chin. "I'm going to Utah."

Trish gave her shoulders a squeeze. "That's my girl."

Chapter 4

Bernie
April 16, 1861
Shulerville, South Carolina

Bernie knotted and twisted the quilt in her hand as she stared up at the ceiling. A strand of moonlight broke through inky darkness to cast a single beam of light on the wall. Like a beacon shining the way forward. Though in her own life, she couldn't see a way forward. Not in this fog of confusion. Not here. Not now.

It seemed the entire world had gone mad. And here they were, caught up in the fray.

War.

Didn't anyone understand what that meant? Why were the lot of menfolk touting the word as if it were some grand adventure? "Off to lick some Yankees and be back by supper." They thought it would last a month or two and then they'd be back with their families, spouting stories of triumph. Perhaps they were right. But what if they were wrong?

Sometimes war cost far more than anyone bargained for when they fired the first shots.

And sometimes, even when your side won, you lost.

After all, Grandpa had returned from fighting the War of 1812 victorious. A hero. Beloved and lauded. And a shell of the man he once was.

Her mother told stories of a kind and tender man, one who taught his children to trap and fish, one who filled their home with laughter. But Bernie had never met that man. She'd tried once to draw him out. He had to be in there somewhere, didn't he? If her mother had gotten a piece of him, why shouldn't she? So, she'd climbed on his lap, kissed his prickly beard, and peered into his honey-brown eyes, longing to see in them at least a glimpse of the man she'd heard stories about.

With a grunt, he pushed her off. She fell to the floor. Scraped her knee. The sting of the scrape matched the sting of tears in her eyes as she gasped in shock. She scrambled to her feet and cast one look at his hardened face before fleeing to her mother.

Her mom held her and dried her tears with a handkerchief. "That's what war does to good men, Bernie. When you grow up, don't you ever let war get ahold of your man's heart. You keep that for yourself, you hear?"

She'd nodded, though she hadn't understood. A few years later, he'd moved in with them. Any joy that had been in the home vanished. No longer could she explore in the creek, catching crawdads and lizards. Instead, under her grandfather's watchful gaze, she had to act the part of a proper young lady. Prim and refined. Without air and light. Without love.

Bernie's mother cowered under Grandfather's rule, while Bernie's father relished the strict discipline kept during his long hours at the office. His house was now in order. His little girl tamed.

"I'm so sorry," her mother would say. "He wasn't always like this. He used to be a gentle man."

Had the shrapnel shredded all such tenderness from him? Because Bernie found not an ounce. A year before she came of age, they'd buried that bitter man. A year after that, they'd buried her mother. But she'd never buried the promise she made. She'd married a good man and would keep hold of his heart. War wasn't going to steal it away, not if she could help it

Her good and kind Hermann fighting in a war? And for what? Southern independence? For the right to own slaves? He hailed from Michigan originally. His extended family lived in the North. Like most farmers, they owned none. What was worth risking everything? Surely not his reputation. *Oh Lord, let him not be swayed by pressure from men. Let him seek Your will alone.*

The knot in her stomach failed to ease and pressure built at her temples, even as Hermann snored peacefully beside her. He couldn't leave. She couldn't lose him now. They had a future to build here together. Plans to expand the farm, to bring in Merino sheep in addition to their Tunis fold. Plans to start a family. Two years of marriage and she'd not yet been with child, but surely it would come soon. It must. But only if they were here, together.

Oh Lord! Keep him here, safe and sound.

Because she could not live with the thought of things any other way.

Her eyes only closed for half an hour the rest of the night, making the next day a struggle. In the evening, she knitted on the settee by the front window, trying to work the needles with trembling hands. After every fifth stitch, she glanced up, though it was a ridiculous notion. She'd hear Hermann's horse, Dolly, trotting down the road before she'd see the pair. Still, why was the meeting in Shulerville carrying on so long? She'd expected him to return hours ago.

She'd prepared him for what he might encounter: pressure to join the war effort. She'd equipped him with an appropriate sympathetic response. *"I wish I could join you, fellas, but the Confederate army is going to need meat and wool. It's imperative I keep operations going on the home front. It's the best way to show my sincerest support."* A diplomatic move that wouldn't brand him as a traitor to "the cause" and would keep him from danger. A way to keep peace with the men and the wife. So, if he had gone to town, said his piece, and gracefully bowed out, why hadn't he returned?

Her fingers worked at a frantic pace. She'd knit thousands of socks for Southern soldiers if she needed to, if that was what it took to keep her husband safe at home. She'd scrimp and save, donate every bit of excess they could scrape together. She'd cover herself with a sheet so soldiers in the field could have her quilt. Whatever it took, she'd do it. *Just please, dear God, don't take my husband from me.*

A stiff breeze rattled the windowpane. Outside, white blossoms from dogwoods fluttered and flew. Her babies bleated in the distance, and the tin cans Hermann had hung as wind chimes pinged their melody. The serene scene before her spoke peace, yet the world shouted war. What a cruel, ugly world to trample this haven they'd built together.

A whinny in the distance made her ears perk. She settled her knitting in the basket and went to the porch, craning her neck to witness her husband's arrival. Her smile spread at the safe sight of him, but as he neared, her throat went dry. Those weren't the clothes he'd left in, were they? She'd washed and dried his light blue shirt yesterday. Helped him to tuck it in proper before he left, praying he'd make a good impression. Did he look like a traitor? No. He looked respectable. Honorable. With that assurance, she'd sent him off.

But the man who rode toward her now wore gray.

Her hand flew to her throat. No. It couldn't be. Not her husband. He would not—*could not*—be wearing a Confederate uniform.

And yet he was. His furrowed brow and frown confirmed it as much as his attire. She forced a dry swallow as he dismounted from his horse. Forced a tight smile as he walked toward her. Perhaps it wasn't set in stone. Perhaps she could still persuade him otherwise.

Her voice came out pinched. "Hermann, what did you do?"

He took the ridiculous army hat off and turned it in his hands. "Now, Bernie—"

Was it a sob that escaped her? Surely not. She wasn't prone to hysterics. It had to be a groan. It came from deep inside her, a place where icy fingers wrenched everything from her grasp. A feral place of wilderness and ache and anger. She pressed her fists to her gut to stanch the blood that had to be flowing from her—had to be because she'd never felt such agonizing pain.

"Bernie," Hermann tried again, taking a step toward her, then away again when she shot him a wide-eyed gaze. "You've got to understand. They need every able-bodied man to fight. If I don't enlist, they'll only end up drafting me. How can I let my neighbors fight while I stay behind? What kind of man would I be?"

The kind of man who promised to have and to hold her for better or for worse until death do them part. That's the kind of man who would stay by her side rather than risk his hide for a cause he didn't believe in.

She spoke through clenched teeth, "And what of me? What do you expect me to do while you go and blow fellow Americans bloody?"

"Tend to the farm, of course. The sheep will keep you company. I'll be back before you know it. They say this war will be over in a matter of a couple of months. It's an easy victory." His lip trembled. How he'd always hated confrontation.

"You are joining a company of fools." She spat out her words, then turned and stormed into the house.

He was slow to follow. She'd already plunked on the settee and managed a row of knitting despite shaking hands before the door creaked shut behind her. She pressed her lips together. If her goal was for him to stay, best to swallow the fiery words that bubbled up her throat. They'd send her tender husband scampering faster than anything. *Oh Lord! This cannot be happening. Please, God! Intervene.* He had to stay. She couldn't bear to see him go. What could she possibly say to convince him? Fear beat a rapid rhythm in the pulse in her neck. Could she tug at his compassionate heart?

She moistened her lips and gazed up at him, lower lip trembling. "This is a mighty large farm to tend to all on my lonesome. However will I manage?"

There. The lines around his eyes dipped in empathy. "Oh, Bernie."

He came and sat beside her, draping an arm around her shoulders. She hunched forward as if burdened by the immense weight of responsibility that would be left to her in his absence though it bothered her not a bit. The weight that pressed on her chest was that of losing the man she loved. In body, perhaps. In soul, most certainly.

He mirrored her posture. "I'll swing by McEvens's place on my way out. Ask him to look in on you. Help out if need be. With his sight failing as it is, he won't enlist."

She couldn't contain the growl that emitted from her. Half-blind McEvens? A perfectly acceptable substitute for her husband? She shucked the knitting back into the basket and folded her arms around herself. "And when do you plan to leave?"

He lowered his gaze as if studying his boots. "Within the hour."

She gasped. Jumped to her feet. "Within the—"

"Now, Bernie—" He stood and spread out his hands in front of him.

"Would you rightly stop with that? Why are you in such a blasted hurry? The war will be there tomorrow. Next week. Can't you take longer than a few minutes to say goodbye to your wife, whom you may never see again?"

"Tuffle's Brigade is only passing through Shulerville before going to Honey Hill and then Pineville. No need to stay long in a town this size."

"You could catch up with them later. Or there will be other opportunities to enlist."

"If I'm going to fight, I want to do it with my neighbors. My friends. I want to watch out for them. I don't want to join a different company filled with strangers."

"Watch out for *them*? What about me? Your wife?" Heat inflamed her face, her hands, her senses. She shook with it.

Hermann sat again with an air of defeat, dropping his head into his hands. His body heaved with a long, slow exhale. He mumbled as if to himself. She stooped closer to hear. "I don't know what to do."

Fury began a slow leak from inside of her as she lowered herself beside him and grabbed his hand.

"I can't be a coward." He turned red-rimmed eyes toward her. "I can't hide away while my neighbors go off and fight. How could I live with myself when they return? How could I live with myself if they do not return?"

She gave his hand a gentle squeeze.

"Do you care about 'the cause'?"

He shook his head. "I care about the men. The ones who helped us put out that brush fire before it consumed our barn. The ones who helped us find Hilda when that stubborn ole cow ran off. The ones who've helped with the shearin' when I've been in over my head. Us neighbors, we look out for each other. Always have. They're going into battle, and I can't stand aside as Yankees try and take their lives." He stared at her then, trailed a rough finger along her cheekbone. "I'd do the same for you if you were in danger. But you'll be safe here. And I'll come home to you straightaway."

Bernie's throat tightened. "You can't promise that."

He lifted a sad half smile. "We'll have to trust the Good Lord, then, won't we?"

Trust the Lord. That was well and good, but surely the Almighty valued those who worked their part in their own salvation. Because she would die a bitter death before she sat in this house and did nothing.

Her gaze fell on the sofa table where a copy of *Fanny Campbell, the Female Pirate Captain* lay. Fragments of a plan formulated, easing the tension in her chest and neck a fraction. Enough for her to look her husband in the eye and see the battle waged there. These might be the last moments she spent with him. No, she couldn't think that way. But … if they were, how would she want to remember them? With bitter arguing and accusations?

"Oh, Hermann." She leaned into his embrace and kissed his bearded cheek. He turned his mouth to hers and captured it, cupping the back of her head. His kiss spoke of apology, the regret he couldn't quite voice, the longing to be all she wished him to be for her, and the hope that all they'd built and dreamed together would be here when he returned.

And she would do everything in her power to make sure this man—this sweet, loving, tenderhearted man—didn't get lost among the horrors of war.

Chapter 5

Sahara
Present Day
Georgetown, South Carolina

Sahara paced back and forth in her living room, phone in hand. Her bare feet plodded on the cool hardwood, then sank into the plush rug, then landed on the hardwood again. One, two, three, four, five, six, turn. One, two, three, four, five, six, turn. Her pulse throbbed in her neck. Maybe she could email instead? No. She needed to call. She had to talk to Rhonda, and she had to do it within the next—she checked her watch—ten minutes, or the office would close.

Okay, she could do this. It was only a phone call. No big deal. She'd known Rhonda for years. They'd always been amiable. It'd be fine. Where had she put her water bottle? There, on the kitchen counter. She snatched it and guzzled nearly twenty ounces at once.

All right. Now or never.

She dialed and once again forced a smile.

"Frost Construction."

Deep breath. "Hi, Rhonda. It's Sahara."

"Oh, Sahara! How great to hear from you. It's been forever. Oh my gosh, did Jaxon tell you he got the Emmerson bid? For the mountain getaway?"

A pang shot through her chest. "Yeah. He did."

"You must be bursting with pride. He's doing well. Making a name for himself. Soon, Frost Construction will be known nationwide. I'm telling you, your husband is going places."

Frost Construction. What a name for a company run by a South Carolina native. Of course, he'd think it hilarious to name his business after his favorite poet. She bit her lip. Focus, Sahara. Focus.

"Actually, I'm wondering if you could help me with something."

"Sure, dear. Anything for you."

Pain. Oh, she was clenching her hand so tight her nails had made marks in her palm. Deep breath. Relax. "I want to come to Utah and work on Jaxon's crew. Only I don't want him to know I'm coming."

A nervous chuckle. "You what?"

"I want to surprise him."

"Oh?"

"I want to work on the"—What had she called it?— "Emmerson place. With him. Under him. As part of the crew."

Silence.

Sahara squeezed her eyes shut. *Please let this work.* Was she praying? Whatever worked.

"I wasn't aware you knew anything about construction. I thought you were an accountant."

"I am. I was. I took a leave of absence to pursue this other endeavor. Of construction. Of which I am … equally passionate about."

"Oh."

"Could you arrange for me to be on the crew?"

Rhonda's voice came out pinched. "He has a full crew already in place, but—"

"More hands can always be helpful, right?"

"I assume so."

Oh my gosh, this was awkward. Sahara spun around and locked eyes with Bernie's picture. Such strength in that woman's expression. She needed to buck up. Be strong. Be brave. "Look, I miss my husband. I need to be near him. If he won't come to me, then I'll go to him. Please help me make this happen."

Papers shuffled in the background as Sahara held her breath.

"When should I tell him this new crew member will arrive?"

Sahara exhaled and pressed a hand to her chest. Thank heavens. "In two weeks."

"Okay. Is your email the same?" The women chatted about details for a few minutes before Sahara hung up and did a little happy dance around her living room. Her plan had worked! She was going to Utah to win back her husband.

She only had to learn something about construction first.

~

Was getting a haircut the most pressing item on her to-do list? Definitely not. But it was the easiest. Procrastinating was normally Jaxon's thing, not hers, and yet the enormity of the plan she'd set in motion overwhelmed her. So, yeah. She'd start in the hairstylist's chair.

"How much do you want off?" Maggie, her go-to gal, asked.

Sahara winced. "All of it." She shuddered. "Not all of it, of course. I'm not going bald. Do you think I'd look ridiculous in a pixie cut?"

Maggie's jaw dropped. "You're not serious."

Sahara stared at her own grimacing face, surrounded by beautiful, long, flowing ginger hair. "Is that a yes? I'd look ridiculous?"

Maggie spun the chair around to face her. "I've cut your hair for fifteen years." She held a finger up. "No, cut isn't the right word. Trimmed. I've only ever *trimmed* from a half inch to two inches off your sassy little head. The craziest you've ever gotten was that one time when I put in a few layers. And now you want to go pixie on me?"

Sahara rolled her eyes. "Not on you. On Jaxon."

"Excuse me?"

"Jaxon likes to shake things up. He despises the same old same old. I look the exact same as I did the day he met me. I need to catch his eye."

A slow smile spread across Maggie's face. "Oh. I see." Her gaze turned predatory. "That I can do."

"Why are you looking at me like that?"

Maggie ran her hands through Sahara's hair. "I've wanted to play with this beauty for a long time."

Sahara squeezed her eyes shut. "I can't watch."

"We'll keep you turned away from the mirror, then."

Sahara shivered as a fine mist of water coated her hair and seeped through to her neck. Maggie combed through her mane with methodical, even strokes, just how Sahara liked it.

"You're looking to knock Jax out of the park for his homecoming, huh? It's been what? Eight months?"

"Actually, he's not coming home. I'm going for a visit. An extended visit."

Maggie's hand stilled. "Not coming home?"

A burning sensation clawed at her throat. "No." She swallowed. "He got another offer out there and decided to stay for a second project."

"Oh. Wow." The combing recommenced.

She pushed out the words. "It's a great opportunity for him."

"Of course."

Oh my gosh, Maggie knew. She knew Sahara's marriage was imploding. Did everyone know? Could they tell by looking at Sahara's plastered-on smile? Was she fodder for town gossip? Her stomach clenched. She had to fix this.

"Naturally, I have to go out there to see him. We can't stand being apart from each other another minute." There. That sounded convincing, didn't it?

"Aw. How sweet. He invited you out there for what, a weekend?"

"No, I think I'm staying a month. Maybe more."

Maggie ducked in front of her and met her gaze. "No way."

Sahara forced a smile. "Yep."

Slipping behind her again, Maggie pulled a section of Sahara's hair between her fingers and sliced the scissors shut. Sahara's stomach dropped as weight plummeted off her. What was she doing? "Stop." She gulped in a breath. "What was that?"

Maggie bent and retrieved the lock of burnished bronze. It had to be six inches long. "I'm not giving you a pixie cut. I'm going with a graduated stacked bob. It'll look great on you."

Was the air-conditioning even on? Stifling heat pressed in on her. She wrestled her hand free from under the cape and waved it in front of her face. She came for a haircut. A drastic one. This was why she was here. "Okay. Yeah. Go ahead."

It took a couple more snips before her breathing slowed to normal.

"What about your job?" Maggie asked.

"It's my slow season." A niggle of guilt threaded through her. Okay, so she'd criticized Jaxon for using that same phrase, but this was different. As a tax accountant, of course, she'd have a busy time of year and a time when things slowed down. *Just like construction.* The difference was, she took on side jobs to make up for the lag. She didn't lounge on the couch or insist on midday hikes, midweek rafting excursions, or other endeavors that didn't pay the bills. If she didn't take on as many side jobs this season, it didn't mean she was irresponsible. She had a marriage to save.

"I have a couple of accounts I can work on remotely from there, but others I passed on to another business."

"And your new house? Is someone looking in on things for you?"

"Myra, of course. And a lawn care company." She'd had to work out those details.

"Do you love living in the historic district?"

"Yes. It's a dream." She didn't have to look in the mirror to know her smile didn't reach her eyes. What good was achieving this lifelong dream if she had no one to share it with? Sure, she loved the period bay windows, arched doorways, screened-in back porch, and cozy fireplaces. She loved the history that came with a home built in 1899, not to mention the brass doorknobs and creaky floors. She loved to imagine all who came before and research the furnishings of that era. But she didn't *love* doing it alone.

She'd imagined her and Jax strolling hand in hand along the moss-draped sidewalks, the scent of roses heavy in the air, to the restaurant where they'd had their first date. They'd choose the same table they'd sat in that day. Maybe they'd have to wait a half hour for it to open, but it'd be fine. They'd sit on the bench in the sunshine and talk like they used to. Maybe he'd even recite a poem or two for old times' sake. After dinner, they'd indulge in peanut butter pie and then stroll the Harborwalk. He'd tease her about how he'd never seen a gator, despite the numerous posted signs warning him against feeding the monsters. She'd quip that he hadn't been paying enough attention. They'd end up in front of the Kiminski House where they got married, and he'd kiss her like he used to when he still believed nothing she could say or do could scare him away.

"Does your house have one of those plaques?" Maggie's voice interrupted the daydream.

"Yeah. A white one." The coveted historical place markers of the historic district.

"How cool. You are living the dream, my friend."

The bridge of her nose burned. "Yep." And there came the stinging behind her eyes. Better change the subject. Quick. "Do you like the cookware your mom got you for Christmas? Is it holding up well?"

That did the trick. Focus off Sahara and on to Maggie's delving into the culinary arts. Thank heavens.

When Maggie swiveled the chair around to face the mirror, Sahara's jaw dropped. Who was the woman staring back at her? Someone who could take risks, perhaps. And not only ones that were carefully calculated, planned out in excruciating detail. Someone who could be more carefree? Let some things slide? Not nag her man to death? She bit her lip as her fingertips grazed the ends of her bob. Knowing she needed to make changes and actually making them were two separate things. But she could do anything she set her mind to, couldn't she? Hadn't she always? And look. She'd taken this first crucial step.

She caught Maggie's wince in the mirror. "I can't tell whether you like it or not."

"Yeah. It's great. You did an amazing job."

"Oh good. I think it would look even better with highlights."

Highlights? Would those make her more eye-catching? "Okay. Fine."

Maggie clapped. "Really?"

Sahara shrugged. "Why not. I've gone this far." Might as well clinch the deal. Because she was not coming home a loser.

Chapter 6

Bernie
April 17, 1861
Shulerville, South Carolina

A knock on the door caused Bernie to jump the morning after Hermann set off with Tuffle's Brigade. Hermann was nothing if not a man of his word, so of course, it had to be Russell McEvens coming to check on her. Since Hermann had disappeared over the horizon, she'd thought long and hard, screamed into her pillow, paced the floor until she'd nearly worn a track through the hardwood. And she stayed up late rereading *Fanny Campbell, the Female Pirate Captain.* The stirring novel about a woman, disguised as a man, who became the commander of a pirate ship to rescue her fiancé enraptured her. What other solution was there?

She couldn't keep her husband at home, couldn't shelter his heart from within the four walls of their beloved farmhouse. So be it. She'd have to enact a far more drastic plan. Lord help her. It would be risky. Illegal. Whom could she trust? She'd prayed late into the night, begged God that McEvens would aid her. Whom else could she go to? She had to keep her circle small. Very small. The fewer who knew the truth, the better.

And now, he was here. On her doorstep. Her hand grasped the knob with sweaty palms. She swung it open and flashed a bright smile. "Good morning, Mr. McEvens."

Wispy hair poked out from under his hat and hung almost to his shoulders, gray under the brim, light brown at the ends. His long coat hung open, dusty along the bottom hem. His solid frame leaned slightly against his hand-carved cane. He looked at her with translucent blue eyes. Nearly eye to eye, such a good match they were in height. Yes. He would do nicely.

"Good morning, Mrs. Reisenfeld." He tipped his hat. "Your husband asked me to check in on you, ma'am, and I'm much obliged to do so."

"Thank you kindly. Do come in." She opened the door wide and waved him forward with an exaggerated gesture.

He shuffled inside. "I'm mighty thankful Hermann saw fit to lick them filthy Yankees. They best leave us alone. Let us govern ourselves. That's what I say."

Bernie turned to him with a tight smile. "Your patriotism is refreshing. May I take your coat?"

He shrugged it off and handed it to her. She hung it on the peg and turned back to him, hands clasped at her waist. "Would you like tea?"

"That sounds marvelous, thank you."

He followed her to the kitchen where she heated water on the wooden cookstove. With a large sweep of her arm, she motioned for him to sit. "Do make yourself comfortable, Mr. McEvens."

They both sat, her back straight and ankles crossed, him bent forward with forehead creased in concern. "How are you faring, Mrs. Reisenfeld?"

How to answer? She desperately needed his sympathies. She heaved a deep sigh. "I miss my Hermann terribly."

She could let down her guard. Allow fear and sorrow to mingle, gurgle forth, reach her eyes. If she would but allow herself a moment of vulnerability, she might win him to her side through a watery-eyed plea. She worked her jaw. No. If she acted like a mere woman, he'd not think her up to the task at hand. She stiffened her spine and tried for a conspiratorial glint to her eye instead.

"I do envy him." The lie tasted filthy in her mouth, but she'd best get used to it. If her plan worked, she'd have to produce many more. All for the greater good. "Just think. In a matter of days, perhaps, he might teach those Yankees a thing or two."

"I'll say! Wish I could join 'im."

"So, do I. In fact," she said as she leaned forward and turned her head this way and that as if ensuring they were alone, "I thought maybe I would."

The left side of his mouth twitched. "What's that, you say?"

"You've heard, of course, of women disguising themselves as men to join the ranks."

His brow furrowed. "Hearsay."

She straightened, shoulders taut. Tension climbed her backbone and stretched through her neck. Had she misjudged him? Told the wrong person? She stuffed her fear under an aloof demeanor. "It's been done before. Why should I let my husband have all the fun? I'm as much of a patriot as he."

His glassy eyes looked past her. She suppressed a shiver. Focused her gaze on his narrow nose.

"You mean to tell me you want to enlist? To join up as a … man?" His mouth dropped open, brows lifted, eyes widened. Was the poor man in shock?

Her heart thudded. She could take it back right now. Say it was a joke. Break in with a boisterous laugh, pour the tea, and steer their conversation onto other matters. Perhaps she didn't need his help at all. She could squeeze into Hermann's clothes. No one had to know of her plans. Blast. Why did she have to marry a man smaller in stature than herself? Maybe she didn't have to even go. She could stay home like a good little wife and knit socks for the soldiers. Take care of the sheep. Wait for Hermann's letters.

She sat stone still as words fled her. What to say? How to reply?

The jostling of the kettle startled her. She jumped to her feet with a nervous laugh. "Let me see to your tea." Her hands trembled as she placed the teacups on saucers. She avoided meeting McEvens's gaze until she set the tray on the table. "Here we are." She forced a smile.

He met her with one of his own. "I must say, Mrs. Reisenfeld, you done shocked the whiskers off me. I'll be. A woman soldier."

A sharp breath whooshed out of her. He wasn't angry? He wouldn't turn her in for suggesting such a thing?

"You really think you can manage the heat of battle? Ain't no place for a lady."

"I'm quite certain I'm capable."

His grin widened to show crooked teeth. "Oh, I've heard you with a rifle. I know you're a good shot." His smile dimmed. "I meant the gore of the battlefield. Men wounded and dying. You've got to have a solid constitution to bear through it."

A muscle tightened in her throat. "I will manage."

He nodded somberly, his pale eyes once again seeming like they saw too much, as if they saw into the future, beyond what she could comprehend. The neckline of her dress suddenly felt too tight. She tugged at it.

McEvens snapped out of his trance-like state. "Tell me now, how's a lady pretty as yourself going to pass as a man?"

She raised a brow. "I'm glad you asked. I hoped you might help me with that."

An hour later, he hobbled away, promising to come back with a change of clothes. He also pledged to look after their farm in her absence, and all she had to offer in return was one cow, two sheep, and a Confederate victory.

~

Bernie stood in front of the mirror, her long brown hair brushed loose around her shoulders, scissors in hand. She bit her lip. This was no time for sentiment. She had to do what needed to be done, and this hair had to go. No matter that her mother had brushed it when she was a child or that Hermann loved to twirl a strand around his finger as they lay in bed at night. She was far too tall and hearty for her figure to have typical feminine appeal, but her hair had always made her feel like a woman.

And that was exactly why it had to go.

The transformation must begin. She would do what had to be done. Always.

With a deep breath, she brought the scissors to chin level. Yawned their jaws around a lock of hair. Squeezed her eyes shut and clamped down. Featherlight weight drifted off. She cracked open one eye. Not bad. She could do this. Relaxing a bit, she grabbed hold of the next lock and, eyes averted but open, snipped. She tilted her head to the right. How much lighter she felt! Air swirled against the side of her neck. All this without pins? She chuckled.

When she finished snipping her hair to chin level, she studied herself in the mirror. She looked entirely different, yet still distinctly female. Perhaps … Yes, she needed to part her hair on the side and then snip around the edges. There. Now she looked like a sloppy, poorly groomed … male. If only she could make her way to Charleston, she could enter a barbershop and receive a proper trim. She sighed. No time for fanciful thinking. She must make herself presentable. Respectable looking.

A knock at the door startled her, and she dropped the scissors with a clank to the floor. Her hand flew to her chest.

Mr. McEvens, surely. But what if it was someone else? Another neighbor come to check on her? Frantically, she searched for her bonnet. She shoved it on her head and tied the laces as she hastened to the door.

McEvens stood on the porch, trousers, shirt, and shoes in hand. She could nearly hug the man she was so relieved.

"Good afternoon, Mrs. Reisenfeld." His eyes lit with mischief.

She ushered him inside. "I do believe you can call me Bernie, seeing as how I no longer look much like a Mrs." She removed her bonnet.

He leaned closer and squinted one eye. A low chuckle rumbled from him, bursting open into an eager laugh.

She huffed. "What is it?"

"Well, Bernie, let's see if I can help you with your cut."

She took a step back. "Mr. McEvens—"

"Russell."

"Russell …" How to state this delicately? "I'm not sure. I don't know if it would be best for you to—"

"You afraid I'll cut your ear off?"

Precisely. "It's just your eyesight is, shall we say, lacking."

"I can see mighty fine right close. It's them far distances that give me trouble."

She sucked her lips in between her teeth. Russell's hair stuck out in all directions, giving no indication of when he'd trimmed it last. His beard, however, was neat and kempt with not a trace of a nick to be seen. If he'd laughed at first sight of her, chances were others might as well. Might laugh her right out of any intention to join up with the army. She needed him, didn't she? But her hands clamped tight at her sides.

"I know the Twenty-third Psalm is a favorite of yours, as it is mine. And what does it say?"

She could picture it then, black lettering on the cream background of Mama's Bible. The Bible she kept on her nightstand so she could read it first thing every morning. The scripted *T* faded from where she'd traced it with her thumb time after time. "'The Lord is my shepherd.'"

He chuckled. "Well, yes. Yes. That's why we shepherds love the psalm, is it not? But I meant the part further down. Verse four, is it? 'Yea, though I walk through the valley of the shadow of death—'"

She finished for him. "'I will fear no evil: for thou art with me.'"

"You will need to keep that verse tucked inside your heart throughout your journey. And you can start right here and now by handing over those scissors." He smiled, and his eyes crinkled at the edges.

She ran her tongue over her teeth. If she was to stand half a chance at this wild plan, she'd have to trust half-blind Russell with a pair of scissors inches from her head. Yea, though she walked through the valley of the shadow of death … or dismemberment.

She swallowed. "I'll get the scissors."

~

Bernie left after the noon meal. Russell's shirt hung baggy against her bandaged chest. Perfect. His pants also hung a bit loose, but the suspenders held them fast. The cut he'd given her, though it set her every nerve on edge, transformed her. Surely, she looked like many young, freckle-faced boys joining up to fight in a war before they had any facial hair to shave. She'd practiced strutting with a male gait and lowering her voice. No one would be able to tell. Tension knotted the back of her neck. *Please God, let no one be able to tell.*

On her way off the farm, she passed through the south field, saying goodbye to her babies. Some fraud she was, for every one of those sheep knew it was her. They gathered to her bleating and nudging her with their heads. She tried out her deep voice on them, but they remained undeterred. It must be her scent. Hopefully, army men wouldn't be able to sniff her out. After a few weeks of living among men, she'd wager she'd end up smelling like one anyway. How often would they bathe? How would she manage to do so? She could only take one day at a time. Do the next thing in front of her.

She must get to Pineville.

Hermann had said Tuffle's regiment would go to Honey Hill first, then to Pineville. A full day had passed since. They might have hung around Honey Hill for a night and attempted to gather as many men as they could before moving on. But they wouldn't have lingered. They'd be headed toward Pineville by now. Honey Hill was a small farming community only slightly larger than Shulerville, and even Pineville was nothing like the big cities of Georgetown and Charleston. How long could one reasonably spend enlisting men in such places? She needed to hurry.

With a last scratch underneath Cecil's chin, Bernie stepped off the land she'd come to as a new bride two years prior and onto the dirt road leading out of town. How naive she'd been about what it would take to help run a farm. But Hermann, whistling his way through every chore and pausing to admire a butterfly or brightly colored bird, was a fresh breeze to the stuffy, oppressive air of her childhood home. She hadn't quite fit there with the straitlaced etiquette, everything prim, proper, and perfect. Tea times and social calls. No, she relished the feeling of dirt sifting through her fingers and rain on her upturned face. The first time she saw an ewe give birth, it struck her with bone-shaking clarity. No mistake about it. She was home. This is where she was meant to be. In this place. With this man.

And now? Now Bernie must walk away. Leave the place she loved soul deep to keep it.

Because if Hermann returned from war the same way Grandpa did, this farm would no longer be her safe place. Bitterness and regret would suck all light and life right out of it, and she'd be right back where she started from. Gasping for air.

She could not let that happen.

She had to fight for what she loved. What she believed in. This land. Her dreams. Her husband.

That was the real war. And it was a battle worth fighting.

Chapter 7

THE TREE THE TEMPEST WITH A CRASH OF WOOD
THROWS DOWN IN FRONT OF US IS NOT TO BAR
OUR PASSAGE TO OUR JOURNEY'S END FOR GOOD,
BUT JUST TO ASK US WHO WE THINK WE ARE,
INSISTING ALWAYS ON OUR OWN WAY SO.

"ON A TREE FALLEN ACROSS THE ROAD" BY ROBERT
FROST

Sahara
Present Day
Georgetown, South Carolina

Sahara blew a strand of her now-far-too-short hair from her face and readjusted her position on the rug in front of the couch. She'd found the used textbook of *Fundamentals of Building Construction* cheap online. She'd always been able to absorb what she read in school and ace every test regardless of the subject. But perhaps she'd overestimated her ability to easily absorb the needed information in this situation. With a week until she was supposed to set foot onto Jax's construction site, she was about fourteen percent ready. And that might be overshooting.

But it was okay. It would be fine. She only needed to watch a few more episodes of *This Old House* and cram in a few dozen more YouTube videos on framing and drywalling, and she'd be set.

"Knock, knock." Myra poked her head in the door. "I come bearing the gifts you requested." A thump resounded as she dropped several bags. "Well, begged for. In your manic, panicked state."

"I wasn't panicked. And it was the coffee."

"Whatever you say." She bent and lifted a red dumbbell. "Five-pound weights so you can get buff within the next six days." She set the weight down. "I don't understand why you won't go to a gym."

"Because there are tons of people at the gym. People I'd rather avoid, thank you."

"There's also tons of equipment. Equipment that will do far more for you than these measly dumbbells. But have it your way."

"Thank you." Sahara stood and stretched her back, arching it like a cat and then rolling her spine. She came to riffle through the bags with her friend. Hammer. Nails. Level. Tape measure.

"Looking for this?" Myra held up a heavy-duty tool belt.

"Yes!" She snatched it and turned it around in her hands. "It's a thing of beauty."

"Okay. That's weird."

Sahara pinched the bridge of her nose. "I've been reading too much."

"How's that going, by the way?"

"Gr-great."

Myra planted her hand on a hip and rolled her eyes. "That good, huh?"

"I just have to figure out if he builds roofs using rafters or trusses. And if he uses rafters, what's the difference between a hip rafter and a valley rafter? And what's a jack rafter? Or is it a barge rafter?" She massaged her temple with her free hand.

"Don't ask me." Myra took the tool belt and dropped it into the bag. "I hired Jaxon to build my house. And if you were on the crew, I would have called off the deal."

"Oh stop. It can't be that hard."

"No. Anyone who watches YouTube can build a house." Myra sashayed into the kitchen. The fridge hissed as it dispensed water. "Have you eaten?"

Shoot. What time was it? Sahara checked her watch. Six. "Nope."

Myra peeked her head around the corner. "You forgot to eat lunch too, didn't you?"

"I got wrapped up in this." She waved a hand around the stack of books on her living room floor.

"Come on. Grab your purse. We're getting food."

But she was in the middle of a chapter. "I really should—"

"You won't be able to carry a two-by-four if you wither away from malnutrition."

Sahara stuck out her tongue. "Fine." She retrieved her shoes from the rack and her purse from the hall closet. "But I get to pick the restaurant."

~

Rhonda called as soon as Sahara stepped through the front door after grabbing a bite to eat. "Okay, I've got you locked in on the Emmerson project. Monday's a holiday, so you're set to start Tuesday morning at eight o'clock. It's a good thing too. We lost a guy two days ago. Family emergency. I snuck you in, no questions asked. You're clear for the full eight months."

Sahara froze in the process of peeling off her shoes. "Clear for what?"

"The entire length of the project. Eight months."

She coughed.

"Is there a problem?"

"No." Not at all. It was only seven months longer than she'd anticipated. About eighty-seven percent more time than she'd planned to spend away from home. Away from her job. What was she going to do about the house? The mortgage?

"The framing itself will take two months, but Jaxon always leaves at least one person behind to assist with cleanup for the other subcontractors. The guy you're replacing was going to fill that role. If you need me to scramble to fill—"

"It'll be fine." Funny. Her confidence didn't even sound forced.

"Wonderful. I'll email you the details right now."

"Great. Thanks. Bye." She couldn't hang up the phone fast enough. She dropped it on the couch cushion like it was on fire.

What had she been thinking? Nothing, clearly. Her mind had to have been devoid of all rational thought. She could stop this right now. Call Rhonda back and say she changed her mind or that something came up at work. As in, she needed to make money to pay the bills. Or she could say she had a family emergency. If she called Mom, something dire would certainly surface. She could buy a cat. Then she'd need to stay to take care of it.

She buried her head in her hands. "Jaxon, you drive me crazy. You always have."

They couldn't afford the mortgage on her dream house without her taking on a full load of clients. She could manage a month off. Maybe two months of light work. Any more than that would put them in serious trouble.

Wait. Was Frost Construction paying her for being a construction worker? Most likely. Surely not as much as she made with her accounting business. She'd have to scour Rhonda's email for details and crunch the numbers.

She scanned the array of books neatly stacked in piles on the living room floor. She should get back to studying. Except all this research had fried her brain. Maybe she should start packing. For an eight-month stay.

Or she could finally hang those shoe pictures on the pathetically bare walls. Yes. That way, the house wouldn't seem lonely while she was gone. She snatched a picture hanger and hammer from the end table and went to work. After placing a picture of Jaxon's work boots into a frame, she hung it next to her great grandmother's picture.

"There, Bernie. Something to keep you company."

She spun around and surveyed the space. Why couldn't she have company stay here while she was gone? Her home would make a great Airbnb with its convenient location, mere blocks from Front Street, and its historic charm. What a practical and efficient solution. She only needed to research how and where to list it and snap a few photos.

Hours later, she uploaded the last photo to the site and the listing went live. There, see? Eight months away would be no problem at all. She'd take on a few more clients and work on their accounts remotely in the evenings. And she'd return *with* her husband to this house, ready to build their future together.

She'd fix this.

Yawning, she closed her laptop and set it aside. Then, she stood from the couch and stretched. A glance at the clock proved it was after midnight. Enough already. Enough researching and working, fixing and fretting. She had to sleep. Next week, she'd be in a different state.

A fragment from her first conversation with Jaxon flitted into her memory.

They'd dined outside on the waterfront of Georgetown. A breeze swirled around them, bringing with it a fishy smell from the harbor. The dating site had an 87 percent approval rating and used a researched-based approach to statistically match prospective users based on their likes and dislikes, interests, hobbies, and goals. Still, Sahara couldn't seem to find common ground with the man sitting in front of her. At least he was pleasant to look at. And when he spouted poetry, common interests didn't seem to matter much.

"So." He'd pointed both fingers at her. "You're not much for amusement parks. What about rock climbing?"

She shook her head.

He downed another fry. "Hiking?"

Hiking? Maybe. She splayed her hands on the table and leaned forward. "If you're talking about walking the hiking trail at the local park, then yes. I'm all about hiking."

He smirked. "Does your hiking involve any sort of gear? A pack, perhaps?"

"A water bottle and sturdy shoes."

His laugh sounded like a melody. Nice.

"Skiing?"

"Never been."

"No?" The edge of his mouth twitched as if he held back a smile. Quirky. Kind of cute.

"Guess I'm a bit of a homebody. I've never traveled outside of this area of South Carolina. My aunt has a sheep farm near Jamestown. That's the farthest I've been."

His eyes had sparkled. "No way. We've got to change that."

Only in twelve years, she hadn't budged, despite Jaxon nudging her to broaden her horizons. The timing had never been right. It'd never been practical. But now…

"Well, Jax, you'll finally get your way."

Chapter 8

THE WEIGHT THAT HANGS UPON OUR EYELIDS—IS OF
LEAD.
MARY BOYKIN CHESNUT

Bernie
April 18, 1861
Pineville, South Carolina

Bernie's stomach sank as she drew close to Pineville. It was quiet. Far too quiet. The air should be punctuated by the chatter of a couple of dozen men, at least. Instead, a whippoorwill called, and another answered. A cow mooed in the distance. A light breeze rustled tree leaves. No voices. No laughter or crude jokes. Nothing.

She stifled a yawn as she came to the center of town. She'd walked until she couldn't see her own feet in the inky darkness. Then, she'd slept in the woods, using her pack as a pillow. When the sun rose, she set off again, eager to make it to Pineville as quickly as she could. Her racing mind hadn't afforded her much sleep. Never mind. She'd made it.

A chapel stood in front of a grove of trees. A woman bustled out the front door, dabbing a handkerchief under her eyes as she made her way toward the trees. Bernie opened her mouth to speak, then shut it again. She had to remember to use a masculine tone. This would be her first test. She must not fail.

She pushed back her shoulders and lifted her chin. "Excuse me, ma'am."

The woman turned with a start and stared at Bernie with wide eyes.

"I didn't mean to frighten you." Bernie put out a hand to reassure the woman, then quickly tucked it back to her side. Though calloused and work worn, her hands might still appear too feminine if scrutinized closely. "Could you tell me if Tuffle's Brigade has been through here? I heard General Tuffle was recruiting for the war effort."

The woman's eyes narrowed. Her lips pursed. "He hasn't been through here."

Why the suspicious expression? Did she suspect Bernie's ruse?

"Where'd you come from, little boy? You're not from around here, I daresay."

The woman thought her a boy. The muscles in the back of Bernie's neck released the pinch of tension they'd held. Bernie nodded in the direction from which she'd come. "Down by Honey Hill. Tuffle recruited my uncle. I'm out to find him. Enlist with him." Her uncle. Yes. That made perfect sense.

"You'd be best gettin' home to your mama. She won't want any Yankee to get ahold of you." The lady's voice faltered on the last word as her eyes took on a watery sheen.

"You got a son fightin', ma'am?" Shoot. She'd allowed her voice to soften with the question. She needed to restore its hard edge. She coughed.

The woman gave a reluctant nod.

"My regards. May the Good Lord bring him back safe to you." Too soft again. Too feminine. What was going on with her? She wasn't given to emotions. Why would she turn to mush at the sight of a mother's tears?

The woman hustled away, handkerchief covering her face. Bernie puffed out her cheeks. What to do now? Perhaps Tuffle's Brigade had lingered at Honey Hill and not yet made their way here. She should wait. They might bound 'round the bend at any moment.

A thousand times, she'd rehearsed what she'd say when Hermann saw her, how she'd react to his shocked expression. If she could manage to steer clear of him until after she'd already enlisted. She would, of course. How difficult that would be depended on how many men they rounded up, how easily she could blend into the crowd. If she could side skirt his scrutinizing eye until Tuffle issued her a uniform and a rifle, she could break the news to him more gently as they marched out to the front together.

He might be angry with her for a moment, but Hermann never stayed riled up for long. More than likely he'd be concerned about her safety, but she'd remind him of what a good shot she was, and he'd chuckle as he agreed. They'd whisper back and forth, then come to a truce. She'd call him Uncle Hermann. When he called her Bernie, everyone would assume her given name was Bernard. No one could deny the bond between them, but they'd assume it familial in a different fashion. Her secret would be locked safe in Hermann's quiet lips.

Lips she wouldn't be able to kiss until they were safely back on their farm, but lips that wouldn't betray her.

She had to do him proud.

Where to wait? She walked a bit farther, passing several homes, a library, and a post office. A few women roamed the streets with small children at their heels, but there were no men to be seen. A somberness hung in the air. She passed an eerily empty tavern. A shiver crept up her spine. Where was everyone in this booming township she'd heard about?

A flyer affixed to the tavern wall stole her attention. It's large block letters shouted at her:

RECRUITS WANTED

FOR GREENMAN'S INFANTRY

TWENTY GOOD ABLE-BODIED MEN WANTED
FOR GALLANT SERVICE
APPLY AT ONCE AT TOWN HALL

Town Hall? She glanced over her shoulder.

"You're not from around here, are ya?"

Bernie spun around to find a brawny barkeeper with wool-white hair and a patch over one eye drying a glass with a towel.

"No, sir. I'm from down by Honey Hill. I heard Tuffle's regiment was recruiting here and came to join up. Have you seen his company?"

"Tuffle?" The man narrowed his good eye. The lines on his forehead deepened. "Haven't heard of him. Greenman's the one you want to join up under." He nodded toward the flyer. "Half the town's down there now. Everyone wants a chance at them Yankees."

Bernie's shoulders slumped. No one had seen or heard of Tuffle? And if there was already someone recruiting here, would another company even bother to come through? Should she walk back toward Honey Hill and hope to meet them on the way? But what if they had gone a different route? What if they'd changed course entirely? How could she ever find them? No, best to wait here. They might come through at any moment.

"Thanks." She managed a weak smile to the barkeeper before exiting the open doors. The steps of the library looked as good a place as any to wait. She slid her haversack off her shoulder as she sat and turned her face toward the sun to soak up its warmth.

A few swigs from her canteen and a couple muffins from her sack did little to ease her anxiety. Where was her husband now? On his way toward her or away from her? How could she get to him?

She sifted through her money pouch. She likely had enough to stay the night at an inn but not much more than that. If he didn't come by tomorrow, what would she do? Go back home? Call it quits on the whole charade? She laughed without humor. How would she explain her appearance to the neighbors? No. She'd come too far to go back now. She had to follow this course through.

If she couldn't enlist in his company, she'd have to find him along the way. Surely, Tuffle and Greenman would fight in the same battles. She'd find him on the battlefield. Find a way to switch regiments when she did. It was a small world, wasn't it? And a small, quick war. How hard could it be to find each other?

Her stomach roiled, and she forced a drink down her dry throat. A few young men in uniform dashed past, faces bright as they chatted and laughed together. As if just noticing her out of the corner of their eyes, they slowed.

One craned his neck to peer at her. A blonde tuft of hair peeked out from beneath his cap. "What are you doing sitting there?"

She shrugged. Should she ask them about Tuffle's Brigade?

"Get on down to Town Hall and do your patriotic duty. As soon as we get a few more men, we can be off."

"I'm waitin' for someone." She squinted against the sun's glare.

"Well, if he don't show, he's a yellow belly."

She jutted out her chin. "He ain't a coward."

"A traitor, then."

Fire rolled through her chest. Is this what Hermann had to put up with? Is this why he felt such pressure to join? "He sure ain't a traitor. He signed up before the lot of you did."

"Then where is he? And why are you waiting for him?"

She explained the situation and asked if they'd heard of or seen Tuffle's Brigade. They shook their heads. "You might as well sign up with Greenman. We're all fighting for the same thing anyway."

Fighting for the same thing? Oh no they weren't. Not at all.

But she nodded. "I might see you boys tomorrow. If he don't show."

Blondie tipped his head to her in acknowledgement, and they continued on their way, hearty laughter following as if they'd joined up for a game of cards. Fools. Eager to fire a gun at another human being. Not thinking ahead to what their family would do when a fella in blue aimed a barrel right back. Fools, the whole lot of them. And she was throwing her hat in the same ring. How was she any better? At least she knew what she was truly fighting for, instead of spouting forth propaganda she'd read in the paper.

The day stretched on, then the sun curled up to sleep, and still no sight of Hermann. She got a room for the night and awoke early the next morning, taking her vigil on the library steps again, her gaze steady on the entrance to town. Noon came and went, and with it, the last of the biscuits she'd brought from home. Her hopes sank as the afternoon wore on.

Suddenly, Blondie was directly in front of her. Had she fallen asleep there on the library steps? "No sign of your uncle?" he asked.

She shook her head.

"Well, c'mon, then." He stretched out a hand to help her up. "Let's get you down there to enlist."

Gravel sifted in her gut. She eyed his outstretched hand. Should she wait a little longer? But for what? He wasn't coming. They must have made alternative plans. If they were coming here, they'd have been here by now. Was she going to wait on these steps like a vagabond, watching for a man who would never come? She took his hand and stood.

"Walter." He smiled.

"Bernie." She tried to return the gesture, but her mouth wouldn't cooperate.

He gave a playful slap to her back. "C'mon, Bernie. Let's sign you up. It'll win me a bet."

That explained his eagerness. She suppressed a sigh and gave one last, longing look over her shoulder before following Walter toward Town Hall. This wasn't at all how she'd pictured things playing out. She'd been going to war to save her husband. Now, she would go to war to find him.

Find him. Then save him.

And along the way, she had to make sure not to lose herself.

~

Bernie pushed through a sea of men—some dressed in top hats and overcoats, others in uniform—toward the wide-open doors of Town Hall. A banner waved gently overhead, promising a hundred-dollar bounty and thirteen dollars a month to all able-bodied men who enlisted. Thirteen dollars a month! My, what she could do with that lot of money. Three times as much as she could make doing any other job normally afforded to her sex. She hadn't come here for the financial incentive, but it sure could help launch their dreams to expand the farm. *Their farm.* Would it be safe under McEvens's care? What if another coyote came? She should be there defending her babies. Her steps nearly faltered, but Walter's hot breath at the back of her neck prodded her forward.

"Make way." Her newfound friend's voice sounded overloud in her ears. "This fella wants to sign up."

She forced a smile even as her insides tumbled. Hermann. Where was Hermann? Would every step she took bring her closer to him or farther away? But what else could she do now? She took the steps with a confident gait. If they looked for a trace of fear in her as a sign she wasn't fit for service, they'd not find it. She walled off the traces of worry worming through her heart. No room for that here and now. She must prove herself to be a soldier ready for battle.

A man with an inky-black wiry mustache sat behind a mahogany table, pen poised over an inkwell. "Here to enlist?" he asked with an eager smile.

Bernie tried to match his enthusiasm. "Yes, sir."

"Name, birthdate, and place of residence."

She cleared her throat to cover a moment's hesitation. She'd already determined to give her true name, the one she went by anyway. Best not to fabricate a different last name if she was to play by the ruse of trying to find her uncle. But she needed to shave a few years off her age to account for the lack of facial hair. And should she give them her correct residence? What if someone along the line recognized it?

"Bernie Reisenfeld. July 12, 1839. Shulerville." She hadn't time to think of another location. She swallowed. If anyone came along who knew of their small farming village, they'd know there was only one Bernie in Shulerville, and she most definitely did not belong in the army. But what were the odds? Most wouldn't even remember such an insignificant place and an insignificant woman in it.

"Wait right there for your medical examination." The man nodded to a row of chairs to his right.

Bernie sat, careful not to cross her legs or ankles. A few men from the steps outside looked in, seeming to scrutinize her. What did they see? A young boy full of patriotism and pride, ready to vanquish abolitionist invaders? *Please God, let them not see through my ruse.* Her chest heated at that prayer. Was it right to ask the Good Lord to aid in a deception? But it was for a good cause. The best of intentions. She'd recited Psalm 27 often as a young girl, and its words flooded her mind now.

> *For in the time of trouble he shall hide me in his pavilion: In the secret of his tabernacle shall he hide me; he shall set me up upon a rock.*

Hide me, Lord.

As long as they didn't make her strip for the medical examination—

"Bernie Reisenfeld?" A man in uniform poked his head out of the door a few feet away from her. She rose, shook his hand, and followed him into a room with only an examination table and two chairs. "It's my job today to ensure you are fit for active duty in the Confederate army. Do you suffer from any conditions or ailments I need to be aware of?" The doctor eyed Bernie with raised brows.

Was being female a condition or ailment? A muscle near her jaw twitched. "No, sir."

"Alright, then. Let me get a look at your teeth."

Her teeth? Surely her teeth wouldn't give her away. She bared them, and the doctor peered at her mouth thoughtfully. "Very good. Two opposing teeth are necessary to bite the cartridge and load the rifle. Now, let me examine your eyes."

Bernie widened her gaze and blinked back at him as he studied her right eye with an ophthalmoscope.

"Good. You'll need to be able to see out of your right eye to aim. Now, let me see your hands."

Her hands. Would they give her away? She willed them to be steady as she spread them out in front of her.

He tapped her right pointer finger and smiled. "Trigger finger intact. Marvelous. Now, flex your fingers." Gladly. The movement eased her tension. He stepped back and glanced her over from head to foot. What was he looking for? What did he see? Her chest ached from where the bandage was wrapped tightly around her and that made it hard to get a full breath. "You've got both arms and legs. Wonderful. Now, please hop on one leg in a circle to demonstrate your balance."

"Yes, sir." She bounded around the room as if in a circus act. Had Hermann performed such antics when he enlisted? The thought of her husband bouncing around made the edges of her mouth twitch upward. If only she could have seen that performance.

"Excellent." The doctor gave two short claps.

She stopped hopping and stood ramrod straight, her gaze trained on his face.

He held out a hand. "Welcome to the Confederate army."

~

May 1861
A month later

"Right face!"

Bernie turned, relief coursing through her when all her fellow soldiers faced right this time. Gone were the wild-eyed, panicked expressions of her comrades who hadn't known their left from their right in those weeks. Finally, they moved as a unit.

"Forward march!"

Bernie marched with her back straight and shoulders square, though her muscles screamed with exhaustion. Drill. Drill. Drill. Her first three weeks in the army had been full of nothing but drills. Turns and facings. Loading and handling their Springfield rifle muskets. And of course, marching. Sometimes all day. Sometimes all night. Some nights they'd march through the darkness, no matter the weather. Some nights they'd sleep on the ground with a single blanket, only to resume marching in the morning.

The men grumbled, sputtered, and cussed. The language she'd been subjected to in camp was enough to make her ears bleed. But she said not a word of complaint. Each time a whine or whimper would snake its way up her throat, she'd think of Hermann. Of why she marched and drilled here. Of why she would fight.

"At least this afternoon, we'll get to drill with bayonets," Walter whispered out of the side of his mouth.

She curbed a smile. Now *that* was fun. Stepping and lunging. Thrusting this way, swinging that way. Jumping out of the way of an oncoming blade, striking in the opposite direction. Bayonet practice broke up the monotony. A few cuts and scrapes were a small price to pay.

"Think you can best me this time?" she teased.

"I'll beat you so good, you'll go crying to your mama."

She snorted. Crying? That was one thing she sure couldn't do. Not when her body screamed from every demand stacked on it. Not when lonely nights stretched on without the man she loved next to her. Not when she imagined the impossibility of the task that loomed before her.

And not even when she realized she'd missed her monthly.

If only she could go crying to her mama. If only the precious woman was alive, a ready wellspring of wisdom and advice. Because what was Bernie to do about this? Two years she'd waited and longed to get pregnant. Two years she'd poured herself into her sheep, calling them her babies because the Good Lord hadn't seen it fit to make her a mother. And now? Had she put on the clothing of a man and gained the privilege of a woman?

Or had the strenuous work of drilling caused her cycle to dry up? Perhaps there was no life within her at all. Only bitter parched ground and sorrow. Perhaps everything feminine in her had given up when she paraded about as a man.

But if it was a baby …

She should quit. Desert. Disappear into the woods one night and never return to camp. She'd disgrace her name—her *real* name—but she'd give the tiny life growing inside her a chance.

Every mile marched, every day without adequate nutrition, and every night without rest put her child at risk. This child she had waited and prayed for. Hermann's child.

If there was a child.

There might not be. And how could she be certain when she couldn't see a physician without revealing her deception and risking imprisonment?

She'd have to wait and see if her stomach grew, pray the war would end quickly and her bulky uniform would disguise a growing midsection until then.

"Do you think your uncle has any idea?" Walter's hushed voice shook her from her ponderings.

Her pulse quickened. "Hmm?" Could he hear her thoughts? Had she accidentally spoken out loud?

"You think he's got a clue his nephew can handle a bayonet like a general?"

She released a shaky breath. "Nah. He'd be surprised." That put it mildly. Hermann would fall flat over if he knew a lick of what she'd been up to these past few weeks. The disguise or the drills or bayonet matches. The games of dominos, checkers, and poker that she participated in at night. The lively round of baseball she'd taken part in on Sunday afternoon. How would he feel if he knew she might have done it all with an extra secret harbored inside her belly?

He'd be none too pleased.

It'd been easier than she'd feared to convince an entire company of men she was one of them. She merely had to observe and imitate. They thought her a modest chap for not wanting to use the company sinks and instead excusing herself to the woods to take care of private matters, but she wasn't the only one. Camp latrines were filthy. Who could blame her? They'd yet to bathe and went to bed fully dressed. Not one had eyed her with suspicion. Yes, hoodwinking the menfolk had been surprisingly, delightfully easy.

But carrying her secret alone, without even one person to confide in? That proved far more difficult.

Chapter 9

Sahara
Present Day
Provo, Utah

Sahara couldn't stop gaping. She'd never felt so small in her life. People here lived with those towering, majestic mountains in their backyards? Did they take them for granted? A honk sounded, and she snapped her attention back to the road. Okay, then. She'd go ahead and drive. She needed to make a right in two blocks, then take that road a quarter of a mile, and she'd be there.

She worried her lip as her heart raced. In a few minutes, she'd see him. What was the plan again? Cool confidence? Yeah. Definitely. Suave sophistication. She'd sling her tool belt over her shoulder, jut out her hip, and say, "Hey, handsome." No. That was ridiculous. She was liable to knock herself out with her hammer doing such a thing.

But no playing it shy, no giving him a clue as to the jumbled mess of nerves balled up inside her. Jaxon liked daring and adventurous. Well, here she was. Halfway around the country doing something she'd never dreamed of. Maybe she could say, "How do you like me now?" Oh, that was good. Shades. She needed to wear her sunglasses and scoot them down slightly when she spoke. Then give a little hair toss. Would that even work with her new do? Or would she look like she had a nervous tic? Okay, nix the head toss. Keep the shades.

What was the rest of her carefully rehearsed speech? She clamored for it in her memory but found nothing. Not a word. She'd have to wing this one. She swallowed hard. Sahara Dawn fly by the seat of her pants? Heavens, no.

But she *had* flown. For the first time in her life, she'd braved the vast, chaotic airport. There'd been entirely too many people in that thing, but she hadn't panicked. No. She'd managed to maneuver through the crowd without bumping into more than a few dozen people, find her way to her gate, and board with her heart rate barely reaching the cardio zone. Her headphones kept the passenger next to her from attempting to carry on a conversation. No matter that she hadn't even bothered to turn on her audiobook with her thoughts whirling. She'd kept a white-knuckled grip on the armrest during takeoff but found herself relaxing enough to do a sudoku. And when the flight attendant wheeled the cart of refreshments down the aisle, what the heck, she ordered a Coke in honor of Jaxon. She hadn't finished the disgusting syrup—it'd been like scooping tablespoons of pure sugar into her mouth—but no matter. It was the thought that counted. And she'd done it. She'd found her wings.

There it was. A big gaping hole near the side of a mountain that begged for Jaxon to fill it with his artistic brilliance. A dozen cars were parked at the far side of the lot. She pulled in beside one and wiped sweaty palms on her skinny jeans. She could do this, right? Nothing more than hammering nails and confronting the empty spaces in a floundering marriage. Easy. The backs of her eyes began to burn. Oh no. No way. No how. She shook her head, snapped open the glove box, and grabbed her lipstick. Using the rearview mirror, she glided it on. Cool confidence. No room for pesky emotions here. This was a construction site. She tossed the lipstick back in the glove compartment and slammed it shut. It was time to roll.

Stepping out of her car, she adjusted her aqua-blue V-necked T-shirt and retrieved the tool belt from the back seat. She snapped it around her waist and made confident strides toward where a group of men gathered. After three steps, she remembered her sunglasses and spun around to grab them. Ready now, she approached the other workers, scanning the area. Where was Jax?

Heads turned as she came near.

"You must be the new guy, er, gal." A stocky, curly-haired kid who looked barely out of high school stuck out his hand. "I'm Miguel."

She took his hand and shook it as panic wedged through her chest. Oh no. What should she say? If she told them her name, they'd know she was Jaxon's wife. Not exactly a common name. They'd know she was here before he did. Not good. He couldn't find out through the other workers. The edge of her mouth twitched. "Dawn."

"Nice to meet you." His dimple testified to the fact he told the truth. He was happy to have her there. Would her husband feel the same way?

"I'm Tony." A young man with a buzz cut gave a small wave, then pointed to the other crew members. "Leo, Chris, Tom, Lucas." One by one, they lifted a finger or hand and smiled. Tony pointed to a middle-aged gentleman a few yards away whose thin muscle shirt did little to hide his protruding middle. The man stared blankly at the empty space in front of him. "That's Gabriel."

"Ah." Point taken. Gabriel was the crazy one. There always had to be a crazy one.

"Jaxon's not on-site yet. We call him Boss Man. He's tough but fair." Tough? Her poetry-loving, spontaneous husband who loved moonlit walks on the beach? Tough to live with, maybe, but tough to work for?

"Oh?"

Tony put a warm hand on her shoulder. "Don't worry. Follow our lead, and you'll be fine."

"I'm not worried. I'm sure I can handle him." Hopefully, the guy couldn't tell her insides quivered like Jell-O.

He dropped his hand. How was that even more awkward? She crossed her arms over her chest. "What's the plan?"

Miguel scrubbed at a nonexistent beard as he spoke. "As you can see, we've already got a foundation laid. Braventon Construction had this gig first. They got all the permits, cleared the land, and poured the foundation. Then the owner changed his mind 'bout what he wanted, and Braventon wouldn't budge from the original agreement, so they terminated the contract."

"And Ja—Frost Construction picked it up?"

"Yep. One dreamer to another. Should be interesting."

What did that mean? "One dreamer …"

Tony splayed a hand in the air in front of him. "We don't just build homes," he started.

The others chimed in, "We build dreams."

"Ah. A motto?" How come she hadn't heard it before?

"More like a mantra." Miguel smirked.

Tony smacked him lightly on the arm. "And if Emmerson changes his mind a dozen times after we've already started to build, and if we have to readjust our plans over and over again, Boss Man will say—"

"We're chasing the dream," Miguel finished.

And that was her cue to leave. To go home, and not to the hotel she'd stayed in last night. Rhonda had asked if she wanted a temporary apartment near the other workers from out of town, but naturally, she'd stay with Jax. Once he knew she was here. But now she should flee. Because an ever-changing agenda sounded like pure torture.

The men laughed and turned toward the makeshift worktables and concrete slab. "Better get to work," one of them—was it Santiago?—said.

Sahara's feet remained frozen in place.

Miguel stopped a yard or so ahead of her and looked back. "Come on. It's not so bad."

Oh, great. She must have looked as terrified as she felt. What happened to suave sophistication?

"The constant changes can drive you crazy, but we get paid by the hour. Who cares? We do what Boss Man says and collect at the end of the week."

Yeah, okay. She forced breath into her lungs. Fresh, clean mountain air. Thin, but pure. The scent of pine lingered in the air. There were worse places to be. She could do this. She walked forward and fell into step beside Miguel.

He gave her a knowing glance. "You new to the trade?"

"Newish."

He grinned. "Yeah, okay."

"What?"

"It's gonna get hot. You might want to wear cargo pants."

She shrugged.

He stifled a laugh. "And your makeup might melt."

She scoffed.

He spread his hands out in front of him and grinned wide. "Just sayin'."

They approached a giant metal box and he threw her a vest from inside. "For the lady." Power saws turned. He handed her a pair of safety glasses. Oh yeah. Forget the suave shades, then. Dorky work goggles it was. "I know. They're a pain, but Boss Man is big on safety protocols."

She nearly spit out a laugh but covered it with a cough. Her Jaxon? Concerned with safety? The man who wanted to cliff dive for their fifth anniversary. Were they talking about the same guy?

Miguel tossed her a hard hat. "Grab a nail gun, and let's get framing."

Framing. Yeah. She'd read about that. "Let's do it." Wait, what had he said? A nail … gun? She fingered the hammer that hung from her tool belt.

He had already taken a few steps toward the work area. She peered into the box. What did a nail gun look like? She sneaked a glance at Miguel to ascertain what was in his hand, but it was hard to tell from that angle. She picked one up. Was this contraption what she needed? No, that had to be some kind of a saw. What about this thing?

"You don't know what a nail gun is, do you?" Miguel's voice startled her, and her hip jammed against the side of the box. His mouth tipped in a half smile.

She rocked back on her heels. "I normally work the old-fashioned way. Good ole hammer and nails." She flashed a grin. Was he convinced?

"Well, unless you want this project to take over a year, you'll need one of these." He hefted a tool that looked somewhat like a drill with a metal bar attached to it and handed it to her. Her biceps protested under the weight. What in the world? The thing weighed a ton. She was supposed to lug that gun around all day? Completely impractical.

"You load the nails like this." He grabbed a nail rack and demonstrated how to insert it into the gun.

She patted her tool belt. "But I brought my own nails."

She pulled a few out to show him. Their red tips gleamed in the sunlight. Galvanized, they were called, and she'd spent over two hours researching them. This brand of nails got the highest reviews on three trusted sites. They were said to increase job-site efficiency. The ones Miguel had loaded weren't color-coated and, therefore, not galvanized. Leave it to her husband to neglect his research.

"Those loose nails are fine to use here and there, but these racks work with the guns."

Okay, then. She'd make a trip to the hardware store during her first break to find galvanized nails that came in those rack thingies.

~

Four hours in, and it was as if she'd taken a shower in her clothes. Sweat trickled down the back of her neck like an ever-dripping faucet. At least she'd accomplished something. The mud sill was down, and they'd started on the floor joists on the left wing of the house.

During a break two hours ago, she'd rushed to the hardware store and found exactly what she needed. The red-tipped nails packaged especially for nail guns. She'd zipped back and attacked those boards with renewed gusto. She was now increasing job-site efficiency. Good for her.

She managed not to stand out as the lone dimwit who had never used a nail gun before. It helped that the guys were too busy teasing each other to pay much attention to her. Save an occasional query into how she was coming along, no one seemed to notice her, much less scrutinize her work. Good thing. Those first few dozen nails didn't go in too smoothly, but she was getting the hang of things now.

And probably looked like a sweaty pig.

The sound of gravel crunching stole her attention from the task at hand. Shoot. Ouch. The nail clipped the side of her thumb. She bit her lip to keep from crying out.

Jaxon's electric blue Jeep pulled into her line of sight, and her stomach dropped. Her nail gun fell with a clatter. He parked and hopped out, surveying the area with a wide smile. Sahara ducked her head, pulse throbbing in her neck. She angled away from him as her breath caught. She should hide. Where could she hide?

"Hey, Boss Man!" Tony's voice called out. "We've made good progress."

"I can see that."

"We got a new crew member."

"I heard."

Oh no. Oh no. They walked toward her. *Think, Sahara. Think.* What had she planned to say?

Tony's attempt to lower his voice flopped. "It's a woman. Dawn."

Crunch. Crunch.

"Really? Rhonda didn't mention that."

With only seconds to spare, Sahara swallowed, straightened, and pasted on a confident smile. She spun around and looked into wide eyes. Goodness, if those baby blues didn't still send shockwaves pulsing through her. He had no right to be that attractive.

"Hi, Jax."

His mouth parted. He tilted his head.

Tony froze, looking back and forth between them. "You know each other?"

Jaxon threw up a hand but didn't break eye contact with Sahara. "Give us a minute, will you?"

"Sure thing, Boss Man." Tony backed away, brows raised.

"What are you doing here?" His voice held question, not accusation exactly, but neither did it hold welcome.

She held her smile. "Framing."

"Framing?" Why was he looking at her like she'd said she was hunting for aliens?

"Yep."

He pressed his lips together and stared at her. Opened his mouth as if he were about to say something, then closed it again. Shook his head. Blew out a breath. Ran his hand through his hair. Opened his mouth again, but no words came forth. The man was exasperating.

"Look, you wouldn't come to me, so I came to you."

"This is—"

"Completely impractical. Oh, I know."

There. The tiniest lift to the corner of his mouth.

"What did you do to your hair?"

Her hand instinctively went to graze the ends of her cut. "Do you like it?"

"I can't believe you do."

She shrugged. What did that matter?

"How long are you here for?"

She narrowed her eyes. "As long as it takes."

"What about our house?"

"My house."

"Our house." He crossed his arms and hardened his stance.

"I think for it to be considered your house too, you'd have to stay in it."

"I help pay the mortgage. It's as much my house as yours."

"When you come home, I'll concede."

"Will you answer my question?"

"I'm renting it out as an Airbnb. Myra's managing things."

"What about your job?"

"I'll work a couple accounts remotely in the evenings."

"You'll stay until this is finished?" He tossed a glance over his shoulder to the foundation behind him.

"I'll stay until you come home."

"If you stay until it's finished, I'll come home."

She worked her jaw. Sounded fair. "Promise?"

"Promise."

She stuck out her hand. "Deal."

He shook it, firm and strong. All business. Her heart twisted. He turned to walk away but spun back around. "One more thing."

She blinked back at him.

He spread his arms out around him. "This is my domain. Here, *I'm* always right."

Oh, it pierced like a knife. But she nodded.

"Great. Glad to have you on board, *Dawn*."

She reached inside her to push another suave, sophisticated smile to the surface. "Call me Sahara."

~

Jaxon's insides shook as he turned and walked away from Sahara. Sahara? Here? His mind reeled. It took everything in him to keep his shoulders square, his expression confident. His crew needed a strong leader. The success of this job depended on him being who he'd fully become in this environment— decisive, sure of himself, someone people could and would follow. He could not collapse under the pressure of his wife's penetrating gaze.

Why did she have to come and slam his past life into his new one? Why did she have to stand there as a bleak, dark spot in the middle of his bright new life? A glaring reminder of his biggest failure.

Miguel sidled up next to him, brows raised skyward.

He firmed his jaw. "Don't ask."

Miguel's wide eyes portrayed innocence. "Wouldn't dream of prying into your personal business."

"Of course, you wouldn't." But the man had to be dying to know what in the world was going on. Who this new team member was, how he knew her, and why on earth tension seeped from their interaction? "She doesn't know a thing about construction."

"I gathered that. She didn't know how to handle a nail gun."

He let out a humorless laugh.

"But you're keeping her on, Boss Man?"

He shouldn't. No good businessman in his right mind who had a top-notch crew would jeopardize this important project by bringing on a novice. One mistake could cost them big time. Not to mention the fact he'd have work with his insides in a knot for eight months. Moments ago he'd been carefree, basking in this place and time where he'd found the success he'd always craved. Now, it was as if a storm cloud blew in and parked itself directly over his head. He should have sent her home the moment she opened her mouth.

Why hadn't he? And why on earth did he encourage her to stick it out for the entire project? His gut twisted. She'd spun the thinnest thread of hope, and he, like a fool, had grasped onto it. The faintest whisper of *what if* echoed. What if things could be different? What if, when she saw him here at the top of his game, she finally respected him? What if she finally opened up to him? Stupid, really. After this many years and so much rejection, he was an utter fool to open himself up to that again. Hadn't she hurt him enough? He was done trying. Done. Still …

"Boss Man?"

What? Oh yeah. Miguel had asked a question. He shook himself from the deluge of thoughts. "Yeah, I'm keeping her on. For now."

He could see how things went. Give it a fair trial. If at any time, he didn't like the direction things were headed, he could send her home. Fire her. He was the boss after all.

The edge of his mouth twitched. After twelve years, the woman had chopped off her hair. His hand itched to run through it, feel the difference. The beauty that struck him when he'd first met her had only grown throughout the years. Pain knifed through him. Loving her felt like death. Easier from a distance. Much harder up close. Even as he positioned himself as far away from her as he could, his senses heightened in awareness of her presence. Could he even do this? Keep his head on straight with her near? With a knife plunging into his heart? He might bleed out.

~

Sahara spun around and let her fake smile drop as Jaxon walked away. Well, that had gone … how had it gone? He hadn't sent her packing. But neither had he swept her away in a breathless kiss. He'd shaken her hand—*shaken her hand*—and all she'd felt was his cool palm against her sweaty one. Weren't there supposed to be tingles or sparks or something? Then again, when had there ever been?

She toed the ground with her boot. That wasn't fair. They hadn't started out intoxicated on love—or she hadn't—and they certainly weren't there now, but there was that sweet spot in the middle. That time when she'd let her guard down enough for him to rope her into glow-in-the-dark zip-lining. She'd screamed her brains out, and then he caught her behind a tree and kissed her senseless. Tingles? Sparks? More like flames.

Or that time they'd played paintball and she'd feigned injury. He came to her, concerned she was hurt, only to have her ambush him. But as he gripped his chest, hamming up the mock betrayal, something flipped inside her. Suddenly, she didn't care who won, who lost, who took home a trophy. She only needed him, his mouth on hers, his hands in her hair. She scaled the barricade and toppled over, right on top of him, slamming him to the ground.

"Wrong sport," he'd eked out.

She'd laughed. They'd kissed. And kept kissing until their teammates found them. A roaring bonfire of heat.

They'd had that once. When had things changed?

Sighing, she grabbed her nail gun and set back to work. It didn't matter. All that mattered was getting things back to where they needed to be. Building—or rebuilding—a marriage couldn't be much different from building a house. A sequence of systematic steps would lead to a desired outcome. One board at a time. One nail at a time.

She could do this.

Their lunch break came and went, and Jaxon didn't say another word to her. She'd brought a chef salad in her cooler and ate it in the back of Tony's pickup with a couple of the guys who scarfed down pastrami on rye and ham and cheese sandwiches. He was avoiding her. It couldn't be more obvious. He wouldn't even glance in her direction. Though Miguel stuck closer by her now, peeking over her shoulder and surveying her work. Jax must have told him to keep an eye on her. He probably didn't trust her not to mess up his precious project. Didn't he know how capable she was? Then again, if he was truly concerned, he'd toss her out of there. That'd be preferable to this hold-her-at-a-distance cold shoulder routine.

She wiped her damp brow with a napkin and guzzled nearly half of a bottled water. If he was going to be like that, she'd have to be more direct.

Tomorrow.

She'd give him a minute to adjust first.

"So," Miguel said as he brushed chip crumbs from his hands, "how do you know Boss Man?"

She ran her tongue over her teeth. Okay, yeah. This had to come out eventually. "That's easy. We're married."

Miguel coughed. Tony threw back his head and laughed. A string of Spanish ensued, followed by a chorus of nervous chuckles and unbelieving statements.

"No way. You're the wife?" Gabriel, who had stood by the pickup, came and peered over the side of it at her.

She put both hands out in front of her. "That's me."

Gabriel's bushy brows knit together. "You're what he's running from? A pretty little thing like you?"

Miguel glared at the older man. "Boss Man's not runnin'."

Gabriel scoffed. "What do you know? You're not even old enough to shave. He's running for sure. Just don't know why." He eyed her with suspicion.

Sahara wiggled under his scrutiny.

"Don't listen to him." Tony flicked a dismissive look in his direction. "Your husband's a genius at this stuff." He waved a hand toward the infantile structure beside them. "He's in high demand. More and more people will see what he can do, and they'll beat down his doors, beg him to build them homes." He took a swig of Gatorade. "He's not running away from anything. He's running toward a bright future." He flashed her a smile before hopping off the truck bed.

Miguel stuffed left over wrappers and paper into an empty bag. Sahara tucked her Tupperware back into her cooler and then gathered other trash to help.

"He didn't tell us you were coming."

She lifted a shoulder. "He didn't know. I surprised him."

"Quite a surprise, huh?" His gaze scanned the distance between Jaxon and Sahara. A gulf. A chasm.

Her lip quivered. "Not everyone likes surprises." Only, Jaxon did. He loved surprises, big ones, little ones. Presents and gatherings. She was the one who didn't like being taken aback. He loved everything spontaneous. Unless the spontaneous gift was … her.

Miguel offered a small, kind smile. "He'll come around."

"I hope so." Because if he didn't, she might forget what it felt like to ever be loved at all.

~

Sahara's anxiety increased the closer it came to the end of the day. When the guys packed up their things, her heart rate kicked up a notch. She took her time gathering her tools and kept an eye on Jaxon the entire time.

Miguel, the only other worker left on-site, had just climbed into his Jeep when Jaxon finally strode to her.

The backdrop of the sunset and the mountains behind her husband nearly took her breath away. He looked at home here, in this majestic place with peaks as high as his dreams. His sunglasses covered those piercing blue eyes. Completely unfair. He could see through her, but she couldn't do the same to him.

"How'd you get here?" His brow furrowed. She stuck her hands in her pockets to keep from tracing the lines on his forehead with her fingers like she used to.

She held back a beam of pride. This was cool, sophisticated Sahara. The one who racked up frequent flyer miles like loyalty points to the container store. "I flew."

"You flew?"

She nodded.

"In a plane?"

She let the corners of her mouth tip upward only slightly. "Cheaper than a hot-air balloon ride for a two-thousand-mile jaunt, so yes."

What? Not even a half smile?

"You know Dreamboat wouldn't have made the drive."

A breath of a laugh. Something at least. "How are you getting around here?"

"I bought a used car off Craigslist. Figure I can clean it up. Flip it when I leave. A business deal."

"You bought a—" He shaded his eyes and scanned the parking lot. He cursed under his breath. "You've got to be kidding me. How old is it?"

"It's an '89."

"You don't know the first thing about cars."

She held up a finger. "Correction. I didn't know the first thing about cars. After inundating myself with YouTube videos, I know perhaps the first and second things about cars. Not much more than that, but I do know it runs, and the engine is not smoking. Currently."

"If you would have let me buy you a—"

"I would have missed out on an educational flight experience." He stared at her. Shook his head. Opened his mouth. She beat him to it. "I'm fine, really."

He folded his arms across his chest. "You've got a place to stay, right? Rhonda set you up?"

She instinctively stepped back. What was he saying? "Well, yeah, but—"

"Good. I don't want you to sleep in some shady hotel to save a few bucks."

A hot lump formed at the base of her throat. "Jaxon, I'm your wife."

"Yeah." His gaze landed on his wedding band and lingered.

"I thought … I assumed I'd stay with you."

He exhaled deep and long. Stupid shades. She should rip them off his face right now. Then maybe she'd be able to see a hint of connection in those eyes. Longing. Regret. Something.

"I'm not ready for that, Sahara."

Her jaw dropped. "Not ready? We've been married nearly twelve years, and you're not ready to live with me?"

"Give me a break. You completely bulldozed me here. I had no clue about any of this." He waved a hand in her direction. "You can't expect me to jump on board your ship just like that." He snapped his fingers.

"*My* ship? Oh, excuse me. I thought it was *our* marriage. *Our* ship."

"You have always had an agenda all your own. And Lord help anyone who gets in your way."

"So, don't get in my way." Why did this man have to be so difficult?

"Look where you're standing, sweetheart." He spit the pet name out with as much affection as a rival sports team. "I think this would qualify as *you* getting in *my* way."

His words hit her like a punch to the gut. She winced. That's all she was to him, then? A nuisance? A pesky interference? She ran her tongue over gritted teeth.

"I'll stay in the hotel tonight and contact Rhonda about the apartment in the morning." She spun around and stomped to her car. Gravel crunched under her steps. Blood rushed in her ears. She pressed her lips together so tight they were surely white. With each step, she willed him to call out to her, stop her, apologize. Take her in his arms. *Come on, Jaxon. Fight for me.*

But no voice came. As she pulled away, she glanced in the rearview mirror to see him standing where she'd left him, a cold, immovable mountain where the man who'd loved her had once been.

~

She was on her third cup of coffee when she pulled onto the construction site the next morning. Because she hadn't slept more than thirty fitful minutes at a time, she needed the caffeine to pry her eyelids open. A heartbroken, sleep-deprived amateur with a nail gun. What could go wrong?

As soon as she exited her vehicle, it became clear something was, indeed, wrong. Every head snapped in her direction and all conversation ceased. She'd expected Jaxon to continue to ignore her today, but he stormed in her direction. She braced herself against her car door. She felt dozens of eyes on them. Oh gosh. Public confrontation. Could she make a run for it? Hide … where? Behind that tree?

"ACQ-approved nails, Sahara."

She stared back at his reddened face with wide eyes. What was he talking about?

"You can only use ACQ-approved nails when you're working with ACQ lumber."

She bit her lip. "AC …?"

He threw up his hands. "Alkaline copper quaternary. Did you not come across that term in your *research*?" He used air quotes. Rude. "The mud sill is made of treated lumber. You used standard framing nails, which will corrode when they come into contact with ACQ lumber."

Oh. Shoot.

"What I don't understand is why. Miguel gave you the proper nails."

She grimaced. "I thought I'd use my own. That I bought." She needed to stop talking. Now. Before she told him her nails got better reviews. Something told her he wouldn't be impressed.

"Well, your little stunt set us back because now we have to go back over all those spots with the correct ones."

She swallowed. "I'll do that. I'll fix it."

He huffed. "I'm afraid to let you anywhere near it."

"Please. I might have things to learn, but I can do this." She could do anything. Right?

He let out a humorless laugh. "I should fire you."

She narrowed her eyes. Was he talking about the job only? Or about their marriage as well? Had she messed up one too many times for both?

"I can fix it." Her whisper contained every ounce of fierce determination she could muster. She stuffed all other emotion underneath it. "Give me another chance."

"I'm not sure you deserve it."

Irrelevant. She stared him down.

His shoulders drooped a fraction of an inch. "Fine. But I'm going to have Miguel babysit you while you replace every single nail."

Miguel. Babysit her? She was nearly old enough to be his mother. She bit back her snarky responses and nodded.

Was that a glint in his eye? The brat. He enjoyed this. "The men around here normally say, 'Yes, Boss Man,' when I give them an order."

She shifted her jaw. "I bet they do."

He took a step closer. She caught a whiff of his woodsy cologne, and her heart skidded to a stop. Oh, heavens. Why the torture?

"Why don't you try it?"

Try what? Oh, yeah. The *Yes, Boss Man* thing. She coughed to dislodge the scent and past memories. "That was a statement, not an order."

He raised a brow.

"You said you'd have Miguel babysit me while I replaced the nails. You didn't ask a question, and you didn't give a command."

He crossed his arms and rocked back on his heels. The eagle tattoo peeked out from underneath his sleeve. Her stomach wobbled.

"Get over there and start replacing the nails, Sahara."

The men whispered and jested in the background.

Nerves taut and mind screaming, she forced a stiff smile and saluted. "Yes, Boss Man." She pivoted and turned her gaze to the group of gawking guys, who quickly averted their eyes and busied themselves with their work. She made a beeline toward Miguel and hooked her arm through his elbow. "Come on, babysitter. Do your job."

~

After shooting plain, stupid ungalvanized nails next to her beautiful high-quality ones, a long soak in the hotel tub sounded heavenly. Yes, the hotel tub, because she couldn't bring herself to call Rhonda about hooking her up with the apartment. Not yet. Jaxon needed time to adjust to the idea of her being here, that's all. He'd come around. She'd bide her time at the hotel another night or so until he did.

A long soak and a good book, that was what she needed. Too bad *The Power of Charm: How to Win Anyone Over in Any Situation* wouldn't arrive until tomorrow night after six o'clock. She normally didn't give much credence to any book with less than a 4.4 rating on Goodreads, but this one sounded promising.

Or maybe she was desperate.

She could *not* lose the battle for her husband's heart. She could not.

Her wounded pride smarted. To think she'd been about to ask Jaxon to go to dinner with her tonight. Nix that plan. He thought of her more like a child than a dinner date. Her shoulders sagged as she stacked her tools in the job box. She needed to get her head on straight before she even attempted to talk to the exasperating man again.

"You did good today." Miguel removed his hard hat and wiped sweat from his brow.

She tried for a smile. "I'm pretty good at fixing things I mess up." Was it even true? Sure didn't seem like she was making any strides in repairing her broken marriage.

Miguel looked from her to Jaxon, where he stood conversing with Gabriel. "He didn't fire you. Says something."

"Maybe." Looking at the man sent a pang through her. Her gaze dropped to her boots. "I'd better go. Thanks. Have a good night." She tossed her hard hat into the box and nearly sprinted to the car.

"Sahara."

Jaxon's voice stopped her in her tracks. Her heart hammered as she turned. Two car lengths stood between them. An abyss. The air swirled. Tousled his hair. Tossed hers. His clear blue eyes were softer now. The corner of his mouth lifted a fraction. It was enough.

A flitter of hope filled her chest.

"Good job." He sounded … sincere.

Her own gentle smile bloomed. "Sure thing." Her words came out husky. She pushed the next ones out with more strength. "Boss Man." She spun around and slipped into her car.

When she glanced in the rearview mirror, he stared in her direction. Maybe she wasn't so easily forgotten after all.

Chapter 10

Bernie
June 1861
A month later

Bernie crept through the woods back toward the tent she shared with Walter and Barneby. She'd excused herself to use the privy, then hightailed it to the far end of the creek—an area secluded by trees and brush. Far enough from camp that she could nearly—nearly—take a full, relaxed breath as she washed herself, her shirt, and the bandages that bound her chest. Still, despite the distance, she kept glancing over her shoulder. Kept willing her rapid pulse to slow. Her ears stood as sentinels, listening for the slightest noise to alert her of an intruder. Thankfully, the only rustle of leaves had been from a squirrel, and she'd left the area a far cry fresher than she'd come. It was a wonder the men didn't fall over dead at their own stench.

She'd grown accustomed to a great many things she'd have shuddered at months ago. Words that once would have set her ears on fire were so common to her now that she barely noticed them. Men spit tobacco juice inches from her foot, and she didn't as much as flinch. And the vulgar way they talked about women! But the sour smell of hundreds of unwashed bodies, rank with sweat, still twisted her stomach.

As she slinked over twigs and brush, through oaks and maples, a low cadence of voices pricked her ears. She slowed her steps. The voices didn't come from the direction of camp, but from the woods to her right.

"Massa thinks I be fine diggin' ditches. He thinks I haven't a lick of sense in my head to be able to tell what this war is really about."

Bernie's breath caught. Were these Sammy Cutchington's slaves? The ones he'd brought with him to help with the war effort? In the distance, a faint orange glow shone. A fire, no doubt. Were they cooking a meal? But why out here? She stilled and inclined her ear in their direction.

"Soon as we get in spitting distance of them Yankees, I'm hightailin' it out of here. I'll fall on my knees before Lincoln himself and beg for my freedom."

"And he'll give it to you. That's for sure. He'll give it to the lot of us, you wait and see. Mr. Lincoln is a good man. He knows 'bout our suffering. He's Moses come to lead us to our promised land."

The sun sank lower through the trees, and Bernie could just make out two forms sitting on what appeared to be a log, bent over a soft glow. Slaves. She'd never heard any speak so freely before, never been around many, truth be told. Her family had never owned any, and Hermann's family certainly hadn't, with him being from up north. They were far too poor to own a slave. But if they'd had the means, would they? She'd never thought of it before. Never had reason to.

When one was born and raised a South Carolinian, owning slaves was as natural as breathing air. And one did not question breathing.

"You almost finished?"

The chirping of crickets was the only reply.

"Bob, I said, you almost finished?"

"Oh. Yes. Sorry. Got caught up in a freedom dream, I guess."

A soft chuckle. "Soon, it'll be more than a dream. Finish them beans, now. We best get back before Massa be missin' us."

A scraping and clanging sound ensued, probably a utensil against a tin can.

"They can fight to keep us in bondage, Abram, but we're gonna break free."

"That's right. It's comin'."

"Freedom's comin'."

A hiss and sizzle sliced the air as they extinguished the fire. Their voices and footsteps trailed off. Bernie stood, as if frozen in place.

Fight to keep them in bondage? Is that what she was doing? She pressed her lips together. No. Of course not. She'd joined the war to find her husband. Not a bone in her body wanted to aid the cause of slavery. This war wasn't about such for her. Maybe for others, but not for her. Her sole focus was on Hermann's heart. On their marriage. Their dreams together. On sheltering that ember lest it snuff out with the wild winds of war.

Uncertainty snaked through her middle as she looked down at her uniform. Weren't her efforts, however noble, advancing "the cause" that those men spoke against? Those *men*. Something lit in her chest at that word. Because she'd never been close enough to dark-skinned people to understand the difference. They'd always been *slaves* to her. But there, standing hidden by shadows mere feet away, she'd seen not slaves but *men*.

People. Who had dreams for their future just as she had for hers. People whom others thought unintelligent but who seemed mighty sharp to her. Bob and Abram. Two men whose masters dragged them along and forced them to dig trenches to keep her safe in this war while she fought to keep them enslaved. A wave of nausea crested. She leaned over and vomited on moss and leaves. She straightened. Pressed the back of her hand against her trembling mouth.

No. She would not blame herself. Their predicament wasn't her fault. She was only one woman. She had no bearing on the outcome of this war. The only thing that mattered was finding Hermann and bringing him, and his heart, home in one piece. Let everything else be counted as a casualty of war.

~

July 1861
A month later

"Whoo-hoo! Pack your bag, Bernie. We're finally gonna get to see action." Walter loped into the tent wearing a goofy grin.

Bernie grumbled and threw an arm over her eyes to block the sun's glare. "I've heard that before."

There'd been rumors of the regiment moving out for a month, but they'd yet to leave camp. Every day brought the same monotony. Drilling. Then feeble attempts to pass the time with cards, games, and pranks. Everyone was restless. Most looked forward to battle. At least they could pass the time writing letters to loved ones and reading missives from home. Mail call was a sacred time of the day. For everyone but her. Had Hermann written to her at the farm? Was he worried that she hadn't written back?

"This time, it's for certain. We're headed out bright and early tomorrow. Hope you like Virginia."

"Never been."

"That's about to change." He whooped. "Let's go spank some Yanks!" He galloped out, shouting up a storm, and the tent flap fell closed.

Bernie dropped her arm from her face to her middle. Did it feel thicker than before? If anything, it seemed she'd lost weight. No surprise with such meager rations. But if that was the case, why did her britches seem to fit better than they did at the start? Or was it only her imagination? Most days, she tried not to think about the possibility of a stowaway under her uniform. Hard to do when there was little action to occupy her mind. But now they were moving toward battle, toward danger. Would she be moving a baby with her?

Perhaps this was another rumor. Maybe they weren't moving at all. She heaved a sigh. No, that wasn't what she wanted. She had to find Hermann, and the only way to do so was to move toward a battle. That was where other regiments would be. That was where she'd find him. Certainly not napping in her tent.

If she was with child, the best course of action would be to find Hermann and tell him. Surely, he'd see reason to take leave. They both could take leave and … never come back.

Being branded as deserters tasted like bile in her mouth. She wasn't a quitter. Yet, what did she feel about this war anyhow? Because the other scenario running through her mind—winning a decisive victory at this battle in Virginia that ended the war and brought all soldiers home—didn't sit well with her either when the faces of Bob and Abram crested to the forefront.

~

After eleven days of marching, General Greenman informed them they'd arrived at Manassas, Virginia. Relief pooled in her chest when the general allowed them to rest as several colonels and generals conferred. A light breeze provided a reprieve from the heat, though the sun barreled down on them. Soldiers from other companies milled about, some lying on the grass, some tossing a baseball, some bent over paper writing letters to home.

Bernie leaned back on her elbows, stretching her legs out in front of her. She rolled her neck back and forth, attempting to ease her stiff muscles. As her head turned right, a soldier caught her eye. One sitting slumped against a tree. She squinted to make him out more clearly. There was something different about him. Something almost as familiar as her own kitchen. She pushed herself to standing. Stretched. Walked a few steps closer.

Did she know him? That was a dangerous thought, for if she knew him, he would recognize her. Could blow her charade. But it wasn't that kind of familiar. She couldn't pin it down, but … no, she'd never seen this person before. And yet …

She closed the distance between them. Crouched. Stuck out her hand. "Hello. I'm Bernie."

The soldier's gaze snapped to hers, brows pinched as if he, too, was trying to figure out a riddle. "Henry."

She took the soldier's hand, and her breath hitched. It hid in the smoothness behind the rough worn callouses. She searched the face, the eyes. Eyes that studied her in much the same way. The lines around the sides of this soldier's eyes and mouth were distinctly … feminine. Could it be? She swallowed. What if she was wrong? What if she'd misjudged and this was a young, clean-faced boy? But a wave of longing to be known crested in her throat and overrode any fear lodged there.

"Bernie," she said again, still holding the soldier's hand in her own. Then she lowered her voice. "Bernice."

Her heart thudded in her ears and seconds stretched. The soldier's eyes rounded. Bernie's stomach plummeted. Oh no. Oh goodness. What had she done?

The soldier leaned forward a fraction and whispered, "Henrietta."

A mixture of a laugh and a sob bubbled up from within her. She clasped a hand over her mouth, glancing around to see if anyone looked on. But everyone else seemed occupied elsewhere. She lowered to her knees next to her new friend.

"I can't believe it," she said. "I didn't think I'd find anyone else …"

One side of Henrietta's mouth tipped in a smile. "There are more of us out there than you'd think. I've met three others already, not including you."

"No?"

"I promise you. You're not alone."

The back of Bernie's eyes burned with that statement. Oh, how she needed to hear that. She'd felt nothing but alone these past couple of months away from home. Away from Hermann. Away from everything familiar and safe. She blinked quickly to push back the threat of tears.

"I've so wanted someone to talk to."

"Tired of trying to be one of the boys?" Henrietta plucked a blade of grass and ran it through her fingers.

Bernie twisted her lips. Could she divulge her secret without giving in to tears? But it pushed hot against her chest. How could she keep it in? "I haven't had my monthly since I enlisted. I fear I might be … fear is not the proper word … but what if I am w-with child?"

Henrietta's gaze filled with compassion. Compassion. What a precious resource such a thing was. She soaked it up, feeling it penetrate portions of her heart that had grown brittle during the past weeks. "I stopped having my cycles, and I assure you it's not for maternal reasons. I've heard the rigor of army life and lack of nourishment can do that to a woman."

Bernie frowned. "Yes, I heard that as well. I wish I could know for sure."

"I suppose time will tell."

Bernie nodded, though disappointment billowed. What had she hoped? That this fellow woman soldier was also a doctor? That she could do an examination and give Bernie the needed assurance? Still, her shoulders felt a mite lighter from having shared the burden, even if there was nothing that could be done about it.

"You married, then?" Henrietta squinted against the sun's glare. "You one of them gals who couldn't stand to be away from your beau? Had to follow him into the ravages of war?"

Not exactly. Her reasons for enlisting had expansive roots. But she answered with, "Something like that. You?"

"Nah. I'm not married. Not yet. My family needed money, and this seemed to be the surest bet in being able to send some back to them."

"They know about your ruse?"

"Sure do. Weren't too happy 'bout it at first, but the money helps. They don't complain anymore." She grinned, then cast a glance around the yard. "Where's your husband?"

Her shoulders sagged. "Not here. He signed up with Tuffle's Brigade. I'm hunting for him. Figure my best chance of reconnecting will be in battle."

"Where are you from?"

"South Carolina."

"I'll keep an ear out for divisions from South Carolina."

"Thanks."

"Henry!" A man waved his cap over his head, snatching their attention.

Henry waved back.

"We're about to have a tobacco spitting contest. You in?"

"You bet I am." Henrietta grinned.

Bernie sputtered. "You? In a tobacco spitting contest?"

Henrietta stood and brushed off her backside. "You got to blend in, don't ya? I've gotten quite good. Won me a pretty penny at these matches. Want to participate?"

Bernie laughed. "I've never chewed tobacco in my life."

"I'll have to teach you later." And with a wink, Henrietta jogged off to join a group of men that had gathered.

Later. Thank goodness there was a later to be had. Time to forge a friendship with this woman who knew what it took for the battle at hand.

Chapter 11

"FIRE AND ICE" BY ROBERT FROST

Sahara
Present Day
Provo, Utah

Who would have thought two words could be so powerful? Yet, Sahara lived off the power of "Good job" for nearly twenty-four hours. When nerves ping-ponged around inside her at the prospect of asking him to dinner, she replayed those two words, and the chaos settled. She could do this. She could be so utterly delightful Jaxon would fall madly back in love with her. He wouldn't be able to stand being away from her another minute. Yes. She could be irresistible.

She waited until everyone else left before she sauntered up to Jaxon. Just in case he did reject her, no need for an audience. But he wouldn't, would he?

He was rolling up a set of blueprints as she approached. She smiled at him. "Hey."

"Hey."

"What are you doing for dinner?"

"Cooking."

"Cooking?"

"I make a pretty good chimichanga."

Her smile wobbled. "I remember." Memories flashed of candlelit dinners in their dining room. Him cooking. Them dining, then dancing. Then … Her cheeks warmed. She shook herself from the bittersweet scene. "I want to take you out to dinner tonight. There's a Peruvian restaurant I want to try."

He raised a brow. "Peruvian?"

She nodded, straight-faced. "My treat. My boss doesn't pay great, but I can afford a dinner out."

His mouth tipped.

"I hear they have octopus."

"Octopus." So, they were doing the thing where he repeated her every word?

"Someone recommended I try it." Several times, actually. Jaxon had bribed and nearly begged her to take a small bite to see if she liked it, but that was one thing she'd never do, even for him. Until now.

The corners of his eyes crinkled. "This I've got to see."

"Yes? You'll come?"

"I'll go to dinner with you."

"That's all I'm asking." For now.

"Text me the address. I'll meet you there in an hour."

"You got it, Boss Man." She held herself together until safely out of his line of sight. Then she did a happy shuffle. She had herself a date.

~

Sahara sat in the booth across from her husband and perused the menu, trying not to notice how awkward the entire situation felt. It should be normal, going out to dinner with the man she'd been married to for twelve years. The mixture of tension and butterflies was odd. Was it more tension or butterflies? Perhaps sixty-three percent tension, thirty-seven percent butterflies. Did he feel the same thing? A glance told her he was looking at her and not his menu. Staring at her, not as if he was smitten, but as if she were a curiosity.

She swigged down a gulp of water. Coughed. Pointed at the laminated sheet in front of her. "Where's the octopus on this menu? Do you see it?"

He folded his hands on the table in front of him. "You, a small-town girl from coastal South Carolina, came all the way to Utah to eat octopus? You could throw a rock out of our bedroom window and hit an octopus on the head."

"That's a gross exaggeration."

"Oh, really? Like a ninety-three percent exaggeration?"

"Don't mock me." On second glance, yeah, nothing on the menu looked edible. Wonderful. Well, she'd hold her nose and gag it down if she had to. She'd eat anything, do anything, if it meant she'd have her husband back with her where he belonged. "Fine. You want me to try something Utahonian? What do they eat out here? Buffalo? Wildebeest? Bear? Mountain lion? What's the craziest item on the menu? Bring it on."

The waitress stopped by to take their drink orders. Jaxon ordered a chicha, whatever that was. She ordered a sweet tea.

As the waitress breezed away, Jaxon narrowed his eyes at Sahara. "A sweet tea? As in, they control the amount of sugar in the tea, not you? I feel faint."

"Might as well go all out. What was your order?"

"A juice infusion with dry purple corn, pineapple, cinnamon, and lime."

Okay, yeah. He made her branching out look lame.

Uncomfortable silence hovered. Around them, silverware clinked. Laughter sprinkled throughout the restaurant. Her stomach lurched. She needed something to fill the void between them, so she blurted out the lines she'd memorized.

> Wild Nights – Wild Nights!
> Were I with thee
> Wild Nights should be
> Our luxury!
> Futile – the Winds –
> To a Heart in port –
> Done with the Compass –
> Done with the Chart!
> Rowing in Eden –
> Ah, the Sea!
> Might I but moor – tonight –
> In Thee!

She bit her lip. Did she get it right? She'd stayed up far past her bedtime memorizing it.

He blinked back at her. "You're throwing down Emily Dickinson now?"

She shrugged. "It's not Robert Frost, but it'll do."

Wait, why didn't he look pleased?

"Who are you?"

"Excuse me?"

"You're trying too hard, Sahara. I don't like this pining, grasping version of you. Grappling for a sliver of light from a cracked window."

A what now?

He spun a finger around in a circle. "This whole thing is ridiculous." He stood, fished out his wallet, and threw a twenty on the table.

Her jaw dropped. "I said I was paying."

"It's not for you. That's a tip for the waiter."

"A twenty-dollar tip?"

He leaned over and braced his palms on the table. "Yes, because he does his job. He hasn't messed anything up."

"Okay, ouc—"

"And he hasn't barged in on someone else's job and distracted them from the very important thing they're supposed to be doing. So, yes. He gets a tip. And my highest praises."

Jaxon spun around and stormed out. Sahara dug out another twenty and slid it on the table before following. She caught up with him as he pushed his way outside the double doors into the fresh air, much cooler with the sun lowering on the horizon.

"Is that all I am to you, Jaxon? A distraction from something more important?"

He turned around so fast she nearly collided into him. "You're impossible, you know it?" Then he pivoted back around and continued to his Jeep.

She followed. "*I'm* impossible?"

He opened the Jeep door.

She put a hand on his arm. "You don't like the version of me that tries too hard. You obviously don't like the version of me that stays at home and doesn't try hard enough. What can I do to make you happy, Jaxon? What hoops do I need to jump through to be the version of myself that you could love again?"

His shoulders drooped as his gaze caressed her face. Lines depend at the corners of his eyes. He reached out and fingered the ends of her cropped hair. His voice came out soft and husky. "You really don't get it." His thumb grazed her chin, and she sucked in a breath. Fluttering filled her chest as she leaned toward his touch. If only she could get closer. "I never stopped loving you."

He loved her? Still? Would he kiss her now? She closed her eyes, held her breath, and waited, clinging to his words, but air swirled in the space he'd once inhabited. The Jeep door shut. The engine revved. She opened her eyes to find him backing away, creeping farther and farther from her turbulent heart.

She took giant strides after the retreating vehicle. "You love me, huh? Kind of hard to tell." She jogged after the electric blue form. "Strange way of showing it." He turned left out of the lot.

Her shoulders sagged as she spun back around and shuffled to her car. A mother and her teenage daughter stood by their car. Had they seen the whole thing while arriving at the restaurant?

"I'm right, aren't I?" she asked the bewildered mother. "If he loves me, he has a funny way of showing it."

The woman merely stared back at her.

"We're married, me and that guy."

A slight nod.

"I'm trying to win him back." She pressed the unlock button on her key fob.

The teenager's gaze went from her mom to Sahara and back again as she took a tentative step in the direction of the front door.

"Not doing a great job right now. But that's okay. I'll fix this." She ducked into her car, leaving the two ladies to whisper to each other as they walked into the restaurant.

But how could she fix something when she didn't know how it had broken in the first place?

~

Jaxon

Jaxon drove aimlessly. His turbulent emotions needed the release of pushing the pedal to the gas. He'd overreacted and ruined what could have been a decent dinner date. *Octopus.* The woman wanted to order octopus. And drink sweet tea. What had gotten into her?

He still remembered the first time he saw her tear those little sugar packets and pour them into her unsweetened tea. Affection had surged in his heart for her then, for the particular way she did things, for those precise systems she had in place. It was part of what made her unique. And now she tossed that away? For what? Because she thought it would make him like her more? Did she not know him at all?

That must be it. Clearly. After twelve years, he could recite her nightly bedtime routine to the minute, remember all her favorite television shows since she was five, and predict what items she would order from Amazon based on their ratings and reviews, yet she didn't know him at all. Because she thought he wanted her to change. She thought she needed to change for him to love her.

He ran a hand through his hair and yanked at the ends. Oh yeah. He was going to pull his hair out. This woman drove him crazy. How many times had he told her he loved her just the way she was? She never listened, so he stopped wasting his breath. Sahara reciting poetry? He snorted. That was as un-Saharalike as her drinking Coke while splatter painting to heavy metal music. If he'd wanted a woman who recited poetry, he would have dated one of the girls he met from the poetry open mic nights he used to go to before he met Sahara. But no. He wanted *her*.

He wanted Sahara just as she was, not trying to change to fit some preconceived notion of what she thought he wanted. Not trying to be something she wasn't. He wanted the woman he'd always loved. But he wanted all of her, not a dangling carrot here and there. He wanted into her very heart and soul. And for her, that seemed too much to ask.

He circled back around the block. The Peruvian restaurant's sign shone ahead on the right. Frowning, he pulled in the parking lot and parked. The ridiculous car Sahara had bought off Craigslist was gone. Should he go in? He had nothing better to do, and his stomach cramped with hunger.

The hostess led him to a table mere feet away from the booth they'd sat in less than an hour before. He stared at the place Sahara had recently occupied and pictured the way her new haircut fell softly around her face.

The waitress approached. "I'm Mary. Can I start you off with something to drink?"

He couldn't yank his gaze away from Sahara's spot. "A sweet tea, please."

"Sure thing. Do you know what you'd like to eat, or do you need a minute?"

He fingered his menu. "I heard you serve octopus here. I'd like that." Perhaps he could keep a piece of her with him even though she was long gone.

~

Sahara lay low on Friday and for the entire next week, nursing her wounds and strategizing her next move. And moving. It only made economic sense to move into the apartment for the time being. But she was on a month-to-month lease, and she didn't plan to sign again. This time next month, she'd be snuggled up with Jaxon in his place—er, their place.

She devoured *The Power of Charm* in one sitting. Not hard, as it was an easy read, but still. Knowing the concepts needed to win Jaxon over was one thing. Putting them into practice might prove slightly more difficult.

Those who have charm usually get listened to and often get second chances. They are given opportunities others may never get. They can be forgiven for things others would be crucified for.

Yep. Exactly what she needed. She'd spent the week putting step one into practice from a safe distance. She smiled at Jaxon whenever she had a chance, forced her face to say, *"It's great to see you,"* even as her heart twisted at the distance between them. She flashed him a grin when she pulled on-site each morning, and whenever she could manage to meet his gaze throughout the day. Step one: acceptance. Check. The book didn't say whether the person was supposed to smile back, so it shouldn't matter, right? Because he mostly looked at her as if she were an oddity. A polar bear who'd shown up to work in the desert heat. He'd nodded once. An acknowledgement, at least. If she kept doing the steps, surely, she'd get the results she was after.

Step two—appreciation—proved more difficult, mostly because she had to get within arm's length of the man to show him gratitude for anything. Every time she took two steps in his direction, he conveniently altered his course. No subtle avoidance here. He might as well wear a blinking neon sign that said *Stay Away*. All she had to do was get close enough to him to say, "Thank you," and she could check this step off the list. But thank you for what? For not firing her? For not berating her in public? He ignored her day in and day out. His laughter wafted to her ears as he joked with the men, somehow maintaining authority and respect while constantly bantering. How could he have a better relationship with these men than with his wife?

She'd racked her brain for something to appreciate about the man in these circumstances. Maybe the guys could help her out.

Sahara met Tony as he grabbed a Gatorade from the cooler that next Monday. She snatched a bottled water for herself. "Two full weeks of work. Coming along good, wouldn't you say?"

"I'd say so."

All right. Time to cut to the chase. "Why do you like working for Jaxon?"

His forehead dimpled as he took a swig.

"What do you appreciate about him?" And now, she sounded like a teenager scoping out a story for the high school paper.

He wiped his mouth with the back of his arm. "What's not to appreciate?"

She shrugged. The cold shoulder. Moodiness. Blatant disregard for her feelings.

"The drinks, for one." He pointed to the cooler. "He keeps us stocked. Doesn't want any of his guys—uh, workers—getting dehydrated."

"Jaxon stocks the drinks?" She'd never given any thought to where they came from.

"Yep. Every day."

"Huh." Well, there was something.

"He's a good man. Pays fair. Works fair. Won't do you wrong, you know?"

No, she didn't. She'd thought the same, but now?

Tony gave her a playful punch on the shoulder. "You're doing good. Catching on." He pointed to a wall they'd just raised.

"Thanks." She flashed a smile, which he returned.

Good. If she couldn't charm her husband, maybe she could charm his crew. They seemed to carry weight with him. Couldn't hurt.

Now, she only had to figure out how to—wait, there he was. Jaxon stood not five feet away, alone, flipping through papers on a clipboard. If she hurried, she could catch him before he had the wits to dodge her. She made a beeline in his direction.

"Hey." There she went again, Susie Sunshine, smile bright as the morning.

He startled, then blinked back at her. "Hey."

"I wanted to say thank you."

"For what?"

She held the bottled water up as if it were a trophy. "For the water. It's generous of you. Providing the drinks for everyone every day. Really great of you."

A low sound emanated from his throat as he looked back down to his clipboard. "You hate drinking water."

"Uh, yeah. I did. But that was before all this heavy labor out in the heat. I appreciate it now. I appreciate you. Providing the water."

He flipped a paper over. Oh, gosh. Not more uncomfortable silence. Should she walk away? Say something else?

"I'd probably like tea more, actually." Uh oh. Criticizing was one of the top *do nots* if you wanted to charm someone. Why couldn't she keep her mouth shut? Stop while she was ahead? "But the water is great. Healthier, I'm sure."

The corner of his eye twitched. She needed to exit this conversation. Quickly.

"Anyway, thanks." She spun around and nearly jogged back to her place beside Miguel.

She took several quick, deep breaths. She needed to read that book again because she certainly hadn't been prepared for this kind of response. Charmed? He seemed so far from charmed it was ridiculous. He could obviously barely tolerate her.

Maybe she needed to push through to steps three, four, and five: approval, admiration, and attention. To do that, though, she'd have to convince him to spend time with her. Could she smile and thank her way into another date? Not likely.

She could try poetry. True, her last attempt had ended in disaster. Maybe he didn't care for Emily Dickinson. What if she wrote a poem herself? Yeah, that was it. She could write a poem asking him on another date.

She snorted.

Miguel raised his brows. "What's so funny?"

"Nothing. Let's get these studs in." She could laugh at the idea of her writing a poem later.

~

She arrived the next morning with a handwritten poem in her pocket, but she couldn't give it to Jaxon. There was no way. She'd feel too vulnerable. He'd given her absolutely no indication he had any interest in restoring their relationship. The only thing she'd received since she landed in Utah was one rejection after another. Laying her heart bare before this man? Nope. Couldn't do it. Entirely too risky.

Besides, it sounded more like Dr. Seuss than a sonnet. He'd laugh in her face. She'd have to think of something else. Something more up her alley.

"The left wing! Isn't she a beauty?" Miguel called out.

"Quite lovely." She grinned. "What are we up to today?"

"We'll start on the next section."

"Exciting." A twinge of satisfaction shot through her. No wonder Jaxon loved this job. Seeing something take shape before your eyes. It almost made her forget about her sore muscles. She stretched. Almost.

Taking her place next to her babysitter, she bent to grab a rack of nails from the box and load them into her gun.

"Oh, wait. No, these ones are for you." Miguel handed her a separate box.

She opened it, and her breath caught. Galvanized red tips. She ran her fingers over their colorful ends. She looked at Miguel in question.

"He thought you might like girly nails, I guess."

He? As in Jaxon? "I do," she whispered, her voice scratchy. It had nothing to do with feminine color preference, and she opened her mouth to tell him so, but cleared her throat instead. What did it matter what Miguel thought? Jaxon understood. "Tell him thank you for me."

Biting her lip, she scanned the distance. There he was, speaking with Gabriel, waving his hand in the air as if it were a magic wand. The corner of her mouth wobbled. Her hand flew to her back pocket. Didn't she bring … Yes, there was her miniature notepad tucked in there, just in case she had any brilliant ideas for another stanza or a better poem altogether. She grabbed it and snapped it open, then took a nail. With the pretty pointy edge, she etched *Thank You* onto the paper. Okay, so this was a bit high schoolish, but … "Will you go give this to him?" She tossed Miguel a sheepish smile.

"Yeah. Sure." He took the note and dashed to Jaxon, slipping it into her husband's hand. They exchanged a few words she couldn't hear before he jogged back.

"Now," Miguel said, "let's see how well those girly nails hold this house together."

~

When she took a break a couple hours later, she made her way to the cooler. When she opened it, her eyes zeroed in on one brown glass bottle in the middle of the bottles of water and blue Gatorade. Tea. Her stomach flipped. A pink sticky note was attached to it. She peeled it off as she picked up the drink that had to be for her. In Jaxon's chicken scratch handwriting, it said, *"You're welcome"*. Tears sprang to her eyes, and she couldn't react fast enough to push them down. She clutched the ice-cold bottle to her heart and pressed her trembling lips together. Sniffling, she scanned the area until her watery gaze met his.

Thank you, she mouthed.

His soft, gentle smile soothed her like a balm.

Heavens, she still loved him. After all this time, after everything they'd been through, after all he'd done recently to push her away, she loved him. Her heart leapt toward him. Her poem burned in her pocket. Maybe she could? But what if he thought her ridiculous? Yet, those piercing blue eyes, the ones that saw so much, the ones that roped her in from their first date, they lapped soothing waves toward her now. No turbulent storm. Maybe she could entrust her heart to him, like this.

She took one step and then another, never breaking eye contact. Heart hammering, tears trailing down her cheeks, she drew close. She pulled the folded square from her jean shorts and handed it to him.

He took it.

"Let me know," she whispered.

He nodded.

She couldn't bear to stand there and watch him read it. Couldn't stand to see his reaction. She turned and sped to her car where she fished tissues from her glove box and worked on steadying her breathing. She recited the poem in her head.

> Give me another chance
> Though at first glance
> I may not be worthy of such a luxury
> Please grant me
> Space in your heart, in your day
> Please find a way
> To make room for me again
> Can't we both win?
> You and me together
> The way it used to be when we said forever

Underneath, she had written *Jaxon, will you go hiking with me?*

Her pulse thrummed in her ears as she exited her car. He must have read it by now. If she turned around, she might see his reaction. But she couldn't make herself. What a stupid poem. She was no English major. She was an accountant. A closet fanatic who alphabetized the books on her bookshelf. He had nearly every poem from the twentieth century memorized. He was probably laughing.

Behind her, gravel crunched. She swiped at her eyes with a tissue again before turning straight into Jaxon's chest.

He cupped her face with his hands and pressed his forehead to hers. All breath left her.

"Yes." He pressed a light kiss to her lips.

She leaned forward, hungering for more.

"Yes, I'll go hiking with you. This weekend. I'll take you to Bear Lake."

He captured her lips with his own. Warm. Welcome. One of his thumbs trailed along her jawline while the other teased the hair at the nape of her neck. He tasted sweet and salty and too good to back away from, but she had to breathe.

Through the fog of delight, she found words. "Will I need any kind of gear for this hike? A pack, perhaps?"

He chuckled. "A water bottle and sturdy shoes." He kissed her forehead. Took two steps back. Two steps too many. "And a jacket."

"A jacket? It's a hundred degrees outside."

His smile widened. "Not in the mountains." He backed away farther.

"Okay."

"You're still trying too hard."

She winced. "I'll try really hard not to try so hard."

Oh, she loved the crinkles on the sides of his eyes. "Now get back to work."

"Yes, Boss Man."

She nearly skipped back toward Miguel. She had another date. Another chance. She could execute steps three, four, and five. As long as she praised him, complimented him, and gave him her full attention, she could charm him back in love with her. She wasn't going to mess up this chance like she had the last one. She couldn't afford to throw something this special away.

Chapter 12

Bernie
July 21, 1861
Manassas, Virginia

"Fall back!" The command issued from Colonel Hampton himself, and Bernie would be a fool not to obey. Gasping, she melted into the sea of soldiers that fled from the Robinson farm lane to the safety of the woods. Heat breathed down her neck like the fires of hell. Men shouted. Cussed. Cried out. They'd done well, fought bravely as the only organized Confederate resistance of the field. During the battle, red dust from the parched roads rose all around, mingling with the blue smoke of artillery and cannons for an otherworldly scene. But their position on Matthew's Hill collapsed, and it wasn't enough. Muskets continued to fire in their direction, and they were no match. They were on the brink of defeat.

Bernie rounded a tree and leaned back against it, catching her breath. The rough bark scratched through her uniform and irritated her skin. What had just happened? A few hours ago, Henrietta had told her the arriving reinforcements were South

Carolinians. Thinking Hermann might be among them, she'd sneaked away to the Robinson house to investigate. Next thing she knew, she was fighting with the group of them as bullets and cannonballs zinged past. Those soldiers from her home state had just arrived in Manassas from a thirty-hour train ride. Exhaustion was written in the dark bags under their eyes and sagging lines around their cheekbones, yet so was an eagerness to join the fray. There were hundreds of them, but so far, no trace of Hermann.

Heaving breaths full of gunpowder, she pushed off from the tree and continued the retreat. With her eyes trained straight ahead, she stumbled over a log and nearly tumbled to the ground. Wait. No. It wasn't a log. It was a man. A wide stain darkened the breast of his uniform. Unfocused, glassy eyes looked heavenward. His chest rose and fell slightly as a soft wheeze emanated. He was alive, but barely. Bernie bit her lip. What was she to do? Leave him there. Of course, that was the necessary answer, yet her heart clanged in resistance. How could she? But this was war. She must. Hundreds of men would die today. There was nothing she could do for this one. She must focus on the task at hand. Get to safety. Regroup. See if there was a way to turn this battle around. *Find Hermann.* Yes, that was the most important task of all. If he was here, she had to find him.

Hermann. Her sweet, tender Hermann. What would he do if he were here, looking into the hollow eyes of a man fading from this world? Would he—could he—turn a blind eye? Soldier on as expected? Everything good and right in him would forbid it. Unless … unless the war had already stolen that from him. Her throat constricted. No. It couldn't have. She couldn't be too late.

An ache to wrap her arms around her husband swelled inside her, overwhelming her senses. She needed him, the gentle man with soft edges, more than she needed air not tinged with sulfur. If she couldn't find him among the sea of

South Carolinian soldiers, perhaps she could find him here. Within herself.

She dropped to her knees, inches from the man's sallow face, and clasped his clammy hand. Damp, dark curls framed his youthful face. So young. He couldn't be older than eighteen. From this distance, the extent of his wound glared. Dragging him deeper into the woods would do little good. He would not recover from this blow. "Would you like me to pray with you?"

His nod was so slight, she'd have missed it if she blinked.

"'Our Father, which art in heaven …'" As she recited the prayer, his lips moved to her words. The lines on his face eased. Peace in the face of death. When his jaw slackened, her stomach knotted. She removed her hand from his limp grasp and closed his eyes. "Rest in peace, soldier."

Rising, she cast one last look at the boy before she left and pushed on. When would his mama find out she'd lost a son?

An image of Hermann lying bloody and forlorn in a field flashed in her mind, and a shiver crawled up her spine. *Lord, protect my husband. Put Your angels around my Hermann. Let every bullet miss.* Artillery continued to fire in the background. *And while You're at it, Lord, would You keep me alive as well?*

~

They had rallied. The command came moments later. "My boys, at them again! Victory or death! See how Jackson stands there like a stone wall!" And they had rallied.

Now, sweltering heat pressed down on Bernie as she held her ground with Hampton's Brigade on Henry Hill. Cannons blasted and bullets ricocheted around her, knocking up pillars of dirt. The air hung heavy with giant columns of smoke. Sulfur coated her mouth and throat. The dry, still air scratched at her nostrils.

Bernie's ears perked up. Was that a woman's voice coming from inside the Henry House? It sounded like a female cried out. She shook her head. Who could tell amidst the roar of guns and cannons? The shouts of the victorious and the groans of the wounded? The rattle of musketry? Her mind must be playing tricks on her.

A bullet zinged not an inch from her head, snapping her back into focus. Her heart hammered as she reloaded her rifle. How many times had she nearly died today? How many men had she seen collapse in a heap around her? But no, she couldn't think about that. She had to fire before she was fired upon. Kill or be killed. She must shut her ears to the moans of wounded men. Because she had to make it out of here alive. She couldn't stomach the thought of Hermann returning home from war to find her gone, never knowing what had become of her. No. That simply wouldn't do. She had to survive. Find him. Bring him home. With every shot she fired, she repeated the mantra: Survive. Find him. Bring him home. Survive. Find him. Bring him home. Minute after minute, hour after hour, she blinded herself to everything save her sole mission.

Her mind hazed as the soldiers in front of her blurred into a mist of chaos. Confusion gripped her as bayonets gleamed in the sun's glare. Wait. Were those men in blue friend or foe? There were hundreds of different uniforms, and while Greenman's regiment wore gray, not all Confederates did. Some southern companies were outfitted in navy. Soldiers on both sides wore red or pinstripes. Even Confederate General Jackson wore Union blue. Distinguishing the enemy on outfit alone proved nearly impossible.

If only there were a breeze, she might be able to distinguish the flags. But on a windless day, both Union and Confederate flags looked much the same, the red, white, and blue indistinguishable. She hesitated, not wanting to impose friendly fire. When someone fired at her and barely missed her left knee, she had her answer, and her target. That group in navy blue was most certainly the enemy.

"Look, they're retreating," the soldier to her right said. Relief dripped from his voice. She felt it in her bones.

Hope surged within her as she saw it was true. The Confederates continued to press forward, and the Yankees were falling back. Could it be? Was the battle nearly over? Her vision blurred, and she blinked to clear it. Was there ever a more welcome sight than their retreating forms? She heaved in a ragged breath.

"Don't just stand there. Pursue them." This was from an officer of another company. She'd best comply.

"Yes, sir." And off she went to rout the enemy.

~

Bernie made her way back over Henry Hill toward the Robinson farm road where groups of soldiers had gathered. She needed to find Greenman's company and Henrietta. After routing the Union army, some soldiers returned singing rowdy songs, drunk on their victory. Others, like her, stumbled back in a daze.

In the heat of battle, with her pulse skittering and her mind occupied on staying alive minute by minute, reality hadn't settled in. Now, she scanned the battlefield, and her stomach clenched. Men of all ages in uniforms of all colors lay with their faces in the dirt. The necks and limbs of some were bent at unnatural angles. Puddles of blood still oozed. The stench of death hung in the air, stifling, nearly choking her. So, this was war.

All energy drained from her, and she forced her feet to plod forward. There was no way this was a quick, decisive war. They may have won this battle, but it had also shown them the tenacity of their opponents. The Yankees would not give in so easily. A ninety-day war? Dread coated her throat. No. There would likely be battlefield after battlefield like this one, strewn with dead men from both sides. How long would it drag on? Years? How many lives would be lost?

Pain sliced through her abdomen, and she doubled over. She must need to drink something, eat something. She hadn't given her own nourishment a thought in the thick of the fray. When she stood to uncap her canteen, she swayed.

"Whoa, soldier. You best sit." A man with a long, brown beard grabbed her arm and guided her to sit on a stump. "Where were you wounded?"

Bernie peered up at him, her mind murky. "Huh?"

He pointed at her leg. "You got blood on your pants there, but I can't see a bullet hole."

Blood on her … Her gaze snapped down to her pants leg. Alarm pulsed through her at the sight of crimson soaking through her inseam. She coughed. "No. Not wounded. Rubbed off from someone else. I'm fine." She waved him off.

His forehead puckered. "You sure? You don't need me to fetch a doctor?"

"I'm fine." She forced a smile and held up her canteen. "Needed water is all."

Though he looked far from convinced, he nodded and continued on.

As soon as his back was turned, she inspected her trousers with wide eyes. Yes, blood trailed the length of her inside pants leg. She hadn't been shot. The only pain came from her stomach, which cramped something fierce. Had she finally had her monthly? Or had … No. She couldn't think of it. She could not conceive of another life lost on the battlefield this day.

Henrietta. She had to find Henrietta.

After one last swig from her canteen, she rose and, wincing against the pain, rushed toward the sea of men, aiming for a group in dark coats and pants. *Please, Lord. Let me find her.* She wove her way through swarms of men, some smiling and joking, others with pale, somber faces.

"Henry," she called, again and again. Dozens of faces turned up to meet hers. She dismissed each one. What if her friend had been killed in battle? What if they'd just met only to be separated forever in this life? Worry niggled and her breaths came in quick succession until finally a hand gripped her elbow.

"Bernie, what's wrong?"

"Henry, you're alive." Her hand flew to her heart, even as another pain seized her. Wrapping her arms around her middle, she clenched her jaw to keep from crying out.

Henrietta's gaze dropped to her stomach, then came back up to meet Bernie's eyes with understanding. "Let's take a walk, shall we?" She guided Bernie away from the throng of men and toward the woods.

When they were out of earshot, she whispered, "Is it the baby?"

Bernie shook her head. "No. It can't be the baby. There is no baby to lose." Tears rimmed her eyes, and try as she might to staunch their flow, they persisted.

Henrietta guided Bernie behind a pine and encouraged her to sit. Lowering on her knees in front of her, Henrietta's concerned gaze roamed the trail of blood down Bernie's leg. "Cramping?"

Bernie nodded.

"More so than is usual during your monthly?"

"Yes," she conceded.

"I'll go fetch rags."

In a flash, she disappeared through the trees, and left Bernie alone to mourn the loss of her very heart. A life planted in her by the man she loved. A long-awaited dream. All she'd truly wanted was to build a family with him in their safe haven of a farm. Other aspirations of Merino sheep and an expanded herd paled in comparison to that beautiful dream. A child. Woven together from the best parts of Hermann and the best parts of her—and perhaps a bit of the impish pieces of both. What could be more lovely, more sacred, than this golden-spun hope?

How could she stand to see it perish? So far from her husband. He knew not of the child's existence, much less its passing into the next life. Here, where thousands of men lay wounded and dying. And her child would be another nameless life lost, buried in an unmarked grave. No, this wasn't right. It wasn't fair. Her flesh and blood should have a grave marker on their property. A name etched in stone. A place to lay flowers. A place to remember. A sob wrenched through her. Why had she come here? If only she had stayed home. The baby might have thrived with proper care. If she hadn't pushed her body to the point of exhaustion. If she'd taken care of herself, this would likely have never happened. Hermann could have returned from the front to meet his child.

But now? Her body shook with weeping. This loss had turned her inside out, made her raw and vulnerable. She could not survive this way. Not here. She must get to work erecting fortified walls. She must will herself to harden, just as she did on the battlefield earlier.

A thought struck, then sank down roots. What if Hermann wasn't the one who returned embittered by this war?

~

By the time Henrietta returned with rags, Bernie held a child's miniature form in her palm. The cramping had intensified, nearly unbearable, to where she'd had to bite down on a stick as blood flowed from her. Blood and something else, something— or rather someone—undeniable. So small, a mere bean of a thing, yet she could no longer say there had been nothing to lose. She held the imperceptible weight in her hand, and it was heavy.

"Oh, Bernie." Henrietta dropped to her knees as tears brimmed in her eyes.

Rags dropped into the brush as she cradled her hands under Bernie's. As if she paid no mind to the blood that coated them. She let silence hang between them as their hitched breaths created a sort of lullaby for this child born asleep. Time stretched with Bernie's aching lungs.

Finally, Henrietta spoke. "We can bury her."

Bernie could only nod.

Henrietta stood and brushed off her knees as she surveyed the ground around them. She scuffed at rocks and sticks with the toe of her boot. "What about here?" She pointed to the base of a pine.

"Sure." Bernie's voice broke with the simple word.

Heavy footsteps approached. The women locked wide-eyed gazes. Bernie closed her fingers around her stillborn child and dropped her hand to her side.

"Who's here?" a gruff voice called out. The trees obscured Bernie's view of the man.

"Just us, sir," Henrietta answered with a salute. "Private Henry Frontenac and Private Bernie …"

"Reisenfeld," she supplied.

An older gentleman with a full gray beard peeked around the pine. Or were his hair and beard merely tinged with smoke from the battle? Perhaps he wasn't as old as he seemed. Blood splatters and dirt marred his uniform.

"Are you injured?"

Her gaze dropped to her blood encrusted hands and uniform. She gave a single nod.

His brow furrowed as he peered at her. "Your color looks good. I'll fetch a doctor."

She opened her mouth to tell him … to tell him what? Not to bother? Any protest would only further rouse suspicions. She clamped it shut and turned a pleading gaze to Henrietta.

Henrietta put a finger to her mouth, and they listened as footsteps retreated. Then she bent close and whispered, "Let's bury the baby right quick, then we need to get out of here before a doctor comes looking. We'll head to the creek and get you cleaned up and back to your regiment."

"Okay," Bernie said, but a pang coursed through her at the thought of being separated from her new friend. But who knew? Maybe their companies would travel together? Perhaps they'd meet again at another battle. She hadn't time to contemplate the brevity of this friendship. She had only a moment to mourn the loss of her child.

Henrietta dug at the thirsty ground with a stick until the indentation reached deep enough an animal likely wouldn't be digging up the tiny body. Bernie lay the miniature form inside. Both women pushed dirt to cover over the child.

"Lord," Henrietta prayed, "look over this precious child. Welcome this baby into Your kingdom."

"They're right back here." The overloud voice broke into their solemn vigil.

Bernie gasped. "Do we run?" She glanced around wildly.

Henrietta's shoulders slumped. "They'd see us."

Bernie clutched her friend's arm, pulse thrumming in her ears, breath coming in quick bursts. "What do we do?"

"There's nothing we can do." Henrietta frowned. The corners of her eyes sagged. "We fess up."

"Fess up?" Had her friend gone mad? "And get sent home?"

Henrietta patted Bernie on the back. "It'll be all right. Trust me." She stood.

Trust her? She was about to blow their cover, everything Bernie had worked so hard to protect, and she wanted Bernie to simply trust her? She hadn't even known the woman for a full twenty-four hours. If they sent Bernie home now, was everything for naught? The nights away from home, sleeping on hard ground, putting herself in the line of danger, the deception, the men she killed, the baby she lost—was it all for nothing? She swallowed as footsteps crunched closer. It couldn't be for nothing. It couldn't.

But what choice did she have? They were too close for her to flee. Henrietta was right. They'd find her. And then what? She could say she wasn't injured. State that she was fine, that she didn't need a doctor. Perhaps they would ignore the blood that covered her. Or perhaps the doctor would be stumped if he examined her leg and found no bullet wound. There was a chance he wouldn't discover her secret. She could continue with the ruse in hopes—

The gray-tinged man appeared, accompanied by a young man with spectacles who was carrying a doctor's bag.

"Oh my," the doctor said as he peered down at her over his glasses. "What's the nature of your injury?"

Her mouth parted, but no words came forth.

Henrietta filled the silence. "This soldier is uninjured, sir. We are Private Reisenfeld and Frontenac, two soldiers who fought bravely today in the heat of battle." She squared her shoulders and tilted up her chin. "Two female soldierssir."

Chapter 13

Sahara
Present Day
Provo, Utah

Sahara was ready when Jaxon pulled up outside her apartment at eight that Saturday morning, right on time. She wore a hunter-green V-necked tee that drew out the color of her eyes while looking appropriately sporty. She'd vacillated between shorts and jeans, finally settling on khaki capris with a matching jacket. Okay, sporty wasn't the right word, but she looked cute.

She hopped up into the passenger's seat and nearly sat on a Bible. She stilled. What in the world? *Acceptance. Appreciation. Approval. Admiration. Attention.* No, she would not comment on the Bible. Wouldn't ask questions. Her conversations with Trish around the topic of religion never ended well. Better to ignore it altogether. She placed it on the back seat without a word.

"Good morning." He flashed her a smile. If he noticed her noticing the Bible, he avoided the subject as well.

"Good morning to you." She placed her backpack purse at her feet. "Where are we going?"

"My favorite place in Utah thus far. Bear Lake. It's about three hours away. Sit back and enjoy the ride."

"Three hours? What's so amazing about this place that you want to drive three hours? There are mountains everywhere. Isn't there somewhere closer? I mean, this is—"

"Completely impractical?"

She clamped her mouth shut. *Acceptance. Appreciation. Approval. Admiration. Attention.*

"Don't worry. You'll love it."

She brushed imaginary crumbs off her pants. She could look at the bright side. A couple days ago, Jaxon couldn't stand to be around her for more than two minutes. Now, he wanted to spend three hours stuck in a car with her. That had to bode well, right? She only had to make it through a three-hour ride without saying something stupid.

"Utah sure is beautiful. I see why you didn't want to come home."

Jaxon's hands tightened on the steering wheel.

Great start, Sahara.

"I mean, you're building something beautiful in a gorgeous location. Well, I think it's beautiful. Not sure what it looks like exactly. But it's big. Lots of floor joists."

"You haven't seen the plans?"

"Nope."

"I didn't realize … You have no idea what you're working on?"

She shrugged.

He reached behind him with his right hand and grappled for papers on the back seat. "There. Take a look." He handed them to her.

She unrolled the blueprints and her breath caught. She trailed a finger over the details. The floor-to-ceiling windows on both stories. The wrap-around porches. The stone pillars. What a unique design. It looked like something from out of a fairy tale. Something from a dream. "Oh wow, Jax. This is magnificent. I knew you had a gift, but this?"

"The owner spent most of his life working long hours and neglecting his family. Now he regrets it. He wanted to build a place where they could gather, wanted to draw them together. See how the open concept is circular?" He pointed to the center of the blueprint. "Everything centers around gathering his family around him. There will be six guest bedrooms, besides the master suite, and they circle the grand staircase. The movie theatre will be on the lower level, to the right of your thumb."

She moved her hand to see. A movie theatre. Yes. Great idea for gathering the family.

"Where's the pool?"

"Huh?"

"If he wants his family to hang out there, he should put in an indoor pool."

"I don't think he's much for swimming. He's more of a skier."

"Yeah, but it's not about him. It's about his family, right? Trust me. He's going to want a pool. He has the money."

"Huh. Interesting."

"It just makes sense."

"You're right. It does."

"Oh." She sat back. "Are we outside the proximity of your domain? I'm allowed to be right?"

He chuckled.

She ran her hand over the plans in her lap. "It's amazing. What you're building."

"What we're building."

"Yeah." She snorted. "I'm an integral part of the process."

"I couldn't do it without you."

If only he meant it.

Her gaze studied the intricate designs for a few more minutes before she rolled them back up and turned to place them back on the seat behind her. Her hand brushed something. What was it? She reached farther and grasped onto a straw hat with a green ribbon.

"What's this?" She brought it around and held it on her lap.

"It's for you. I figured you probably didn't have a hat. In the Utah sun, you need one."

A warm sensation filled her chest. He'd bought this for her?

"I don't have one."

"I prefer ball caps myself, but a lot of the ladies around here wear these. I thought it'd look cute on you. I cut the tag off."

He what? She checked inside. Sure enough, only the hint of a seam. "You were very thorough." Her voice sounded hoarse. Ridiculous to get choked up over a silly tag on a hat. She swallowed the emotion, placed the hat on her head, and flipped down the mirror on the visor. "It kind of does look cute on me. But also somewhat ridculous. Perhaps forty-two percent ridiculous and fifty-eight percent cute? What do you think?"

He tossed her a glance, and his smile widened. "One hundred percent cute."

Her face heated with her grin. He was flirting? Oh, she liked this Jaxon.

Appreciation. That was easy when he was like this. "Thank you. This is one hundred percent thoughtful."

"You're welcome."

"I'm going to wait until we're outside to wear it, though." She took the hat off and surveyed her hair in the mirror. Licking a finger, she subdued staticky strands before putting the hat away on the back seat. Next to the Bible. Her gaze zeroed in on that black book.

She shouldn't say a word. Not one word. But a Bible? Her Jaxon. With a Bible.

She pulled it into her lap. "What this about?" The soft leather cover didn't seem worn by excessive use, thank goodness. She fanned through the pages. No obsessive highlighting like Trish's Bible. That was a good sign.

"I was curious."

Curious. Why? She sucked in a breath. They were in Utah. Near Salt Lake City. Oh, heavens. They had got him. She grimaced. "You're a Mormon?"

Laughter burst out of him.

"What?"

He opened his mouth to speak, then dissolved into laughter again. Nerves taut, she waited until he quieted and wiped the edges of his eyes with the back of his hand before speaking. "No, I'm not a Mormon."

She released a pent-up breath.

"There are other churches out here, you know. Other than Mormon temples. Baptist churches, Assemblies of God, Lutheran, nondenominational—"

"And do you go to one of those churches?"

He shrugged. "Not really. I visited one. Been thinking about going back."

The Bible felt cold and hard in her hands. What was the appeal? "Why? Why now?"

His voice came out small. "It feels like something's missing from my life."

She narrowed her eyes. "Maybe it's your wife."

"Sahara …"

"Sorry. I know." *Acceptance. Appreciation. Approval. Admiration. Attention.* She clamped her mouth shut. Nearly chewed on her tongue to keep from speaking. Awkward silence hovered around them. Suffocating. *Acceptance.*

Appreciation. Approval ... She couldn't take it anymore. "Jaxon, are we going to talk about this? It's like you have a giant sore on your arm and I have a giant sore on my arm. We're ignoring this big ugly thing. We can't talk about it because you don't want to face it. You just want to run away."

He scoffed.

"Can you let me know when we can talk about it? I'll put it on my calendar. In a few days, maybe? Or weeks? Sometime next month? Next year? When, Jaxon? After we sign divorce papers? Can you give me a timeline?"

"I don't want to talk about it because there's no talking about this with you. There's only arguing. I don't want to fight with you."

"I don't want to fight either, but we need to face this. We have to work it out together."

"We could try counseling."

Sahara shook her head. "No. No. No. My grandma Bernice didn't go to a counselor. She went to war. She fixed her marriage all by herself. She didn't need anyone from the outside poking their nose into her business."

"Bernice? The Confederate?"

"The side she fought on is irrelevant. The point is, she fought for what mattered. When are you going to fight for what matters?"

"I don't want to fight with you, Sahara. Can't you be in the moment? I want to show you my favorite place in Utah. Can't you forget everything else and just be in the moment with me today?"

She gazed out the window, majestic mountains towering high. Just be with him? She could do that, couldn't she?

"'Do not worry about tomorrow, for tomorrow will worry about its own things,'" he said.

"Sounds familiar. Are you quoting from a poet or something?"

"That one's from the Bible."

"Oh no. You're quoting from that book now?"

"It seemed appropriate."

She moaned.

"You know, my favorite passages to read in there"—he nodded toward the Bible—"are about David. He was a poet. Wrote a whole book of poems called the Psalms."

Her mouth tipped. "Figures."

"You might like him too. He was also a shepherd."

"Oh yeah?"

"'The Lord is my shepherd; I shall not want. He makes me lie down in green pastures.' You heard that one?"

"Oh yeah. Trish has a plaque with that in her dining room."

"David wrote it."

She tossed the Bible into the back seat. "Good for him. Good for you. Don't try to convert me." She held her hands up.

"Wouldn't dream of trying to make you do anything."

"Thank you." They exchanged a tenuous smile. "Speaking of sheep, I saw my babies the other day. You'll never believe what happened."

She regaled him with the coyote story, and he acted appropriately shocked and invested. Good. He still cared about her world, no matter how small. No matter how far removed from a millionaire's mountain mansion. But what about the whole God thing? Was it only a phase? Something he passed through like valleys between mountains? Or was this a new part of him that she'd need to adjust to? Worry niggled.

That was until they neared their destination. Then all thoughts of anything other than awe-inspiring beauty fled her mind. "It's like a mirror. How can the water be such a clear blue?"

"Something about microscopic particles of white-colored calcium carbonate."

"Lime? Fascinating." She'd have to research the phenomenon when she got back to the apartment.

"I thought we'd do the Limber Pine Trail. It's only a mile and a half roundtrip."

She straightened her shoulders. "I can do harder. You want to do a more difficult one? I'm up for it."

His gaze roamed her face. "I don't want anything about today to be difficult. Let's take a leisurely walk on the trail. Then, we can have a picnic on the beach."

She beamed. "Sounds delightful."

And it was. The trail was sparsely populated, which gave them a sense of privacy. They walked side by side in companionable silence, stilling their steps every once in a while to get a glimpse of a skittering rabbit or bird. Vibrant orange and yellow wildflowers filled the space around them. And then, when they turned a bend and Bear Lake came into view below, her breath escaped her. "It's nearly turquoise."

"They call it the Caribbean of the Rockies."

About halfway through the trail, they came to a huge, gnarled tree.

Jaxon nodded to the twisted tree. "It's the limber pine they named the trail after. It's actually five separate trees that grew together for five hundred and sixty years, but scientists didn't figure that out for some time. They're so closely entwined they seem like one tree."

"That's a long time."

He tilted his head. "Not for trees."

But for people. They'd been married a mere twelve years and had yet to tightly entwine. She stretched out her hand. He took it in his, weaving his fingers between hers and grasping tight. What a simple thing—holding hands. Yet, she'd taken it for granted. And now it filled her with lightness and warmth.

She held up her phone. "Let's take a picture." They posed for a selfie in front of the limber pine. Her and Jaxon together. Smiling. Just like old times.

He'd been right about the jacket. She needed it on the trail that was shaded by pines and firs. A cool breeze tumbled over her.

When they came to a fork in the trail, she put to use the only line from a Robert Frost poem she knew by heart. "'Two roads diverged in the wood, and I—I took the one less traveled by, and that has made all the difference.'" She grinned up at him, proud of herself.

He smirked. "Are you sorry you can't travel both?"

She cocked a brow.

"It's from the beginning of the poem."

"Oh." She shrugged. "Not really. I'm happy to be on whatever path you're traveling." And she meant it.

Once they finished the hike and drove to the lake, it became clear he'd been right about the hat, too. The sun beat down relentlessly, but she was covered. Covered by his thoughtfulness. By his love. "I see why you adore this place."

"It's even better with you."

She melted. *This.* This is what she'd been longing for, pining and grasping for, as Jaxon had said. This is what her thirsty heart needed. Just him and her. Forever like this. She could dance on a breeze she felt so light.

They climbed out of the Jeep and went for the cooler Jaxon had packed. He handed her a blanket to carry, hefted the cooler, and proceeded to the beach. Once she picked a prime spot—set back away from the crowd—he presented the fare.

Chicken salad sandwiches with green grapes peeled and cut in half, the way she liked them. SunChips and a bottle of unsweetened iced tea with three sugar packets. How thoughtful. As they ate, he asked her how she'd learned about construction. His smile broadened as she told him of the books she'd poured over and YouTube videos she'd watched. What was that twinkle in his eye? He seemed … enraptured. *Attention.* Wait. She was supposed to ask the questions, hang on his every answer, show him he was the most interesting person on earth. How did this get turned around? He was charming her. And man, was he good.

She needed to get this conversation headed in the right direction. Needed to ask him a question, get him to talk about himself.

She finished off her last chip and brushed crumbs from her lap. "What else do you like to do out here? What other places have you been to?" As soon as the words left her mouth, a slimy aftertaste followed. It sounded like a question one stranger would ask another. A first-date type of question. She swallowed. *Acceptance.* Right. She needed to smile. She pushed a grin to the surface.

He put a hand on her knee, and her stomach flipped. "You've got to go skiing. There are many great spots out here, and if you fulfill your end of the bargain, you'll be around when the slopes open up." His blue eyes danced.

Her smile softened. She'd rather clean bathroom grout than fly down a hill on two pieces of wood in subzero temperatures, but she couldn't say so. Not with him looking at her that way. Like a kid about to open a Christmas present.

"Oh, I'll fulfill my end of the bargain."

"Then I'm taking you skiing."

"As long as you cover the hospital bills for any injuries I suffer."

"I'll go easy on you. It won't cost me more than a tube of ChapStick and a hot chocolate to nurse your wounded pride."

She swatted at him. "You brat."

He laughed, then stood and gestured to the lake. "Come on. Let's get in."

Get in? "I didn't bring a swimsuit."

"We can wade in, at least." He chucked off his shoes, sending them sprawling in the sand.

"All right." She slipped off her tennis shoes and set them on the edge of the blanket, then tucked her socks inside.

He held out a hand to her and hoisted her up. Cool sand sifted between her toes as they walked to where the water gently lapped the shore. Jaxon took two giant strides and was in up to his knees. Water teased the hem of his shorts.

She nudged a toe closer to the edge. "How is it?"

"Cooler than South Carolina."

She bit her lip. "How much cooler?"

"I'm not the numbers geek. I've heard the water temperature here can get up to seventy degrees. What's it back home this time of year? At least eighty? Eighty-five?" He lifted a shoulder.

She pressed her eyes shut, doing the calculations. "About a thirteen percent decrease in temperature from back home."

"You're insane."

"I think you mean insanely intelligent."

"That too." He reached out and grabbed her wrist. "Take a deep breath and leap in. It's not freezing. Just slightly cooler than you're used to."

She shook her head.

"C'mon." He gave a tug. "It's refreshing."

She dug in her heels. "I can enjoy it from here."

He made a puppy dog face. "Join me in the water?"

A breeze sent a chill up her spine. She wrapped her arms around herself. "No thanks."

"Then I'll bring the water to you." Laughing, he reached and scooped a handful of lake into his hands, hurling it toward her.

She screeched and lunged backward, then tripped and splayed face-first in the sand. Grit filled her mouth and stung her eyes. She gasped in air, but it seemed too thin. Not enough. Trembling, she pushed herself up to sitting.

Jaxon's arms wrapped around her. "I'm so sorry."

She shoved him away, stumbling a bit as she stood and marched back to the blanket. Her face warmed. Her throat burned. How embarrassing.

"Sahara, wait," Jaxon called, but she ignored him.

Three feet from the blanket, she tripped again and tumbled forward, her knees grinding into the sand. What in the— Her gaze landed on the culprit. Jaxon's shoes. She let out a humorless laugh. Over two thousand miles from home, and she was still tripping over his shoes. She scooted herself around until she sat on the blanket, arms wrapped around her knees. No, wait. She needed a picture of this.

She leaned back, snatched her phone from its spot by the cooler, and snapped a picture.

She caught Jaxon's gaze. He'd stilled. Now he stared at her with the phone in her hand. His eyes grew stormy. Uh oh. She knew that look. Her tongue ran over her teeth as she scrambled with how to salvage this.

He stomped toward her. "Still?"

Best to feign ignorance. "Huh?"

"After all this time, you're still taking those pictures."

She shrugged. Averted her gaze to the lake beyond him.

He held out his hand. "Let me see your phone."

"What? No."

"Give it to me if you have nothing to hide." Like a vulture, he swooped down and snatched it from her grasp.

She swiped at the air. "It's not like that."

His face reddened as he browsed what must be her gallery. "Quite a collection you have here." Was that vein in his neck going to pop?

She felt too small with him towering above her like that. She stood. Put her hands on her hips. Jutted out her chin. "I happen to like those pictures. In fact, I had a bunch of them enlarged, and they're now hanging in our home."

His eyes narrowed. "They're hanging in our home?"

"Yep."

"While strangers come and stay?"

A fraction of her confidence waned. "Yes."

"Why would they want pictures of shoes on the walls?"

She shifted her jaw. "Gives it character?"

He snorted. "Yeah. It gives the place a lot of character to chronicle in detail my every perceived failure."

What? Her arms slid to her sides. "Jaxon, that wasn't what I was trying to do."

"Do you know how hard it was to live with you? Do you want to know why I don't want to go back? How would you like someone to catalog every single thing you do wrong? To be on the lookout for you to screw up again? And then when you do, they shove a picture in your face with some *Aha, got you now* air of victory. As if I didn't get enough criticism growing up. If that wasn't enough, you wanted to shame me publicly by slapping those pictures on the walls of our home?"

Her jaw dropped. No. No, that wasn't what she meant, wasn't what she was trying to do at all. She opened her mouth to tell him so, but nothing came out. He brushed past her and grabbed his phone from the blanket. What was he going to do? Text his friends and tell them what a horrible wife she was? Heat prickled her cheeks. But no, a minute later, he stuffed earbuds in his ears and sat, his back toward her. Tension rippled off him like waves.

The back of her eyelids stung. Oh, heavens. How had their lovely day gone south so fast? How could he think she wanted to publicly humiliate him? She hadn't gotten the pictures enlarged to flaunt his mistakes, but in a desperate attempt to feel closer to him. To grasp on to what little she had left of him. As to why she'd taken the pictures in the first place … No, there couldn't be truth to what he said. It was too awful. She wasn't like that.

"Jaxon?" She reached a hand toward him but couldn't bring herself to touch him.

He didn't respond. Because he didn't hear her? Doubtful.

She sat and watched the sunlight shimmer on the lake, her stomach like a rock sinking to the bottom of that giant glistening pool.

Minutes inched on. Finally, Jaxon pulled out an earbud and said, "Ready to go?" His tone was even. Controlled. As cold as the lake water.

"Yeah." Did she sound as small as she felt?

Avoiding eye contact, he grabbed the cooler and stomped off to the parking lot.

She bent and shook the sand off the blanket before folding it neatly and tucking it under her arm. Then she grabbed her shoes and sulked toward Jaxon's Jeep. At least he hadn't left without her. Without a word or a glance, he handed over her phone as she got in. They rode the entire way in silence. Sahara pretended to sleep, all the while her mind whirled. Was that truly how he saw her? No wonder he wanted to stay away. Was that truly how she was? A much harder question. One she'd rather not dwell on. But it kept circling her brain like a bird of prey over a carcass.

When he pulled up in front of her apartment, she slung her purse on her shoulder and fiddled with her sun hat. She couldn't leave things like this. But every time she tried to make things better, she seemed to only make them worse. What could she say?

Jaxon stared straight ahead. Sighed in an irritated sort of way. Like he couldn't wait to get rid of her. She couldn't blame him.

"Jaxon, I'm sorry." Her words came out choked on emotion, likely caused by three hours of churning thoughts. "I never wanted to hurt you."

"I didn't think you did." He ran a finger over the dash. "You're good at a lot of things. You don't even have to try."

Gut punched, she clenched her eyes shut and grasped blindly for the door latch. After he rolled away, she released the hot tears. She'd come two thousand miles to completely fall apart.

~

The next day, after Sahara shoved two chocolate eclairs into her face and watched a few reruns of *Jeopardy* to make herself feel less like an idiot, she called Myra. Her friend answered after the first ring.

"What's up?"

"I need you to burn all the shoe pictures."

"Burn them?" She could nearly see her friend's raised brow.

"Yes. As in kerosene and a match. But keep the frames. Cute frames."

"What happened?"

Sahara spilled every detail of the pathetic affair. "He hates me, and I don't blame him. I might hate me too at this point. I'm telling you, as soon as the couple staying there this weekend pulls off the premises, burn those pictures. And send me a video when you do so I can send it to him as proof. Please?"

"What level of crisis is this? Chocolate, Cheetos, or wine?"

She looked at the bag in her lap. "Two out of three. And only because it's Sunday. The state controls any alcohol besides beer, and their stores are closed on Sundays." She dropped her head in her hands. And now she had Cheeto dust in her hair.

"So, you're orange again?"

"Just tell me you're going to burn them. I deleted the pictures from my gallery. Every single one. The only picture I have on my phone now is the one of Grandma Bernie and the one Jaxon and I took at Bear Lake before things went south."

"Well, that's something."

"Not enough to save my marriage, though, is it? What can I do, Myra?"

"You can calm down, for one thing. It can't be as dire as you think. You said you two laughed together and held hands. You said he kissed you."

"And it was magical."

"See? There's got to be something there to salvage."

"For the life of me, I can't figure out how. I know all the steps. I keep repeating them in my mind. Try to do them. But stupid Sahara sneaks out and sabotages everything."

"The steps? Is this one of your self-help books?"

"It said if I did the steps, I could charm anyone."

"Girl, only you would try to navigate love with a manual."

"It seemed foolproof."

"You sure need that. 'Cause you're acting like a fool."

"You tell me what to do, then. How would you fix this mess if you were me?"

"I would—"

Her phone buzzed. "Hold on. I'm getting another call." She glanced at her screen. Ugh. "My mom. Can I call you back?"

"You know you can."

She switched over.

"Who's the blonde, and why is she at your house? And where are you?"

"Mom, I told you this. Do you ever listen? I'm not home. I'm in Utah with Jackson. I'm renting out my home as an Airbnb."

Sahara stood and paced into the kitchen. She never could seem to talk to her mother sitting down.

"You never told me that. Do you think I would have driven all the way here if I would have known? Why are there pictures of shoes hanging up in your living room?"

She massaged her temples. "Tell me you did not bother the guests."

"I didn't bother them. Just asked who they were and what they were doing in my daughter's house."

"Did you have an attitude?"

Her silence spoke volumes.

"I better not get a bad review because of you. I need this income."

"Why are you in Utah?" She spit the state's name out as if it were a frostbitten lima bean.

"Trying to patch things up with Jaxon." She leaned against the counter and wiped her orange fingertips on a paper towel.

"Patch things up? It's going so bad that you had to drive across the country—"

"Fly."

"Fly? You?"

She pinched the bridge of her nose. "Yes."

"You had to fly across the country to talk sense into him?"

"Something like that."

Her mother wheezed and coughed before continuing. "He isn't worth it, honey. No man is. You're better on your own."

"Thanks, Mom. I appreciate that. Now, why were you stopping by?"

"Oh, I wanted to say hi, is all. Haven't seen you in, what? A year?"

"A year and a half. At Christmas."

"That's my daughter. Such a good memory."

"You drove an hour to say hi because you missed me? Not buying it, Mom."

"Okay, I'm a little short on rent money this month. Well, last month's rent money. If I don't get it to him by the end of the week, he's kicking me out."

Tension built at the base of her skull. "Again? Have you been showing up at work?"

"That's another thing."

She groaned. "Don't tell me you got fired."

"No. No. I quit. Someone offered me a better opportunity at a different restaurant, but when I went to apply, management had already filled the position. It was a simple misunderstanding."

"Mom!"

"I don't need your lecture, Sahara. Can you lend me a few hundred or can't you?"

Sahara bit her lip. She shouldn't do it. No way. It was like feeding a stray cat. Her mother would always come back for more. She'd never grow up if Sahara kept helping. And it wasn't even helpful. Isn't that what Jaxon had told her for years? True love was tough love, in this case.

Her mom coughed again. "You know, I could always come and stay with you for a bit while you get back on your feet after the divorce."

Sahara's jaw clenched. "We're not getting divorced."

"Honey, you're always telling me to be realistic. Seems like it's time to take your own advice."

Her hand clenched around the phone. She spoke through gritted teeth. "I'll wire you the money. Stay away from my renters and keep out of my business."

Chapter 14

LOCATE *I*
LOVE YOU SOME-
WHERE IN

TEETH AND
EYES, BITE
IT BUT

TAKE CARE NOT
TO HURT, YOU
WANT SO

MUCH SO
LITTLE. WORDS
SAY EVERYTHING.
LOVE YOU
AGAIN,

THEN WHAT
IS EMPTINESS
FOR. TO

FILL, FILL.
I HEARD WORDS
AND WORDS FULL

OF HOLES
ACHING. SPEECH
IS A MOUTH.

"THE LANGUAGE" BY ROBERT CREELEY

Sahara
Present Day
Provo, Utah

She had to keep plugging away. Show up on the job site, do her job with excellence. She couldn't give Jaxon one iota of a reason to fault her. If she worked hard and bided her time, he'd cool down from the whole shoe pictures thing, and she could attempt to make amends. For now, no hasty moves. No pining and grasping. Just honest, hard work.

He hadn't even shown on the job site Monday. Was she disappointed or relieved? Moot point. She had texted him Myra's video of the enlarged prints going up in flames along with the following message: *The pictures are gone. Off our walls. Off my phone.* When he didn't reply after half an hour, she sent a follow-up *I'm sorry* text. He didn't reply to that either. She left it alone. Anything more would only make her sound desperate. And Jaxon despised desperate.

It was lunch hour on Tuesday, and she, Tony, Gabriel, and Miguel all sat in the bed of Tony's truck, parked in the shade of a maple tree to avoid the oppressive heat barreling down. No sign of Jaxon yet today. She'd just finished her chicken salad sandwich when her phone buzzed in her pocket. Myra. She hopped down and ambled away from the guys.

"Hey, what's up?"

"You never called me back."

Sahara grimaced. "Shoot. Sorry. My mom's call threw me off."

162

"I hope they're okay with you leaving a little early because you have an appointment at five and it looks like it's fifteen minutes away."

"What now?"

"You asked what I would do if I were you. Well, honey, I'd get my behind in counseling. That's what I'd do. I went online and made you an appointment. Covered the cost of your first session. You're welcome."

"Myra! That's ridiculous. Cancel it. I do not need therapy."

"Jaxon suggested it, didn't he?"

"He threw out the idea of couples counseling, yes. But—"

"You've got to start somewhere. Start with you. Go from there."

"This is completely unnecessary. I ordered another book. *How to Improve Your Marriage Without Talking About It.* You know, since Jaxon doesn't want to talk about it."

"Enough with you and your self-help books. Go *talk* to a professional. Give it this one visit. If you hate it and think it was a waste of your time, then fine. Don't go back."

"You infuriate me. You know it?"

"Glad to know the feeling's mutual. I'll text you the address."

Myra hung up, and Sahara stared at her phone. What had just happened? Had she agreed? Was she actually going to spill her personal problems to a complete stranger? It might score points with Jaxon, actually. Once she got back on speaking terms with him. It would prove to him she was willing to change, that she was working on becoming a better version of herself. Even if she only went once, she could technically say she went to counseling. She could endure an hour of interrogation for the leverage it could give her with her husband, couldn't she?

"Everything okay?" Tony called as he shut the bed of his pickup.

"Yep. Everything's great." Or it would be. She inadvertently shivered. If she could endure an hour of vulnerability.

~

She, Miguel, and Tony had just hoisted up a wall when Jaxon's Jeep careened up the drive, spitting gravel. He jumped out and waved his hands over his head. "Stop what you're doing."

"Uh oh," Tony mumbled.

"What?" Sahara bit her lip. Tension radiated from the men around her.

"Take a few deep breaths," Miguel said. "And remember, they're paying you by the hour." He slapped on a tight smile and turned his attention to Jaxon, who stalked toward them. "What's up, Boss Man?"

"Slight change of plans."

Sahara's throat tightened. She took a swig of water. Didn't help.

Jaxon unrolled a set of blueprints, and the men gathered around. She squeezed into a space beside Miguel and tilted her head, trying to make sense of the sketch before her. Where was the wall that she'd helped raise moments before?

"I just met with the owner. He originally wanted his bedroom—the master suite—to face east so he could view the captivating mountain sunrises. After pondering it, however, he's not much of a morning person, and he'd rather have his bedroom face west so he can watch sunsets instead. That means we're going to move the master suite from here to here," Jaxon said as his finger swiveled around the page, "and we're going to make this the family room. The other main alteration we'll make is that the owner wants to add an indoor pool." He glanced pointedly at Sahara. "Right here, where we were going to have the movie theatre. We'll move the theatre to this end of the home."

Tony pointed to the wooden frames that surrounded them. "So, those four walls we raised moments ago—"

"Will have to be moved, unfortunately. And that one, shortened. But guys, we're chasing the dream." He flashed a grin.

Miguel nodded. "Sure thing, Boss Man. We'll get right on it."

Sahara planted her hands on her hips. "He's allowed to change his mind whenever he wants?"

Jaxon's gaze swung back to her. Lingered as he studied her with a neutral expression. Finally, he spoke. "Yes. Because he's the owner. He's paying for our services."

Panic welled in her chest. "Can't he work around what we've already done? We just built that. We got that wall up. We made progress. Now you want us to undo the progress we made?" Her breath came out in quick, tight bursts.

He stroked his beard as he took his time answering. "Sometimes, progress looks like taking something down or moving it around. You are allowed to change your mind. You're allowed to readjust your vision. You're allowed to examine if what you thought you wanted is what you truly want. That's all part of building the life you want."

He turned and left Sahara standing slack-jawed, mind reeling. The life you want? The *life* you want? Not the home. The life. What was he trying to tell her in that veiled way of his?

Tony's voice rang out. "Come on, sister. Help us get this wall down."

Her body went stiff. Every nerved screamed at her to resist, to run. To not cooperate with moving backward. *Push forward. Push forward. Put walls up. Don't tear them down.* But she had a job to do. And that required ripping up a few things to move forward.

~

The color blue was statistically proven to have a calming effect on the central nervous system, which must have been why the counselor's office was bathed in azure and cobalt. It was as if Sahara floated in the middle of an ocean. Intriguing strategy. She remembered reading how after blue lights were installed at seventy-one Japanese train stations, suicides decreased by eighty-four percent. At least she'd be spending an hour with a professional who was up to date on her research. Either that, or it was a fluke.

Her knee bounced wildly as she waited in the foyer. What was she doing here? She could leave. Tell the secretary it was all a big mistake. Admit that her friend blackmailed her. She could agree to come back another time, with Jaxon. She could submit herself to couples therapy, just not to being the only one on the hot seat.

A woman with tight brown curls peeked around the office door. "Sahara?"

She sucked in a breath. Let it out in a quick burst. Raised her hand. "That's me."

The woman's smile broadened. "I'm Jocelyn. Come on in."

Sahara clutched her purse in front of her and followed. Jocelyn sat behind a dark mahogany desk and gestured to a pale-yellow couch. Sahara perched on the edge and piled her purse in her lap, fiddling with the straps.

"Nice to meet you, Sahara. Why don't you start by telling me why you're here?"

Sahara chewed on the edge of her lip. What to say? What to say? A hundred thousand thoughts tumbled through her mind at once. A million steps that led her from her first steps to this point in her life in this office. Which step was the one? Which one step brought her here? Or had they all collided together in a firestorm of calamity?

"I married a man I didn't love. I don't know why I did it. I don't know if he even knows I didn't love him when I walked down the aisle. It's just that … his last name was Raine, and I'm named after a desert, and I thought, hey, Sahara, maybe he's exactly what you need. I plunged in, and I didn't think to second-guess myself. And now my marriage is falling apart."

"Because you're married to a man you don't love?" Jocelyn, who'd been taking notes, tapped an eraser to her chin.

"No. The thing is, I love him now. Desperately love him. I don't know when it happened or how, but he's like my air, and I'm suffocating. Because now I love him, and he doesn't love me anymore. At least, I don't think he does. I don't know. He says he never stopped, but he acts like I've hurt him too much. Too many times."

Sahara jumped to her feet and paced. "Maybe I married him to get away from my mom. She had me when she was fifteen, and she's never grown up. I've had to mother her all my life. And Jaxon, he knew what he wanted, knew how to take the lead." She stopped and turned to the counselor. "Is this okay? Am I supposed to be lying down or something?"

The edges of Jocelyn's eyes crinkled. "Whatever makes you feel most comfortable."

She continued to pace. "The first time I took Jaxon to the sheep farm— My aunt, Trish, has a sheep farm, and she's more like a mother figure than my own mom. That's probably important for you to know. Anyway, the first time I took Jaxon there, he tried his best to learn their names, but he kept fumbling them up." She chuckled. "They liked him, though. They gathered around him and talked to him in their sheep way. They can sense goodness in people, my aunt says. Only *her* sheep, though, 'cause Shetlands are special." Her smile widened. "I knew then I could marry him, even if I didn't fully love him. Because he was a good man."

She stilled and lowered herself onto the couch again. She leaned forward, catching Jocelyn's gaze with her own.

"Jaxon's a good man. I can't lose him. Tell me what I have to do to hold on to him. How can I change? And how long is it going to take for me to change? What's my prognosis?"

Jocelyn tilted her head. "Your prognosis?"

"Yes. How bad is my case? How long is it going to take for me to get better?"

"Do you think you're sick?"

"Maybe sick isn't the right word, but something is wrong with me. Something's wrong because if everything was right, Jaxon would be happy with me, and we'd be together right now instead of me sitting in this office."

"When did the problems in your marriage begin?"

Sahara rolled her head back and whimpered. "That's as difficult as asking when I fell in love with Jaxon in the first place. I can't pinpoint when it unraveled. All of a sudden, it hit me that his jokes didn't seem funny anymore, but I don't remember when I stopped laughing. I've always been the one in charge of the finances. At some point, things we used to be able to work through became a big deal. I don't know when or how or why. And then, I started taking pictures of his shoes." She confessed the whole fiasco to the counselor, who to her credit, didn't gasp in horror. Instead, she nodded sympathetically. "But I deleted them off my phone and had my friend burn the enlarged ones."

"So, you want to change."

"Desperately. I've bought books, listened to podcasts, read articles, and watched documentaries. I'm working on myself... or trying to. But no matter how hard I try, I'm still me." She spread her hands out in front of her.

"Has Jaxon asked you to change?"

She gave a decisive nod. "He made it clear he does not want me taking anymore pictures of his shoes."

"What else has he asked you to change?"

She opened her mouth, but then shut it. Well, nothing, but ... "He speaks in poems and riddles or doesn't speak at all.

He won't answer me straight out in a way I can understand. I'm left to guess what's going on in his head."

Jocelyn's face scrunched. "Guessing at someone's thoughts is never a good solution."

"I guess not." She winced at the unintended pun. "But today, for instance, he said something about having the right to change your mind and your vision and decide if what you thought you wanted is what you truly want. Only at first, I thought he was talking about the owner of the house he's building, and then I realized he meant something more. But what? Did he mean me? *I* have the right to change *my* mind? Or did he mean *he* has the right to change *his*? Does he want me to change my mind? Change my mind about what?" She grabbed her hair by the roots and tugged. "Do you see why he drives me crazy?"

Jocelyn set down her notepad and folded her hands in her lap. "Here's what I suggest. Let's work together to formulate a clear request for Jaxon as to what he wants and needs from your marriage. He may ask for something from you that you feel equipped to give or that you and I can work on together. Or he may ask for something from you that you do not have to give. In that case, though the communication of his need and your lack to be able to provide it would be painful, honesty is better than spinning your wheels guessing."

Something she did not have to give? Her lack to be able to provide what he needed? Her throat closed. She shook her head. "Whatever it is, whatever he needs, I'll make it work."

Jocelyn leaned forward. "You sound determined to make your marriage work, but knowing what you can do and what you can't do is a sign of great maturity."

"I need to be everything my husband needs me to be. He's the one person in this world I have to bend and break for."

"Why do you feel you have to bend and break for your husband?"

"What kind of question is that? Of course I have to."

"Because he needs you to, or because you need to feel successful at this relationship to feel whole?"

Sahara sprung to her feet. Her purse tumbled to the floor. "I knew this was a waste of time. I can't believe I let Myra talk me into this." She snatched her purse and slung it over her shoulder. "Forget it. I'll figure out what Jaxon needs, and I'll figure out how to meet his needs. Because that's what a good wife does."

Jocelyn's soft voice crested like a wave behind her, but she blocked it out. She pushed through the office doors and into the warm evening air.

Chapter 15

IS ANYTHING WORTH IT?
MARY BOYKIN CHESNUT

Bernie
July 22, 1861
Manassa, Virginia

Bernie and Henrietta sauntered down the road, their skirts swishing with each step. Bernie adjusted her bonnet strings. Now unaccustomed to wearing something so frivolous, it felt odd and unnatural.

"Are they still watching?" Bernie whispered.

Henrietta cast a glance over her shoulder. "Greenman is."

Bernie groaned. "Is he going to watch until we get to the station? Why didn't he carry us over his shoulder and put us on the train car himself?"

Henrietta chuckled.

"I don't know what you think is so funny. We've been kicked out of the army! Put in lady clothes. Sent home. I'm disgraced." Bernie hung her head.

"First time, I take it."

"First time what? Getting kicked out of the army?"

"Yes."

"Yes, it was my first time. You?" Bernie looked over at her friend to see a glint of amusement in her gaze.

"Third."

Bernie stopped in her tracks. "You got kicked out two previous times?"

"It's part of the experience. No big deal. We'll find another regiment and reenlist." She shrugged.

"That's what you've done? You got kicked out and enlisted with another company?"

"Sure did. And they were none the wiser." Henrietta tapped Bernie's elbow. "And this way, we can serve together."

A slow grin spread. Oh, that was why she'd asked Bernie to trust her. They resumed their walk toward the station. A sea of soldiers would be there. It would be quite easy to melt into the crowd. Bernie's gaze snagged on her skirt's yellow calico. Well, not dressed like this. "Where will we get more men's clothing?"

Henrietta patted the pack she'd somehow convinced them not to confiscate.

"You have some? In there?"

"Sure do."

"Where'd you get them?"

Henrietta averted her gaze. "Best not ask."

"Off dead men?" Bernie's stomach roiled.

"I said don't ask."

Bernie pressed her lips together. Maybe Henrietta pilfered them from lifeless bodies strewn across the battlefield. Or perhaps she stole them. If Bernie didn't know where they came from, she had no part in the guilt of wearing them, did she? No matter how bad it was, she'd done worse today. She'd stopped men's beating hearts. So what if she took the clothes from their backs. What did it matter, anyway? What did any of it matter?

Grief attempted to roll up her throat, but she swallowed it. She had to leave thoughts of her baby back on the battlefield. Her shoulders weren't broad enough to carry the weight of such a heavy burden. No. She must focus on why she set off to fight this war to begin with. Survive. Find Hermann. Bring him home. Nothing else mattered.

~

Their victory had made the Confederate army lax. In the nearly three months since the battle at Manassas, there'd been far fewer drills. Bernie and Henrietta tented together after they enlisted as chums in the Eighteenth Mississippi. They'd been careful not to so much as whisper their shared secret. Even when they thought no one could hear, snooping ears were everywhere. Instead, they communicated their shared comradery through a look here, a hand on the shoulder there, a chuckle at an odd time. It was enough.

At times, Bernie found herself going through route drills with her mind miles away, buried with the miniature frame of her child. When a command or blast brought her back to the present, grief clawed at her chest. She tampered it down, put on a brave face, and left a piece of herself behind each time.

They'd been in Leesburg, Virginia, since August and hadn't seen any action. On picket duty again, Bernie hunkered against a tree trunk and scanned the area. Her job was to watch out for danger. She'd best be ready in case a Yank tried to start something. Yet, everything remained quiet on the Potomac since Manassas. And though it was possible for a fight to break out, it was far more likely for—

There it was. Bernie's ears perked at a whistle. A Yankee soldier inched forward. Her hand tightened on her rifle until he waved his hat in the air. "Hey ya, boys." He spoke with a strange accent. Was that how Northerners talked? "Would any of you fine gents happen to have tobacco to trade? I've got me coffee to part with."

Bernie cocked her head at the way he said *coffee*. Real coffee? Her stomach rumbled at the thought of it. How long had it been since they'd had anything other than a sorry substitute made with rye, sweet potatoes, or beets?

Henrietta sauntered forward. "Sounds like a fair trade."

Bernie matched her stride. Her friend shouldn't be at the picket line alone.

The Yankee's face lit as Henrietta riffled through her sack and pulled out a tin of tobacco. He produced a bag of coffee from his own sack, and they shook hands. "Nice doin' business with ya," the Yank said.

"Much obliged." Henrietta brought the coffee to her nose and sniffed. A grin spread.

The Yankee settled onto a stump and stuffed a wad of tobacco into the side of his cheek, apparently in no hurry to scurry back to his side. "Any news?"

"None here," Henrietta said. "When will your men make a move?"

The Yankee shrugged. "No tellin'." He pulled sheet iron crackers from his pack. "Hardtack?" He offered one to the women. Bernie took it from his outstretched hand. "You can soften it in your coffee."

She nodded her thanks.

He stretched his long legs out in front of him. "This here's one bear of a war, ain't it? How long do you think it'll last?"

"Not long." Henrietta flashed a sassy smile. "We'll whip you right quick."

Bernie's stomach tripped over itself. If only she could believe that. If only it were true. But dread curled its fingers around the base of her throat.

The Yank laughed. "You Rebs got spunk. I'll give you that." He leaned forward and rested his elbows on his knees, lacing his fingers together. He peered at Bernie then, and when he spoke, it was as if his words went clean through her. "But we got the Almighty on our side. We're on the side of justice and righteousness. Right always wins in the end."

She couldn't breathe. Her lungs refused to function as her conscience scrambled to regain footing. What was he saying? That she was on the side of wrong? The wrong side of the war? The cadence of Abram's and Bob's voices filtered through her memory.

"Both sides read and use the Bible, soldier." Henrietta sounded unaffected, unruffled.

Yes, that was true. Bernie inhaled deeply through her nose. Many God-fearing people owned slaves. Many God-fearing pastors didn't condemn the practice.

"And yet, we cannot both be correct." Though he pointed a finger at Henrietta, his gaze remained fixed on Bernie. The pit in her stomach remained.

Henrietta shrugged. "Thanks for the coffee." She turned and sauntered back to the line of trees. Bernie took a step to follow.

"What are you fighting for?"

She spun back around as his words echoed in her ears. His blue eyes pierced her. "Excuse me?"

"What are you fighting for? Why do you fight in this war?"

She forced words past her tight throat. "I'm fighting for my family."

"I'm fighting for the freedom of a people who've been oppressed for generations. What about their families?"

With a dip of her head, she turned and walked to the shelter of a line of trees, fully aware that his words lodged like shrapnel in her heart.

~

Bernie's ears perked, on high alert for the slightest sound of danger.

"Something's about to happen," Henrietta whispered. They lay in their tent at night in full gear, arms stiff at their sides. "I can feel it in the air, like before lightning strikes in a storm."

Fall lingered in the air, as did rumblings of another fight. "About time." Something had to happen, because if nothing did, this war would stretch on forever. Hermann would remain apart from her forever. Still, her throat went dry at the thought of what the next day might bring. Would she survive it? Her head dropped to the side, and she surveyed her friend who was lying still in the moonlight. If some Yank killed Henrietta, how would she cope?

Where was Hermann tonight? Was he on the eve of a battle somewhere? Was he thinking of her? Endeavoring to make his way home to her? She closed her eyes and tried to envision his smile, his laugh, but other memories crowded it out. Memories of sulfur and smoke, of the tumult of desperate shouts, the shriek of shells, the zing of bullets. She gave her head a slight shake to dislodge the cacophony and find her husband in the fray, find him on their farm among the sheep and cattle. Find him ambling along the fence line, a spring breeze tousling his hair, a song whistling from his lips. But a scream sounded in her mind as a man fell to his death before her. Another doubled over from a wound to his stomach. A cannon blasted mere feet in front of her. Hermann. Where was Hermann? How could she get to him?

She squeezed her eyes tighter. If only this was a dream she could wake from, but she wasn't asleep. Now that the possibility of another battle loomed, the scenes from the last battle played out in her mind day and night. There was no escape. She must push it down. Away from her mind. Because she would likely fight again tomorrow, and she couldn't allow a lick of cowardice. *What are you fighting for?* For him. For Hermann. She could do this job as good as any man, and she would. She would do what she had to do. Survive. Find Hermann. Bring him home. Whatever the cost.

~

Bernie focused her gaze on the force ahead of them as the thunder of boots clomped through the field toward their target. The afternoon sun beat down, and a thin trail of perspiration beaded the nape of her neck. The orders were to attack, and she pushed all else out of her mind. Blood rushed in her ears as her pulse hammered in time to the soldiers' steps. With her eyes trained on the enemy, they neared the middle of the field.

A rustling to her left snagged Bernie's attention. Movement teased her from the corner of her eye. She turned her head just in time to see a large troop emerge from the woods, rifles aimed at her and her company.

"Watch out!" she cried. "To your left!"

But it was too late. Bullets banged and zinged. The man on her left fell to the ground in a heap. Then, the soldier in front of her did the same. Shock melted into rage as heat sizzled through her limbs. She aimed and fired her rifle, watching in triumph as one man went down, then another. Beside her, Henrietta's breath came in short bursts as she fired again and again toward the men in the trees.

Keeping her gaze forward, Bernie leaned close and whispered, "Attagirl. Let's show these boys what we're made of."

A man charged close—was he out of ammunition?—and lunged at her with his bayonet. She spun toward him and brandished her own. Sabers clashed and clanked as she dodged his jabs and delivered some of her own. He slashed with vigor, his wild eyes devoid of anything other than bloodlust. All of a sudden, his foot swiped at her own, and she went down. The ground jumped up to meet her with a hard thump. Her weapon fell from her grasp and thumped in the grass. She looked up at his snickering face as he pressed his bayonet to her chest.

This was it. She was done for. After all she'd been through, she would die in the field this day. And after all her boasts, it would be at the losing end of a bayonet battle. She clamped her eyes shut and prayed it would end swiftly.

A bang sounded, and the pressure to her chest fell away. When she opened her eyes, her opponent lay in a heap near her feet. Henrietta stood, chest heaving, rifle aimed in his direction.

She'd saved her life.

Her friend winked at her. "What are you doing just lying there? We're in the middle of battle, soldier. Get up and fight."

Reeling, she stumbled to her feet. Henrietta handed her rifle back to her.

"Withdraw. Withdraw." The order came, and they scrambled to the top of the hill, several men falling prey to assailing bullets in their retreat.

~

The afternoon wore on. They now fought in the woods toward the ravine, firing from tree to tree. The towering timber obscured any clear view of the enemy. Exactly who were they contending with? How many soldiers opposed them? The trees that hid and sheltered her sheltered them as well, and tension hung thick in the air. A chilly breeze sent a shiver down her arms. Where would the next bullet come from? Anxiety frayed her nerves like a weathered rope. Could they not get a break from this? If only it would end. Weariness pulled at her limbs.

As daylight faded, a tumult arose. Voices called to each other. Frenzied movement. Chaos. Confusion. Suddenly, the Union army turned and swarmed to the Potomac. Around her, Southerners whooped and yelled as they chased their enemies. Her boots pounded through the woods, over open ground, and to the edge of the bluff.

"Drive them to the river! Capture them." The command filtered to her ears, but as the river came into sight, she slowed. Then stilled.

Union soldiers stumbled and tumbled over the bluff, falling into the river, sputtering in the wide waters. Shots fired from Confederate guns pummeled the men as they ran for their lives. Shrieks and groans arose as they collapsed and rolled down the bluff. Southern soldiers captured some men, their heads drooped in defeat. But it was the ones who were drowning before her eyes that made her blood run cold. Four boats waited, but those sank when Confederates shot holes in them. Some soldiers clung to the bluff for dear life. Hands flailed in the air. Heads bobbed to the surface and sank, bobbed and sank, bobbed and … She squeezed her eyes shut as shivers coursed through her body. This had to be a bad dream. She was living a nightmare. Screams assaulted her ears and melted with the rebel cry. When she opened her eyes, reality smacked her in the face.

What was she doing here? Nothing was worth this. This price was far too high to pay. She should have stayed on her farm, watched after her sheep, and waited for her husband to return. Nurtured the life within her. Trusted in her prayers alone to keep him safe.

Leaves crunched beside her, and a hand rested on her shoulder. Henrietta. "Oh, heavens," she whispered, surveying the scene before them.

Bernie couldn't stop trembling. "Bodies are washing down the river." She couldn't bring herself to say *dead bodies*, though surely none of those who floated downstream could survive. Where would they wash up? Who would find them? Report their death to their family?

A Confederate to their left let out a whoop. "Did you see those Yanks run? Another Confederate victory!"

Bernie couldn't force herself to smile. May she never fight in a slaughter like this again.

~

Army life meant so much waiting. Normally, the tedious boredom wore on Bernie, but now waiting in Richmond wasn't a problem. No need to rush back into battle. They'd moved to Culpepper, then Yorktown, and now they'd been in Richmond about a month, reorganizing the regiment. Now requests came for a two-year re-enlistment. Two years! So much for a ninety-day war.

Henrietta didn't hesitate to sign the next two years of her life away, but Bernie wavered. Perhaps she should go home.

Her sheep would welcome her back. There might be letters from Hermann. She could write back, encourage him the best she knew how. Would her words prove purer now that she'd been refined in the fire of battle?

But if she retreated, everything she'd gone through thus far was for naught, including the loss of her child. Hadn't she come too far to turn back now? She spread her hand over her flat stomach, heart echoing the hollow place there. Nothing could return to the way it was before the war. That truth sank deep into her bones. This rift between the states had changed everything and everyone. No one would come out unscathed.

Henrietta and Bernie lounged against a tree. The nearest campfire pushed warmth toward their toes. "Take a look at that soldier. He's a mite handsome, wouldn't you say?" Bernie craned her neck to see the man her friend spoke about. Orange radiance from the fire licked his dark trimmed beard and distinguished brow. "He must be new. I don't recall seeing him before," Henrietta continued.

But Bernie sucked on the inside of her cheek. He looked familiar, though in the dimness of the setting sun, it was hard to tell. Something about his angular jaw.

As if sensing their stares, he turned in their direction. Bernie averted her gaze.

Henrietta spoke out of the corner of her mouth. "Goodness! He's coming this way."

Bernie nudged her. "Remember who you are, *Henry*." Last thing they needed was to be tossed out again because her friend's flirtatiousness gave them away.

She looked up as the man approached and felt the blood drain from her face. Fredrick Rempart. A neighbor from childhood, only a few years older than her. She scrambled to her feet and stuck out her hand, eager to beat Henrietta to the introductions.

"Hello, I'm Bernard." He could not know her last name. She made her handshake firm.

Henrietta's forehead creased, but she smiled slightly. "And I'm Henry."

"Freddy Rempart. Nice to meet you."

"Good to meet you." Bernie's words rushed out too fast.

Henrietta's lopsided grin spoke of an interest Bernie hoped he'd misinterpret. "You're new?"

"Joined up this morning. Had to take care of business back home before I could enlist." His smile wavered. What business? Hopefully, nothing was wrong with his mother. She'd been such a gentle soul.

"Glad to have you on board." Henrietta patted him on the back.

"Thanks. I've been looking for friendly chaps. Seems like you're the welcoming committee."

"That's us." Henrietta roped an arm around Bernie's shoulder, pulling her close.

Bernie forced a grin. "We were about to retire for the night, but perhaps tomorrow, I can best you in a game of checkers." Her laugh came out stiff and awkward.

A sound emanated from Henrietta's throat. Bernie stepped on her toe slightly to keep her from protesting further. Her friend frowned and slid her foot away.

"Retire this early?" Freddy lifted a brow.

"It's been a long day." The excuse fell lamely from her lips.

"We were on night patrol last night," Henrietta added.

"Ah." Freddy nodded. "Understandable. See you tomorrow, then."

The two women were halfway to their tent before Henrietta whispered, "What was that about?"

Bernie cast a worried glance over her shoulder. Coast clear. "I know him."

Henrietta's mouth parted. "You know Freddy?"

"Yes. He was a childhood neighbor."

"What's he doing in the Eighteenth Mississippi?"

Bernie rolled her eyes. "I don't know. What are we doing in the Eighteenth Mississippi?"

"Well, he didn't recognize you. That's good."

"Not yet. But it's dark. What if the resemblance hits him when the lighting's better?" She put a hand on her friend's shoulder. "You cannot call me Bernie. Call me Bernard."

"I'll try. It'll be difficult."

"We have to steer clear of him." Her gaze darted all around. Just in case.

Henrietta smirked. "Then why'd you offer to play him checkers?"

"I didn't want to appear suspicious."

"Don't you think it'll be a bit suspicious when you don't make good on your offer?"

"I haven't thought ahead that far."

Henrietta snorted. "This will be a fun game of cat and mouse."

~

A day full of drills, inspections, a lecture, and a march kept Freddy away from the women. Now, though, the men were free to do as they pleased. Henrietta set to work making coosh for dinner out of bacon and cornmeal while Bernie split more wood for the fire with her bowie knife.

Freddy loped up to them, stretching his arms over his head. "Hiya, boys."

Bernie swallowed and held back a wince. She erased the frown from her face, though she likely never reached a full smile. "Hello, Freddy."

Henrietta waved and patted the stump next to her.

Bernie shot her a glare as Freddy sat, making himself right at home among them.

"So, Freddy," Henrietta said, "where are you from?"

He leaned forward and laced his fingers together. "Corinth, recently, but Charleston originally."

Henrietta sat forward, ignoring the sizzling in the pan. "How interesting—"

"What made you move?" Bernie tried for an air of nonchalance but likely failed. She ceased chopping wood and turned the knife over in her hands for a distraction. The less eye contact she made, the better.

He smiled. "Don't tell me you're a South Carolinian."

She gave a singular nod. "From Honey Hill." He'd known her growing up in Charleston. Had he heard she'd married and moved to Shulerville?

"It's a splendid state. I'd be there still if not for my wife. She hails from Corinth. We live there to be near her family."

So, he had married as well. Good for him. Married and … "Any children?"

He straightened. "One boy. Two years old. Buster."

Her throat constricted. Why had she asked? She forced the words out. "Congratulations. You must be proud."

"Proud as can be." His chest puffed out. "How about you? Married? Children?"

She clenched her jaw while shaking her head. Bile rose in her throat. How could she deny Hermann? Her child? But of course, she must. She couldn't force herself to speak.

He turned to Henrietta. "You?"

She scoffed. "Not me."

"Well, it will come."

Henrietta slid coosh onto two tin plates. "Want some?" she asked Freddy.

"No, I'm all right. I'll have my slave cook me something in a bit. He's laundering my clothes at the present."

Bernie hid a flinch. He'd brought a slave along to make harsh army life more comfortable?

Henrietta continued, not appearing bothered in the least. "Suit yourself."

The women dug in to the dry, tasteless meal.

"You burnt the bacon again," Bernie mumbled.

Henrietta chuckled. She cast a glance at Freddy. "Aren't you disappointed you passed? Bernie and I take turns cooking. You'd have a better meal tomorrow." As if suddenly realizing what she'd said, she paused with her fork halfway to her mouth.

Bernie's breath hitched, but she forced herself to take another bite. Perhaps he wouldn't even notice the use of her nickname.

"Bernie, you say? Is that what you go by, Bernard?"

No such luck.

"That's right." She kept her gaze trained on the last couple of bites of her meal.

He tilted his head. "I used to know a Bernie."

"You don't say." With her dinner finished, she needed something to occupy her hands, her attention. She could not risk looking him in the face. She picked up her knife and tugged a long branch in front of her. She could trim it down to make it ready for the fire.

"It was a girl, actually. Bernice, I'd guess, though I never heard her called anything but Bernie. Plucky little thing." His voice took on a reminiscent air. "She wasn't afraid to get her hands dirty, that's for sure. Caught frogs and lizards. It was nearly like she was one of the boys. Her parents had the hardest time teaching her to be ladylike."

Bernie pressed her lips together as she hacked at the branch with her knife.

"You remind me of her, actually."

Bernie yanked her head up, alarm coursing through her.

"Something about your eyes."

Her eyes? She'd been working to keep her eyes away from his scrutiny. Pain sliced through her then, and she gasped. Her gaze fell to her bloody left thigh, then to the bowie knife in her right hand. She'd cut herself? She'd missed the mark and sliced into her flesh. She sucked in a ragged breath and dropped the knife. It clattered to the ground as Henrietta and Freddy huddled around her.

Henrietta knelt in front of her. "Here. Let me see."

Bernie's leg shook as she stretched it out. How could she have let this happen? She'd survived battles that other men died in only to sustain an injury at her own hands. Ludicrous. Mortifying.

"I'll fetch the doctor." Freddy started to jog away.

"No!" Bernie gritted out. "I'll be fine. I don't need a doctor." It was far too dangerous. The doctor would likely make her undress, and what then?

His brow furrowed. "What do you mean? You have an injury. Of course, you need a doctor."

"No." Henrietta spoke with authority. "She doesn't. We can take care of it. Fetch us bandages, will you?"

"No, I won't. I'm going to get the …" He looked back and forth between them, then zoned in on Bernie's face. He blinked. His jaw dropped. "Bernie?"

Her stomach plummeted. "Please don't tell," she whispered. Her eyes pleaded with him to understand, to have compassion, to keep her secret.

"Bernie?" he repeated, his voice raspy.

She nodded.

"What are you doing here?"

"Fighting for the one I love."

Henrietta stepped close to him and put a hand on his arm. "Now, please go fetch bandages so she can continue to do it."

He shifted his weight from foot to foot, clearly torn. His jaw worked from side to side. Finally, he shoved a hand through his hair and turned to go.

"Do you think he went to get bandages, the doctor, or the colonel?" Bernie bit her lip.

Henrietta shrugged. "I don't know, and we can't worry about that now. Let's take care of this wound."

With a wet handkerchief, Henrietta wiped away excess blood. Bernie pressed the handkerchief to the wound to stop the flow. A few minutes later, Freddy returned with bandages. Bernie's shoulders dipped in relief.

"Thank you." Her heart swelled with gratitude.

"Now, can you help me get her to our tent?"

Henrietta hooked her arm through one of Bernie's and Freddy hooked his through the other. With their support, she managed to limp to her tent.

"Stand guard, will you?" Henrietta asked Freddy.

He gave a solemn nod.

Inside the tent, Henrietta helped Bernie undress, then she wrapped the bandages around her wounded leg. Once her pants were back on, Bernie lay down. Henrietta lifted the flap and went out. Her conversation with Freddy drifted to Bernie's ears.

Freddy's deep voice sounded shaken. "So, are you a-a—"

"Am I a woman, you mean?" Henreitta's voice contained a lilt.

"Yes. I guess that's what I mean."

"I am. But I'm a fine soldier. Bernie and I both are. We fought in Manassas and Ball's Bluff, and we'll fight in whatever other battles we face. Don't you think that because we're women, we're not up to the task."

"I don't know what to think."

"Just don't say anything. We've worked real hard to get where we are. Let us be. Please."

Boots crunched away, and Henrietta ducked into the tent.

Bernie bit her lip. "Do you think he'll tell?"

"No." Henrietta smirked. "Most decisively not."

"How can you be sure?"

"I have a sense about these things." She dropped onto her blanket. "He's handsome. Too bad he's married."

And a slaveholder. But when had that ever bothered her before? She'd grown up in Charleston, for goodness' sake. Though not wealthy enough to own slaves of their own, her family never spoke against it. *She* never spoke against it.

She shook herself from the musings. "You're something else. You didn't have to confess, you know. He'd be none the wiser if you denied it."

She gave a firm shake of the head. "I'm proud of who I am. Wish I didn't have to hide it from anyone." She rolled onto her side and propped onto her elbow. "Can you imagine a world where society acknowledged women as brave and strong instead of merely docile and dutiful?"

Bernie blinked back at her. What a world.

~

Leg throbbing, Bernie shifted onto her side. Crickets serenaded her with their melody in the darkness. A sliver of moonlight crossed the top of her tent. Hushed conversation filtered in from a distance, but mostly the night hung still and quiet. The pain in her thigh amplified without anything to distract from it. A doctor may have given her something to dull the ache. She blew out a breath. Physical discomfort wasn't the only thing keeping rest at bay.

"Can't sleep?" Henrietta's soft voice startled her.

"I didn't know you were awake."

"Too much excitement today, I reckon."

Bernie let out a soft snort. "Shows you how dull our days are between battles."

"Why are you up? Is it your leg?"

"Partly." She bit her lip. Could she divulge what she'd spent hours pondering? The woman beside her knew her biggest secret and kept it faithfully. Surely, she could be trusted to hold Bernie's doubts in her hands without recoiling in revulsion. She took a deep breath, then let her words creep out slow and cautious. "Do you ever wonder … Do you ever think about slavery and whether it's right?"

At Henrietta's pause, a cold stone seemed to weigh heavy on Bernie's chest. Her heartbeat galloped faster and faster as silence stretched.

Finally, her friend spoke. "Whether it's right?" She said the words as if she were tasting them on her tongue for the first time. "What are you? An abolitionist?"

"No." Bernie's answer rushed out too quick and nervous. But she wasn't, was she? An abolitionist spoke out boldly against slavery. She'd only begun to consider. To ponder. "Just thinking."

"It's the way things are." Bernie could hear the shrug in her friend's voice. "Slavery is as old as mankind himself. It's in the Bible. I've never owned a slave myself, but who am I to tell someone else they shouldn't?"

"Hmm." Bernie's mumbling neither assented to Henrietta's assessment nor denied it, but let it swing like a pendulum in front of her. Who was she to challenge an institution as old as time? Who was she?

"Focus on finding and reuniting with your husband. Don't get distracted by anything else." A yawn followed Henrietta's words. Bernie let them rest over the women like a blanket. She was right. Finding Hermann had to be her priority. Her only priority. But Bob and Abram flitted to mind as she drifted to sleep, leaving her unsettled. She had fitful dreams of dark men in chains.

~

September 17, 1862

Stomach cramping with hunger, Bernie marched toward the sound of gunfire. Rumor had it that the battle at Sharpsburg began hours ago. The Eighteenth Mississippi was late to the fray due to the fight at Harpers Ferry. They'd scaled the mountain and fought for a while before the enemy escaped. Now, orders led them here. They'd marched all night, and many men, as well as Henrietta, were too exhausted to go into battle.

But not Bernie. Though weariness pulled at her limbs, there was no way she would miss this chance to reunite with her husband. Nothing would keep her from the possibility of seeing him. Not tiredness or hunger. Not fear of death. She steeled herself for another battle as they neared the West Woods.

The roar of artillery and shouting rolled toward them. The scent of blood and death wafted in the air. She held her breath for a minute before releasing a slow exhale. She would not, could not, die today. She hadn't come this far to lie bloody in the woods. An image of the infant she buried flitted to mind. She swallowed against the ache. No time to dwell on that now. *Please, Lord, sharpen my senses. And help me find Hermann.* He had to be here. From the bits and pieces of conversation she'd overheard, most everyone would be.

If she wanted to find her husband, she needed to break away from her company. Sooner rather than later. Thankfully, she was at the back of the line. Easier to sneak away that way. There. In about twenty paces, she could duck behind a large tree. No. It was too soon, especially with nothing to distract the others. They'd find her out and reprimand her for shirking from battle. Maybe if—

A soldier rushed through the trees to speak with Major Campbell. The regiment stilled as the two conferred. Then Campbell's command rang out. "Pick up the pace, boys. They need us to help thrash New York."

Boots clomped at a steady, rapid pace as the regiment jogged to their assignment. Sticks and leaves crunched under their feet. Rifles clanged against bodies as they ran. A man a few feet ahead of her stumbled on a tree root. His comrades scrambled to steady him before he fell and toppled those coming up behind him. Men swarmed around them but didn't stop. *Now.* Bernie seized the opportunity afforded by the distraction and dashed to the right, holding herself as still as possible behind the oak.

She held her breath. The pounding of footsteps faded into the distance. She waited. Would anyone come looking for her? Surely not. Not until the battle was over. They had far more important things to focus on.

Once convinced the coast was clear, she wove her way through the trees to her right, on the lookout for a soldier from another company. She crunched her way onward, grinding acorns into the dirt with her boots. She was too far back, too far from the heat of the battle. Still, the ground shook with each boom of a cannon. The shaking intensified. She must be nearing a battery.

"Bernie?" The hiss of her name filtered through the trees.

Her breath hitched as she stilled. Who was it? Footsteps crunched closer. Two sets? She craned her neck in the direction of the voice.

"Bernie, is that you?"

From between branches, a face emerged. Freddy. She let out a long exhale. Just Freddy. And … someone clomped behind him. His slave. Her shoulders slumped ever so slightly.

"Yes, it's me," she mumbled her defeat.

"What in the blazes are you doing?" His forehead creased as he searched her face.

"Looking for my husband."

His lips pressed in a firm line. "Fine. I'll help."

"Don't be ridiculous. No sense in both of us getting reprimanded. Get back to our unit."

He shook his head. "I don't like the idea of you trouncing out here alone."

Oh, that was it. She planted a hand on her hip. "You mean because I'm a woman."

The dark man's eyes went wide. Oops. Guess she'd confirmed it. As if saying she was looking for her husband hadn't been enough. Now another person to keep her secret. One more mouth with the potential to betray her.

Freddy scoffed. "No."

Her narrow eyes pinned him down.

"Yes." His exaggerated exhale caused a tuft of hair to lift from his brow. "It's not right for you to be out here unprotected."

"This is war. We're all vulnerable to the enemy."

"We're safer in a company."

She shrugged. Maybe. Maybe not. She didn't have time to argue. She had to find Hermann. "I need to get closer. See if I can find someone who can tell me where the South Carolinians are stationed." She turned from him without a backward glance.

Rifle cocked on her shoulder, she crept forward to the battlefield. What would she find there? Friend or foe? Who claimed the field closest to her? She inched closer, ignoring the echo of footsteps behind her. Smoke hung in the air. The zing of bullets confirmed she was close. Through the branches, the shape of men formed in the haze.

Just then, a man staggard backward and fell in a heap.

"Ziggy!" Another soldier stared at the crumpled body with haunted eyes. "Blasted Yankees." His face reddened. "I'll show you a thing or two."

"Excuse me," Bernie said.

The man's gaze snapped to her as did the barrel of his gun. The footsteps crunched to a halt behind her.

She threw up her hands. "I'm Confederate."

He slowly lowered his weapon.

"I'm looking for the South Carolinians. Do you know where they're stationed?"

"You got separated?"

She nodded. Yes, she did. A long time ago.

"I heard they're behind Dunker Church. Thataway." He pointed to the right.

"Much obliged." She ducked her head in gratitude, then retreated farther into the woods. "Come on." She waved Freddy to follow as she continued her trek.

They walked in silence for a few minutes, pushing branches and leaves from their way so they didn't smack them in the face. Their quiet unnerved her. She cast a side-eyed glance at the dark-skinned man, then at Freddy. "Are you going to tell me his name, or must I refer to him as your slave?" The words tasted bitter on her tongue.

His brow creased in puzzlement for a second before it relaxed. "Oh, this is Jimmy."

"Jimmy," she repeated. Much better.

"How long has Jimmy been with you?" No, the awkwardness remained. Perhaps because she talked about the man right in front of him instead of talking directly to him.

"He was my wife's family's slave. A wedding present."

A wedding present? What was she to say to that? *How nice? Congratulations?* Her in-laws gifted her a tea set for her wedding. Freddy's had gifted them a human being.

The ground rumbled, snapping her thoughts back to the present. She had no time for idle chatter. She must stay alert.

Her stomach growled in protest. When was the last time she'd eaten? A swig of water would have to do. Her teeth chattered against the canteen at the blast of cannons. Another battery? At least it was certain to be friendly fire turned away from her and toward the enemy. Every muscle ached as she pushed her body to continue. How far was Dunker Church? She needed to approach the battle again.

She angled her head in that direction. "Let's check our progress."

They exited the trees and came into a clearing. In front of them stood a battery. A cannoneer pounded the charge into the gun's barrel with his ramrod while the other soldiers stood at the ready. The sergeant moved in and aimed the cannon.

"Prepare," he ordered.

A scurry of activity ensued, and then the men directly beside the cannon leaned to the side and covered one ear.

"Fire!"

A crack blared as the shell flew.

"Excuse me." Bernie inched closer.

Only one man whipped around to meet her gaze. The others must not have heard her. He raised a brow.

"Where am I?"

"This here is Raine's Battery."

She spotted a building up ahead, but it appeared to be a house, not a church. "How far to Dunker Church? I'm looking for the South Carolinians."

He waved a hand in the general direction she'd been traveling. "Past Walker's Division."

"Thanks."

"Thank you, kindly," Freddy echoed.

Once again, they retreated farther back.

Was this madness? Even if she found the South Carolinians by Dunker Church, there was only a slight chance Tuffle's Brigade was among them. They could be anywhere on this massive battlefield, or nowhere at all.

Or he could have already departed from this world. She clenched her jaw. No. She would not give in to that worry. She'd push that thought far from her mind. Survive. Find Hermann. Bring him home. She rehearsed her goal with each step.

Finally, she neared the sound of intense fighting. Muskets rattled and pinged, and men's voices echoed off the trees. Soldiers stood a few feet ahead of her. She made her way to one, swallowing as she stepped over a corpse that reeked of fresh blood to get to him.

"Are you Walker's Division?"

She must have startled him, for he whipped around, nearly knocking into her with his rifle.

"Yeah. You?"

"I got separated from my company of South Carolinians. I'm turned around. They that way?" She pointed.

"Yeah. Be careful. This is madness."

As if on cue, a bullet crested her shoulder. She shuddered. That was close. Too close. She needed to be alert. She took cover behind a tree, then dashed to the next. She had to move closer to the front, closer to the church. Wait. Where were Freddy and Jimmy? A glance around didn't bring them to her line of sight. When had she lost them? She'd been preoccupied in her own thoughts.

She shook her head. No matter. They could take care of themselves. She must continue with her mission. She moved from oak to oak, rifle at the ready. As she came closer, her throat went dry. She couldn't fathom the carnage. The amount of dead and wounded men strewn before her rivaled any battlefield she'd been in thus far. What was happening here? Shots rang out, and two men collapsed in front of her with a collective groan. Her eyes widened. Had she come this far only to die now?

Wait? Could it be? In front of her, a soldier fired away. The familiarity of his wiry frame, the stoop of his shoulders, the curve of his nose …

"Hermann?" she shouted.

Mouth agape, he turned toward her. Her husband. At last. His brow wrinkled. His lip trembled. "Bernie?" His voice wavered.

She broke out in a run toward this man she'd fought a war to find.

The snap of musket fire sounded close. So close it snatched her breath. Hermann cried out, then stumbled and fell to the ground at her feet.

Chapter 16

AND THE SUNLIGHT CLASPS THE EARTH
AND THE MOONBEAMS KISS THE SEA:
WHAT IS ALL THIS SWEET WORK WORTH
IF THOU KISS NOT ME?

"LOVE'S PHILOSOPHY" BY PERCY BYSSHE SHELLEY

Sahara
Present Day
Provo, Utah

Sahara banged on the Geo Metro's dash as if she were a doctor using a defibrillator to shock a patient back to life. "Oh no. No. No. No. Stay with me, little guy. Don't give up on me now!"

But Met—as she had nicknamed him—puttered, uttered a strange clang, and slowed. Good gravy, the car was about to die an overly dramatic death like a soap opera actor right in the middle of the highway. Right here on her way back from counseling. Sahara checked her mirrors, then yanked the steering wheel and veered Met onto the shoulder before he puffed out his last breath.

Cars whizzed by as she forced her shallow breaths to slow. She'd made it safely out of harm's way, though barely. She was okay. But her only means of transportation in this foreign city was dead. And from the sound of it, resurrecting this baby would likely cost far more than he was worth. She'd meant this purchase as a business deal. Buy a cheap car. Drive it for a few months. Shine it up like new. Sell it for a few hundred more than she bought it for. This was not in the plan.

She dropped her head onto the steering wheel. What now? Should she call AAA? Did they still have AAA? That was one domain Jaxon had always handled. She pursed her lips. Should she call him? They weren't exactly on the best terms. But this was an emergency. She blew out a breath and snatched her phone. Her finger hovered over number two on speed dial. He'd thought this a stupid purchase. His disdain for old Met had been palpable. Did she want to sit there and listen to him gloat? Have him shove her face in how naive she'd been to buy a used car when, clearly, she knew nothing about automobiles? She could call a tow truck. Then, an Uber. Then … Then what?

Knee bobbing, she pressed the button and waited. His voicemail picked up on the third ring. She hung up without leaving a message.

Well, that was dumb. Now he'd think she was lonely and desperate. Pathetic. Very charming.

Googling tow services, it was. But as soon as she pulled up the search bar, her phone rang. Jaxon's handsome face flashed on the screen.

"Sahara, saw you called. What's wrong?"

The concern in his voice caused a lump to form in the back of her throat. She swallowed past it. "My car broke down. I'm on the side of the highway."

"Where at?"

Good question. She was still a bit confused with the area. At least she knew the highway she was on and a couple landmarks she'd passed. She relayed what she could remember.

"I think I know where that is. Hang on. I'll be there in about twenty."

Her voice came out scratchy and thin. "Thank you."

"Of course. Do you have water?"

"Water?"

"It's hot. Don't get overheated. If you can't roll down the windows, climb out your passenger door and wait for me in the grass. Don't stay in the stuffy car."

"Okay."

"Be there soon."

A click and he was gone. Before she could say, "I love you." When had she said it last? When was the last time she'd been confident enough to believe he'd say it back? Because now it felt too much like skydiving without knowing for sure whether she had a parachute.

Heat pressed in around her. Suddenly, Met had become an oven. The power of suggestion? Or perhaps it only took minutes without the air conditioner blasting for the desert sun to start talking trash. She took a swig from her water bottle, then shimmied over the gear shift and out the passenger's side door. She dug out her purse, water bottle, phone, utterly useless keys, and last scrap of dignity and plopped down on the grassy knoll a few feet from Met.

The sun beat down on her. Out here under the oppressive glare, it wasn't much cooler than the car. Too bad she didn't have her hat. Without shade, she felt naked under the sun's wrath, sweltering as searing heat beat down on her. Vehicles zipped past, one after the other, so fast the colors blurred. Was her vision hazing over? Exhaustion grappled with her, clutching to her consciousness for a minute before she shook herself from its grasp, only to succumb again. Everything was bright, then orange, then fading …

"Sahara!" A heavy hand shook her shoulder. A deep voice. Familiar. "Oh, dear God, let her be okay." Something cool on her forehead. A dribble of water against her lips. "Sahara, honey, drink."

Jaxon?

His hand cupped the back of her head and lifted it oh so gently. Refreshing liquid coursed through her mouth and down her throat. She sputtered. Her eyes fluttered open. Jaxon. His piercing blue eyes were serious. She swallowed.

How had she … Why was she lying down?

"That's right. Drink. Drink it all." As she did, the lines around his eyes softened. Tension eased from his shoulders. His mouth twitched in a nervous smile. "I told you not to get overheated."

If she had the energy, she'd think up some quippy comeback. Pain seared her temples and her extremities felt like wet noodles.

He pressed the cool rag to her forehead and cheeks again. As he did, his sandalwood scent pirouetted under her nostrils. It pulled on her fragile emotional state and tears brimmed in her eyes.

"Oh, Sahara, come here." Jaxon scooted next to her and pulled her to his chest. She clutched his crisp linen shirt—he must have changed after work—and let the tears fall. Tears for what? Maybe she was crying because she'd passed out on the side of the highway. Or because her car had broken down in a strange city. Perhaps it was because the man who came to rescue her had been so cruel recently. Or because he'd been so kind just now. Was it because of all she had or all she'd lost or all that was in between? Her head swam. Only one thing was clear.

"I love you." She eked it out, then held her breath as sheer terror raced through her veins.

He kissed the top of her head. "I know," he said, and then his phone belted out a ring tone. "Yes, that's right. A burgundy Geo Metro at mile marker …" He stood and took a few steps to the right, shading his eyes as he looked off down the highway.

Her stomach dropped. *I know.* What kind of response was that? He knew she loved him. Great. Glad it was obvious from the fact that she flew across the country to try and win him back. From how she'd studied for hours upon hours learning his stupid trade so she could work with him. From how she kept completely humiliating herself by throwing herself out there for him to reject again and again. *I know.* Wonderful. She'd married a genius.

But what if he'd been about to say it back before he was interrupted? The question nagged at her.

He turned to her with a smile. "Tow truck is almost here." He held out his hand. "We need to get you in the AC."

She took his hand, and he hefted her up, then cradled her elbow. "You okay? Feel steady enough to walk?"

She nodded, then reached down for her things. "Don't worry about that. I'll come back for them." He led her down the hill, taking baby steps, steadying her the couple of times she wobbled. He settled her in his Jeep and turned the vents so they blasted on her before he dashed back up the hill for her things.

Why hadn't he told her he loved her as soon as he hung up with the tow truck company? Did he have that short of an attention span? Had he forgotten already? She worried her lip. Perhaps she was being as naive about this as she'd been about the car.

Jaxon never said what he didn't mean.

Moments later, a tow truck came, and within twenty minutes, old Met faded to a spot in the distance.

"All right." Jaxon slipped into the driver's seat. "Got that taken care of. Now, I'll take you home."

Home. Wouldn't that be nice? But no, he'd take her to the drab one-bedroom apartment she spent evenings in alone. What a sorry excuse for an existence.

She shifted in her seat. "What about the car? Are they going to try to repair it, or do I need to find another one or what?"

"I'm taking care of it."

"What does that mean? You're getting it repaired?"

"It means," he said as he gave her a pointed look, "don't worry about it. I'm taking care of it."

She slammed her eyes shut. Counted to ten. She was too tired to play this game with him.

"I'll have to pick you up for work tomorrow."

Should she point out that it'd make things a whole lot easier if she stayed with him? She gnawed on her tongue. If the man couldn't even say he loved her …

"Okay."

A few beats of silence, and then Jaxon asked, "Where were you coming from anyway?"

She gave a humorless laugh. "Counseling."

He glanced at her with a raised brow. "You're kidding."

"Nope." She studied her cuticles.

"How'd it go?"

"Not great. Turns out she thinks maybe I can't be a good enough wife for you." So much for scoring bonus points with Jaxon.

Why did he look skeptical? "She said that?"

Sahara shrugged. "Not in those exact words."

"Maybe she's right. Maybe you can't be everything I need, and I can't be everything you need. Maybe we both need something more."

Panic swarmed her. *No.* What was he saying? He wanted another woman? Someone who could give him more than she could? She searched his profile with wide eyes.

"Don't look scared, Sahara. I went to church on Sunday."

Church? Her pulse slowed a notch. He was talking about church?

"The pastor spoke on how everyone has this space inside of us only God can fill. We all try to fill it with things and achievements and other people, and we come up empty. Until we're filled with Him, we won't be satisfied."

Her gaze dropped back to her cuticles. God could give her husband something she couldn't. That was … well, better than another woman, but it stung of defeat.

She spoke toward the window. "I don't know how I feel about the whole God thing."

"I know." There were those two words again. "But since you love me, do you think you could make a bit of space for the idea?"

Her mouth twisted. She couldn't make any promises, but … "Maybe."

He smiled. "Thank you."

Jaxon turned on his blinker a block before her exit.

"Why are you getting off here?"

"You need to rest tonight. Rest and stay hydrated. I don't want you to have to cook dinner."

"Oh." She hadn't even thought ahead that far.

"Is Subway okay?"

"Yeah."

He pulled into a strip mall. "Hang tight. I'll be right back. The usual?"

"Yes, please."

His thoughtfulness floored her. But why? Hadn't he always been attentive? The whole nurturing, protecting, providing thing fit Jaxon like a favorite pair of jeans. Had she simply stopped noticing?

Twenty minutes later, Jaxon helped her into her apartment, one arm supporting her elbow, the other toting a bag of sandwiches and her purse.

She opened her mouth to assure him she could manage on her own but clamped it shut. She'd swoon again if it meant he'd stay with her a little longer. Her knees wobbled at the thought. He tightened his grip.

"Almost there." Three more steps, and he paused to dig in her purse for the key.

"Oh, my book arrived." She started to bend and grab the package. Her head swam.

"I'll get it. Hold on." He held the keys out to her. She selected the one for the apartment and handed it back. He swooped up the book and opened the door.

They took two steps inside. His gaze roamed the space, as if taking everything in. How strange her temporary home was unfamiliar to him. He inhaled sharply, then refocused on her.

"Let's get you to the couch."

She let him guide her to the sofa, prop pillows behind her back, and cover her with a blanket. She took a deep breath. Closed her eyes. Her shoulders relaxed, and the pain pulsating through her temples eased.

Jaxon clanged around the kitchen.

She smiled. "What's that noise?"

"You don't have any tea. I've got to make some."

She should tell him not to bother. She needed to drink water, anyway. But exhaustion gripped her and calling out those words didn't seem worth the energy.

A minute later, he set a plate on her lap with a chicken salad sub and SunChips. "Tea's brewing."

"Thanks."

He sat in the chair across from her, plate in his lap. "Nice place."

A wave of homesickness crested for her historic Georgetown house with its creaks and character. This apartment proved functional, but the drab furnishings and cheap art weren't exactly a welcome mat for her soul. "It's fine."

"There's a tree outside your bedroom window." He grinned.

Uh …

"I noticed when I grabbed the blanket."

"So?"

"So? Come on. You know I've always wanted that."

Always wanted … Oh yeah. The memory swirled around her like leaves in autumn. The two of them house hunting. Her with a list of ten practical must-haves in a would-be home. Him with one utterly ridiculous wish: a tree outside the bedroom window.

"From that Robert Frost poem, right?"

He leaned forward and locked eyes with her as he recited,

> "Tree at my window, window tree,
> My sash is lowered when night comes on;
> But let there never be curtain drawn
> Between you and me.
> Vague dream head lifted out of the ground,
> And thing next most diffuse to cloud,
> Not all your light tongues talking aloud
> Could be profound.
> But tree, I have seen you taken and tossed,
> And if you have seen me when I slept,
> You have seen me when I was taken and swept
> And all but lost.
> That day she put our heads together,
> Fate had her imagination about her,
> Your head so much concerned with outer,
> Mine with inner, weather."

She bit her lip. How could those blue eyes contain so much passion? Passion about a tree. "Yeah. That one."

Why had she blown him off? Acted like his request to find a house with a tree outside the bedroom window was stupid and immature? She'd fallen into the role of the adult in the relationship and relegated him to the role of the foolish child. Much like she had in her relationship with her mother. But those dancing eyes, sparkling with life … She'd never meant to dim them.

He sat back and took a bite of his sandwich, spell broken. Meanwhile, her mind reeled. How could she fix this?

"We can plant a tree. Outside our bedroom window." It wasn't the same. Obviously, not the same, because trees took time to grow. Time to etch out the history the poem spoke of. But it was something.

His small, polite smile proved he understood all her solution lacked, yet accepted it anyway. "Okay." He grabbed the remote from the coffee table and turned on the nightly news, a clear signal he'd had enough conversation for one day. At least he felt comfortable enough to make himself at home. When they'd eaten, he cleaned their dishes. Before he left, he made sure she had both tea and water within reach.

"Do you need anything else before I head out?" he asked, hovering over her.

She shook her head, not trusting her voice. She couldn't bear for him to walk out the door.

"Oh, your book. You might want that."

"It's fi—"

But he'd already torn the package open. He studied the book with lips pressed tightly together. "Hmm."

She winced.

"*How to Improve Your Marriage Without Talking About It.*"

"Well, you said you didn't want to talk about it!"

A laugh bubbled out of him. "Only you."

He wasn't mad? Or annoyed, even? She allowed the corners of her mouth to lift. "I'll have you know over a thousand people rated that book on Goodreads. It's not *only me.*"

"Four point four or higher?"

"Well, no, but—"

He mock gasped. "Sahara Dawn lowered her standards."

"Just give me the book."

He set it down next to her tea and pressed a kiss to her forehead. "Let me know how it is. Without talking about it, of course."

"I'll try." She took a deep whiff of his distinctly Jaxon scent before he pulled away.

"But not too hard."

She shook her head, suppressing a smile. "Not too hard."

"I'll pick you up at eight thirty."

And then he was gone.

~

Jaxon's hand lingered on Sahara's doorknob as the evening breeze swirled around him. Perhaps he should stay. Open the door back up and settle in for the night. Just in case she needed anything else.

Ever so slowly, he twisted the knob. It came to an abrupt stop. Oh yeah. He'd locked it behind him. For him to go back inside, he'd need to knock, and Sahara would have to get up from her comfortable position on the couch to let him in... Never mind. He wouldn't bother her. She needed rest more than anything.

It was probably for the best. He'd left on a good note. If he'd stayed much longer, who knew? A fight might have broken out. He'd leave angry. She'd cry. It'd be a mess. Much better to slip out when a tenuous peace reigned. But he waited a few minutes more, listening to make sure all was well, to make sure … what exactly? What would he do if he heard a clatter? Bust down her door because she dropped her plate? He scrubbed his beard. He needed to head home and get a good night's sleep, after doing a bit of internet research on Sahara's car situation. She was fine. She'd be fine. This was a good time to practice trusting God.

A new concept for him and one that didn't come naturally. But when he'd seen her lying in the grass on the side of the highway, his blood chilled. Fear clawed at his chest, and he had to remind himself to breathe. What if he had lost her? What would he do then? He couldn't bear the thought. And for those seconds before he got to her, before he knew whether she was dead or alive, he'd prayed all right. Because this was out of his hands. Bigger than him. And he needed the Lord's strength.

Thank God it was merely heat exhaustion with no permanent damage. He'd never been so relieved. The back of his throat burned as he hopped in his Jeep and started the engine. Nothing was more precious to him than that woman. Nothing. And if he had to give up all he'd built and achieved out here for her, so be it. She was softening, right? Her walls starting to crumble? If she could scale that mountain of fear and insecurity looming in front of her, maybe they could even finally start a family together.

Hope ballooned in his rib cage. A child. *Please, God.* He would have welcomed a honeymoon baby, as unwise as that might have been. She'd put him off for twelve years. Twelve years! Someone should give him a medal for sainthood because it took a whole lot of patience to keep waiting for someday. But maybe someday was finally on the horizon.

Maybe they were finally close to a breakthrough.

~

Sahara woke up at four in the morning and couldn't fall back asleep. Jaxon's words from the day before echoed through her mind. *"Since you love me, do you think you could make a bit of space for the idea?"* The idea of God.

"Maybe," she'd said. After she'd resolved that she would do anything and everything possible to save her marriage, she met Jaxon's honest request with a weak *maybe*.

She would cut her hair and brave an airport. She'd eat an octopus and propel herself down a frigid mountain on skis. But could she stop fighting the deity she'd been resisting all her life? If that's what it took to win back her husband, could she lay down arms?

God hadn't exactly been there for her when she was young. Another absent parent. Yet, she'd let her father walk her down the aisle. Given him a chance to at least stick a big toe into her life on special occasions. Perhaps she could do the same with God. She and Jaxon could be one of those couples who went to church on Christmas and Easter and had a Bible on their shelf. Yeah. That sounded like a fair compromise.

Uncertainty niggled. What if Jaxon wanted more?

Maybe she could see what God had to say for Himself. Not rush into anything. Not make any rash judgments. Just see.

She grabbed her phone from the nightstand: 4:10 a.m. Yeah, she was up for the day now. Back in South Carolina, Aunt Trish would be whipping up breakfast while Robby crowed in the yard. Sahara dialed her number.

"Dawn, how nice to hear from you. Everything okay?" Something sizzled in the background. Sahara's stomach growled.

"Everything's fine. Hey, if one were to, say, read a Bible for the first time, where would that person start? And what kind of Bible? Um, what translation?"

A soft sigh. "Oh, Dawn. I'm delighted."

"Don't start crying, Aunt Trish. It's completely hypothetical."

"Oh, shush. Text me your address. I'll get a Bible in the mail to you right away. In the meantime, you can download an app on your phone." Trish walked her through how to navigate a Bible app and the pros and cons of a couple different translations. "Why don't you read First Corinthians, chapter thirteen? That will tell you about what love looks like."

"Got it. Thanks. Take care of my babies for me."

"I sure will. And I'll be praying for you and Jaxon."

Praying? Well, that couldn't hurt, could it?

As soon as she hung up, she downloaded the app and pulled up the passage her aunt had suggested. Her insides twisted as she read verses four and five.

> "Love is patient, love is kind. It does not envy, it does not boast, it is not proud. It does not dishonor

others, it is not self-seeking, it is not easily angered, it keeps no record of wrongs."

This is what love was supposed to look like? No wonder her marriage was failing. She was doing this all wrong. She'd been impatient and unkind. She'd been jealous of his job success. She boasted in her own accomplishments. Pride? Oh yeah. She was steeped in pride. And she couldn't even count the number of times she'd dishonored Jaxon. When had she not been self-seeking? She *only* ever looked out for herself. Easily angered? Her anger had a quick trigger finger. And she only had to reference the shoe fiasco to prove she'd kept a record of wrongs.

Okay, this was bad, but at least now she had a list. A list of things to do better. A list of how to love Jaxon better. She typed it out in her phone's notepad: be patient, be kind, don't envy, don't boast, don't be proud, don't dishonor him, don't be self-seeking, don't be easily angered, don't keep a record of wrongs. She read further and added protect, trust, hope, persevere, and do not fail.

Why did this list feel impossible? And Jaxon said *she* had too high of standards. This God basically expected His people to be perfect. No wonder she'd avoided Him for so long. She huffed. Forget this. She set down her phone, picked up the marriage book, and began to read.

~

By the time Jaxon picked Sahara up for work, she'd nearly finished the book and planned to put the methods into practice. She'd approach instead of attacking and avoiding. She'd "step into the puddle" with him, empathizing and meeting him where he was. She'd accept his silence, make a physical gesture of unity, and be ready to do something he was good at. And if he shut down, she'd remember he didn't hate her. He was simply overwhelmed.

She glided on cherry lip gloss and slid on her shades before she stepped out the door. Game time.

He jumped out and opened the passenger door for her. "Feeling better today?"

"Much." Though she hadn't gotten enough sleep and could really use some—

"Coffee." He winked as he handed her a Starbucks cup.

"Thanks." She scooted in. He shut her door and jogged back around to his side. He sure was chipper this morning.

Tom Petty's "Free Fallin'" emanated from the speakers. Jaxon sang along. She joined him for the chorus. Lightness filled her chest, her lungs, her heart. She flung an arm out the window and let her hand dance with the breeze.

When the song ended, she turned down the volume.

"What's going on with my car?"

He smiled at her. "I'm taking care of it."

"Okay … What does that mean? You're getting it fixed, or what?"

"It means I'm taking care of it."

"Yeah, but—"

He touched a finger to her lips. Instinctively, she caught his wrist and kissed his finger. Then his palm. Then planted a trail of kisses down his arm. Desire lit a fire within her. It had been a long time since they'd been intimate. There was nothing she wanted more than to make a physical gesture of unity, and do something he was really, really good at. She leaned closer and worked her way back up his arm.

His smile melted into longing. The deep rise and fall of his chest told her he wanted her before he even breathed out her name.

But he was driving. To work, no less. Great timing, Sahara. She pulled back just as he exited the interstate and came to a stop. Better give them both time to cool off.

Suddenly, his hands tangled through her hair, turning her toward him. His lips covered hers, drawing her closer, deeper.

Coffee and peppermint and desperation mingled. Her heart thudded, expanded, stretched toward him. Her arms wrapped around him, pulling him closer as his mouth explored hers.

A honk sounded behind them, and they parted, breathless.

She adjusted her shirt. "Way to make use of a red light."

He blew out a breath, gaze now focused on the road. "Wasn't long enough."

She hesitated. What if he turned her down? But she had to take the risk. After the way he'd responded to her, was it that much of a risk? She pushed her shoulders back and tried for a flirty air. "I'm free later. All night long, actually."

It wasn't true. Or shouldn't be. She had fallen behind on those extra accounts, and she'd planned to catch back up tonight. But this was more important.

He raised a brow. "Is that right?"

And just like that, they were in their twenties again. Young and in love—or at least highly physically attracted—with the only history between them, the one waiting to be built.

A few minutes later, Jaxon dropped her off at the job site with a discreet kiss to the inside of her wrist. Then he drove away.

"Where's Boss Man off to?" Tony asked.

Sahara shrugged. "No idea." Maybe he was dealing with her car. Strange how he was so secretive, but perhaps he wanted her to stop worrying and trust him for once. She could do that if he would reward her tonight. Her toes curled at the thought.

An hour later, she went to find Gabriel to ask him a question and couldn't find him. He'd been there earlier. "Where'd Gabriel go?" she asked Miguel.

"He went to help Boss Man with something."

"With what?"

"Dunno."

Odd.

But right before lunchtime, Jaxon's blue Jeep turned up the drive. Was that Gabriel driving it? A stunning silver Mercedes-Benz followed. She squinted. That was … Jaxon at the wheel. What in the world?

She walked over, mouth agape. What a thing of beauty. Her dream car from the time she was a little girl. Jaxon had wanted to get her one, but that was ridiculous. Dreamboat drove just fine. Two hundred thousand miles and still kicking. Barely, but still kicking. Studies showed it was more economical to keep an older car and pay for repairs than to lease a new one. She'd told Jaxon this, showed him two articles as proof. Eventually, he dropped the subject. So surely, he hadn't bought the Mercedes for her.

Only the twinkle in his eye when he stepped out of the vehicle said otherwise. He dangled the keys and sauntered toward her.

She blinked back at him. "Jaxon?"

"I told you I'd take care of it." He lifted her hand, then dropped the keys in her palm.

Around them, the men whistled and commented. Some came closer to inspect the new car. *Her* new car.

"We can't afford it," she whispered.

"Yes, we can." He closed her fingers around the keys. He leaned closer and tucked a stray hair behind her ear. "I got another job offer out here."

His words tumbled past her ears, settling in her gut. Another offer? No. She sucked in a breath. "But you said—"

He ducked to meet her wide eyes. "I'm not breaking my promise to you. I can still come back to South Carolina in seven months. It'll be under roof by then and in the hands of subcontractors. I'll only need to fly in on a couple weekends to check on things. I'm not breaking my word."

She exhaled long and slow. He would come home. He was still coming home. She closed her eyes. Yes, relief settled, easing some of the tension in her shoulders, but something didn't feel right. Her eyes flew open. She took in the scene around her. A crew of men who clearly respected their boss. Off-the-charts talent that millionaires were beginning to recognize.

"You have a whole life out here. A good life."

Sadness lurked on the edge of his smile. "I've had a good run."

The keys weighed cool and heavy in her hand. Once again, he had given her her dream. And she was taking his away.

Chapter 17

Bernie
September 17, 1862
Sharpsburg, Maryland

Stomach plummeting, Bernie rushed to Hermann's side. "Hermann!" She tucked her arm under his shoulders as her heart thudded.

His face scrunched in pain, but his gaze sought hers.

"I'm here. I'm here." She trailed his grimy cheek with her fingers.

"Bernie," he eked out. "What are you doing here?"

"I came to find you." She scanned his chest, sides, and abdomen. No bullet wound. "Where are you hurt?"

"My leg." Her heart twisted at his pinched voice.

Her gaze dropped to his right thigh. There. Crimson soaked through his uniform. She stilled, awareness tingling in her own leg around that same spot where she'd cut herself with a knife. "Oh, Hermann." She had to staunch the blood flow. She pressed her lips together. What to do? What to use?

In an instant, Freddy knelt beside them. "Here. Use my shirt to bandage the wound." He took off his gray frock coat and discarded it on the ground, then stripped his battle-shirt from over his head and ripped it in two with a fluid motion.

She wrapped it around Hermann's thigh and tied it as Freddy put back on his gray uniform.

"Thank you," Hermann gritted out.

"Where can we take you?" Through the trees, Bernie could barely see the white outline of what she assumed to be Dunker Church, but smoke from muskets surrounded it, and bullets pinged in every direction. There was no way they could make it there for safety.

"We passed a farm about a mile back." Hermann attempted to rise. A hissing sound emitted from between his teeth at the effort. "There was talk of using it as a hospital."

A mile. They'd have to hoof it a mile. Could they do it?

"Put your right arm around my shoulder." Freddy wedged himself next to Hermann, shouldering much of his weight as she helped her husband to stand. "Bernie, come around to his left side."

She did so.

"Jimmy, carry our packs." Freddy tossed his pack into the dust for Jimmy to pick up. Hermann's pack lay in the spot where he'd been.

"Yes, sir." The man scrambled to do Freddy's bidding.

"Here you go, Jimmy." Bernie held out her pack when he'd gathered the other two, making eye contact with the man. "Thank you."

The man dipped his head in acknowledgement. She held his gaze.

The four of them inched forward, the sound of bullets at their back. Hermann hobbled unevenly, his face strained, jaw tight. It wasn't lost on Bernie how he put most of his weight on Freddy, lightening her load as if she couldn't handle the burden. Perhaps she couldn't. She was the reason he'd been wounded, after all. She'd stunned him. Distracted him. Made him a prime target for that ball of lead. Heat prickled the back of her neck. Perhaps that was weight enough to bear.

A boom resounded, and seconds later, fiery dust flung over their heads. They ducked, shielding their faces with their free arms as a cannon ball hit an oak a few yards ahead of them. It knocked the tree sideways as shrapnel rained down.

Smoke invaded Bernie's lungs, and she coughed. Her eyes burned.

Freddy cast her a worried glance. "Let's try to move a bit faster, shall we?"

And they did try, but the closer they got, the more Hermann stumbled. The paler he grew. His shoulders slumped, and his movements faltered. Fatigue must be sucking the life out of his body. Bernie's gaze zeroed in on the makeshift bandage, now soaked through. He was losing blood, too much blood. He must be fighting to stay conscious. She needed to instill in him the will to continue the fight.

"Stay with me, Hermann." She channeled into her voice all the steely determination that had gotten her to this point. "I didn't let half-blind McEvens chop off my hair for nothing."

The corner of his mouth lifted ever so slightly. "You gave Russell a pair of scissors?"

"And let him within an inch of my face. Lord help me, I did."

The softest chuckle propelled her to continue.

"I didn't give up my comfortable bed to sleep on hard ground for nothing. And there's a reason I've been eating dry, tasteless cornbread every day for breakfast, lunch, and dinner. That reason is you, Hermann Reisenfeld. I did all of it because I love you, and now you're going to make it to the doctor and get through this ordeal because you love me right back."

He turned a weak gaze to her that pummeled her heart with his sincerity. "I do love you, Bernie."

Truer words were never spoken. Her heart testified to this fact. Yet, she needed him to press on, so she winked and said, "Prove it. Make it to that farm and recover good as new."

His chin trembled as he managed a smile. "Anything for you, dear."

"Good." She nodded her approval, but worry niggled at her gut. How many men had died of infection in this war? More than had died of bullets themselves. No one could seem to figure out why or how to stop it. How could she ensure Hermann wouldn't be one of those taken by infection from an otherwise nonlethal wound? Would he lose his leg? She shuddered as the image of a physician's bone saw flitted through her mind. What incomprehensible agony.

They emerged from the clump of woods and burst into a clearing. Thank heavens. Now there'd be no more tree roots to stumble over.

"There." Freddy nodded his head toward the buildings in the distance. "A barn and a house. Jimmy, run ahead and ask where to bring him."

"Yes, Massa," Jimmy said, and sprinted away. He returned a few minutes later. "They said to bring him to the barn, Massa."

They slinked toward the barn. As they neared, Bernie's blood chilled as the moans and cries of injured men leaked to her ears. Haunting. When they turned the corner, the stench of blood on unwashed bodies assaulted her. Dozens upon dozens of men lay in rows outside the barn, writhing in agony. Were they waiting for treatment? Would the doctor give Hermann permission to go ahead of these men? She steeled herself as they helped Hermann inside.

Men lay side by side on tattered, bloody blankets on top of hay on both sides of the musty barn. A physician stood in the middle, conversing with a younger man. The steward? A nurse? The doctor pointed to one patient, then another, seeming to give instructions to the assistant. When the physician looked up and met Bernie's gaze, the lines under his eyes spoke of a weariness that went bone deep.

His gaze dropped to Hermann's leg. "Bring him over there." He pointed to a spot in the corner, then pinched the bridge of his nose.

Hermann settled down on the blanket with a stifled moan.

The physician neared. "We'll take it from here. We need every able-bodied man out on that battlefield."

"Yes, sir." Freddy took a step toward the door.

Bernie shook her head. "I'm not leaving him."

The doctor cocked an eyebrow. "Excuse me?"

Freddy stared at the exchange.

"I'm not leaving my … uncle's side, sir. I'll tend to him, and to others here. It appears you could use the help."

His chin dimpled with his frown. Finally, he said, "Fine. We'll take your boy's help too." He pointed to Jimmy, who stood halfway in between Bernie and Freddy.

"He's not my—" Bernie began.

Freddy nodded. "That's fine. Jimmy can help here. I'll check back later." With the briefest of encouraging smiles, he left Bernie with his slave, two dozen writhing, wounded men, and the husband her actions had injured.

Bernie wrung her hands and paced as the doctor examined Hermann's wound for what seemed like an eternity. Why was it taking so long for him to make an assessment? Jimmy had to have given fifteen men a drink of water from the tin ladle by now, and the physician hadn't said a word.

Would her husband lose his leg, or wouldn't he? The Minié ball could splinter a bone like a battering ram splintered a door. Often the best chance of survival in such cases was amputation. At least that was what the men had said. Hermann alive with one leg was a far cry better than Hermann in the grave with two, but how would her husband tend to the farm he loved if he were missing a limb? How would they survive? *Please, Lord. Help us.*

The doctor cleared his throat. Bernie rushed to his side.

"The good news is there's little damage to the bone."

Bernie's shoulders slumped in relief.

"I've removed the missile and bone splinters and given him morphine powder for the pain. Now, we'll cover the wound with cerate and honey." The doctor swabbed a beeswax-like substance over Hermann's wound, followed by a generous dab of honey. He then covered it with a dressing of charred cotton before he rebandaged it with a fresh strip of cloth. "All done." He dipped his hands in a washbasin, then dried them on a towel.

She hated to ask, but she needed to know. "What's the risk of infection, Doctor?"

His frown dipped lower. "Hard to say. We'll hope for the best." Weary eyes trailed the length of the stuffy space.

Bernie knelt beside her husband. "Do you need anything, Uncle Hermann?"

A muscle in his cheek twitched. She could tell he wanted to burst into laughter. If only he had the energy and the privacy.

"Water?"

"Sure," she said, but before she could even rise, Jimmy was at their side with a ladle. The man's dark hands cradled Hermann's matted hair as he helped him raise his head enough to drink. There was a gentleness to his touch, to his manner, as if Hermann's suffering pained him as well. But no, that was ridiculous. She must be imagining it. They didn't know this man, this slave. There was no reason to feel anything toward him, or for him to feel anything toward them. Their paths had crossed much like any of the slaves she'd passed on the streets of Charleston. Just another nameless, dark face.

Only she knew this man's name. Only she'd looked in this man's face.

She reached out her hand and placed it on his. She couldn't mistake his quick intake of breath. "Thank you," she said. "That was kind." Because while he had no choice but to be here working to aid the cause of his enemy, no one could make him do the task with tenderness. Yet, he had.

Now perhaps she could follow his lead and tend to these soldiers with compassion and grace.

~

He was dying. As Bernie wiped his clammy forehead with a damp rag, it was abundantly clear the soldier that lay next to Hermann, the one she'd tended to for the last few hours, was only moments away from death. He drifted in and out of consciousness, too weak to even tell her his name. Who would tell his family he'd passed from this world? She swallowed past the melancholy and rehearsed the Twenty-third Psalm, praying it might bring him a piece of comfort.

When she finished, his chest no longer rose and fell, and hers burned. She met the doctor's eye from where he operated on a new patient across from her.

"Is he gone?"

She nodded.

"Ralph," he called to the assistant. "Take him out to the mass grave. We'll need the room."

Bernie shuddered as the assistant dragged the nameless man off to throw him in a ditch with other nameless bodies. But the doctor wasn't wrong in saying they'd need the room. Another fifty men had arrived over the past few hours, and there wasn't a speck of space for them in the barn or house where two other surgeons operated. Those soldiers deemed to be mortally wounded, the ones they couldn't do anything to save, occupied the space directly outside the barn. Ralph administered opium to them to make them comfortable as they passed from this life to the next. The doctor treated men with arm and leg wounds first, often with a quick and precise amputation.

When she went outside to tend to the men there, she averted her gaze from the pile of limbs stacked against the barn, surrounded by flies and gnats. The smell alone gagged her. One accidental glance had been enough to make her woozy.

She checked on Hermann again. Still sleeping, though fitfully. The morphine powder did the trick.

She stood and brushed off her trousers, scanning the room for a sign of anyone who needed assistance. A commotion out front snagged her attention. A man stumbled into the barn door, holding his shoulder. A grimace covered his face. His familiar face.

"Walter?" His name escaped her lips before her mind caught up to where she knew him from—or what he knew about her. She sucked in a breath as her eyes widened.

"Bernie?"

His face twisted. Was it from pain or disgust or betrayal? Oh no. She hadn't seen him after Greenman had discovered her gender and kicked her out, but he had to have heard. And how had he felt when he found out his friend had lied to him the entire time? Her pulse drummed in her ears. He couldn't rat her out now. She'd only just found her husband. She couldn't lose him again.

"I found my uncle." She flung an arm in Hermann's direction. Did she look as desperate as she felt? Desperate for him to see why she'd done it, why she was still doing it.

He pressed his lips together until they nearly turned white. Then he took a sharp breath and said, "My shoulder."

"Of course." She rushed to his side, grabbed onto his good arm, and steered him to the spot the nameless soldier had just vacated. She steadied him when his steps faltered. "Right this way. The doctor is finishing with another patient. He'll be right with you."

"It hurts like the dickens."

"I'm sure it does." She helped him to settle onto the blanket. "Let me clean the wound so the doctor can have a good look at it."

Bernie peeled his shirt off, refusing to breathe through her nose as the pungent odor of blood wafted. She swiped a sponge over the crimson area, then rinsed it in the basin. The red swirled into the clear water. She checked for an exit wound—none—then resumed cleaning.

"I see it now," he whispered, his mouth so close to her ear it sent a tingle up her spine.

"See what?" she returned at equal volume.

He gave a quiet huff. "I can't believe I didn't see it before."

Oh. She met his gaze. "You weren't looking."

"I was looking for a friend."

She held back a smile. "You were looking to win a bet."

He blinked. "I was looking for a friend, and I found one."

Blood trickled from the wound, and she held a dressing to it with gentle pressure. "Good. I'm glad you found what you were looking for."

"And you did too?" He glanced to where Hermann lay beside him. "You found what you were looking for?"

"I did."

Just then, a loud crash sounded. The barn creaked, splintered, and moaned as a cannon exploded. Heat pushed into her as flames engulfed the opposite side of the barn. She screamed, a girlish scream that melted into the cacophony of other cries. There had been four men lying right there—*right there*—mere seconds ago. Now they were … incinerated.

She jumped to her feet. They must get these men out of here. Now.

Her panicked gaze found Hermann. His mouth hung open; his eyes were wide with fear.

"Help me!" Walter shouted next to him. "Help me out of here!" His hand flew to his not-yet-bandaged wound where blood oozed. He struggled to sit up, then scrambled to his feet.

The dressing—she still held it in her hand. She plunged it toward his shoulder. "Press this to the wound. And hurry!"

He took two faltering steps toward the doors, then turned. "Come on."

She shook her head, sweeping the room with a glance. Dread coated the expressions of every man who lay there, too injured to rise and run for safety. Men who'd had amputations mere hours ago. Men who, like Hermann, were frozen in fear. "I must help these men. Go!"

He frowned as his gaze settled on his bleeding shoulder. Then he hustled away.

What to do? Who to help first? Her husband lay at her feet. She bent and shook him, bringing her face inches from his glassy eyes. "Hermann, get up. You must get out of here!"

His jaw snapped shut. His expression cleared. "Bernie?"

"Let's go."

She grabbed his forearm and pulled with all her might, hoisting him up. Though he wasn't a heavyset man, she grunted under his full weight. Her knees threatened to buckle. They plodded forward with miniature, methodical steps. At this rate, she'd collapse before they made it halfway to the door.

"Help me!" A soldier grasped onto her pants leg as she passed by. His wide eyes begged for mercy as the flames licked closer and closer. Her throat burned. From smoke or the threat of tears? Bernie shook her head. She couldn't help this man, even if she wanted to. She had to save her husband. She must block out the groans, screams, and cries. The scent of burning flesh. She had to focus on the only thing that had mattered all these months: Survive. Save Hermann. Bring him home.

Except with this massive weight pressing down on her, she could barely inch forward. Had she come this far to fail now? No. It couldn't be. But smoke filled her lungs, and it took everything in her to take another breath.

"I've got him." Jimmy's voice startled her. The stupor that hung over her like a thick cloud dissipated as his powerful arms wrapped around her husband's chest, lifting him as if he was a feather. She gaped as Jimmy carried Hermann to safety in six fluid steps.

"Help me!" The desperate soldier at her feet continued to plead. Suddenly emboldened, she bent down and snatched the edge of his blanket.

"Hold on tight." She gritted her teeth and pulled the blanket—and the man on top of it—toward the entrance.

She made it nearly to the door when Jimmy burst through and took over. He leaned forward and scooped the soldier in his arms as if the man were but a child. Then he dashed off.

She spun around to locate who was in gravest danger. There. A legless soldier only feet away from the hungry blaze. Tears streaked his soot-tinged face. She raced over and tugged his blanket away from the inferno. Once again, Jimmy met her at the door and hoisted the man to his shoulders, carting him to safety.

One by one, Bernie dragged the remaining men toward the wide barn doors. One by one, Jimmy carried them farther from the blaze. When they'd freed the last man, Bernie pushed out into the fresh air, sputtering coughs as she attempted to drink in deep, clean breaths. She collapsed in the grass and rolled onto her back. Smoke filtered across the clear blue sky. What had happened? She'd nearly lost Hermann. Again.

And Jimmy had been the one to save his life.

Jimmy. A slave that she—and the rest of the soldiers that he had rescued—fought to keep enslaved.

Her stomach roiled. It wasn't right. It wasn't fair. But what could she, one lone, *illegal* soldier, do about it? This was war with hundreds of thousands of men fighting on both sides.

What are you fighting for?

The Yankee's words from the picket line tumbled through her brain. Hermann fought to protect his neighbors, his friends. She fought to protect Hermann. Many Southerners said they fought for their land, their homes, their rights. Many

Northerners said they fought to preserve the Union. Only a few, it seemed, said they fought this war for or against the right to own another human being. Was that what it was really about? If so, if she had a choice, what side would she want to be on? What side would she fight for?

She must find Jimmy. To thank him. She stood and wove her way through the sea of men lying in the grass in search of him. And where was Hermann?

The physician's assistant plus several women rushed with buckets of water toward the barn. Yes, of course. She should help douse the blaze. And she would. She only needed to find Jimmy and her husband first.

There. A dark figure hunched over a man on the front porch. She hastened her steps. As she neared, the familiarity of the man lying there came into focus. A smile crested her lips. Her Hermann. Safe and sound.

"There she is right now." Jimmy's soulful voice caught her off guard. It held warmth. Respect? Something that didn't seem to be there before.

"Were you talking 'bout me?" She bounded up the porch steps.

Jimmy smiled at her, his face covered in grime and sweat. "He wanted to make sure you made it out of there okay. I told him 'bout how brave you were, getting those men to safety."

"That's my Bernie." Pride laced Hermann's voice. "She's got pluck."

Jimmy winked. "Fo' sure."

"I came to thank you, Jimmy. You saved Hermann's life."

He waved her off.

"No." She put a hand on his shoulder. "Really. Thank you."

He responded with a solemn nod.

"Now, I must help fight the blaze. Take care of my Hermann."

Bernie trusted him to do just that.

~

Hermann, along with hundreds of other wounded men who were well enough for transport, convalesced at a hospital in Winchester. They'd turned nearly every home there into a hospital. Thankfully, Winchester was also where the Eighteenth Mississippi had chosen to rest and recruit. Bernie stayed by Hermann's side as he gained strength day by day. When he slept, she aided other patients alongside Jimmy and some local women who had risen to the occasion and assisted.

She washed men's wounds, offered them sustenance, and assisted them in writing to their family members. It brought her a sense of purpose in the midst of the unfathomable pain this war had wrought.

She'd just finished spooning broth into a young soldier's mouth when Corporal Pembody stepped into the room. "Private Reisenfeld?"

Bernie stood and saluted. "Yes, sir."

"Our unit has orders to move out to Fredericksburg in the morning."

Air whooshed out of her lungs. Move out? Move away? From Hermann? "S-sir." She struggled to keep her breathing even, grappled to keep the strangled panic from her voice. "I have to stay with my uncle." She pointed to where Hermann slept three cots away. "He's still recovering."

His expression and tone remained neutral. Unbothered. "Your contract with the army is not yet fulfilled. We're moving on to Fredericksburg."

"But my uncle—"

"Take it up with Lieutenant Colonel Griffen." With a huff and clack of his heels, he made a swift exit.

Take it up with Griffen? Well, she would. She had to. There was no way she'd found Hermann only to leave him to convalesce in a hospital while she marched off to fight another battle. Surely, Griffen had a seed of compassion she could appeal to. And she must. She could not—would not—lose her husband again. Not now. Never again.

~

Lieutenant Colonel Griffen was an imposing figure. An air of authority emanated from him that made most everyone stand a bit straighter and take notice. But Bernie would not be intimidated. She would stand her ground. Respectfully, of course. Politely, as always. But she had to get her way in this. There was no other option.

Eyes trained on the officer, she marched forward, jaw tight.

"Where you off to, Bernie?" The jovial lilt to Henrietta's voice befuddled her.

She blinked at her friend.

Henrietta rocked back on her heels with her hands stuffed inside her pockets. "Did you hear we're about to move to Fredericksburg? Thank heavens. I've had my fill of lollygagging around this place." She ended her pronouncement with a snort.

Bernie shook her head.

"What?"

Could her friend be so daft? "I can't leave Hermann. I've got to talk with Griffen."

A quiet "Oh," escaped her lips.

Bernie pushed forward. Past other officers. Past propriety. Right to the man who held her fate in his hands.

"Excuse me, sir."

He turned and regarded her with a curious tilt of his head.

"Private Reisenfeld, sir."

"What can I do for you?"

"I've come to request furlough, sir. My uncle was injured in Sharpsburg and is convalescing here. I've been taking care of him, and I request leave to continue to do so"—her throat constricted—"until he's recovered."

Griffen's beard shifted with the twitch of his jaw. "I see."

He did? Of course, he did. He had to see the reason for such a logical request.

"We lost eighty more men at Sharpsburg, Private. We need every soldier who can fight." He raised his chin a notch. "Let the physicians and nurses tend to our wounded. Your uncle is in expert hands. I simply can't grant you leave when the Confederacy needs you."

What? No. No. He could not deny her this.

"Please." Her voice came out in a squeak. "My uncle and I are very close."

His frown deepened. "Look around you. Everyone here has left a loved one to fight for 'the cause.' Every soldier has sacrificed for the South they love. If I were to make an exception for you, I'd have to make an exception for everybody, and we'd have no infantry left. We are not issuing furloughs at this time."

Fear coiled around her insides like a snake, constricting until she couldn't breathe. Eyes wide and pleading, she threw herself down at his feet and clung to his boots. "Please! I beg of you. I beg of you."

Tears pressed against her eyelids and demanded release. She squeezed her eyes shut, holding them back, and scrambled for a scrap of dignity. But no, she'd relinquished that when she'd fallen in the dust.

All fell silent around them, the hum of voices extinguished at her dramatic display.

"Gather yourself together, Reisenfeld."

She gritted words out through clenched teeth, "I can't. Not without my uncle."

"I'll have you written up for this."

He could go ahead and write her up. He could kick her out for all she cared. As long as he didn't force her to move on without her husband.

Wait. Her eyes sprung open and released a watery sheen. That was it. She could get kicked out. Dismissed from the army for good. They wouldn't force her to move on. They wouldn't force her to follow them anywhere, would prevent her from doing so, in fact. All she had to do was confess to the one secret she'd safeguarded this entire time in the Eighteenth Mississippi. They'd put her in a dress and leave her behind while they moved on without her. The perfect scenario. The perfect solution.

She took a deep, trembling breath, then shouted, "I'm a woman!"

Among the many gasps, she distinguished Henrietta's. Hopefully, she hadn't put her friend at risk by association. Murmurs and whispers ensued around her. She managed a glance up at Griffen's reddened face and swallowed.

"You mean to tell me we've had an illegal female soldier in our company this entire time?" A vein protruded from his temple.

She bit her lip and nodded. How would he feel if he knew there were actually two of them?

"This is disgraceful." He spat out the words.

She fought the urge to cringe under his glare.

He turned to the men who stood beside him. "Roger, Sambold, escort her to the magistrate." His gaze leveled at her. "You, young lady, are going to jail."

Chapter 18

Sahara
Present Day
Provo, Utah

Sahara stretched between the sheets. Her smile spread when her bare skin contacted Jaxon's. She checked her watch. Nearly midnight. She must have dozed, but he was still here. She snuggled close to him and nestled her cheek into the crook of his shoulder.

He kissed her hair. "I should buy you a car more often."

She chuckled. Oh, he smelled delicious. A mixture of the sawdust under his fingernails, the soap she'd bought him for Christmas, the fresh air that swirled around him each day, and the cologne he'd worn since she'd met him. A distinctly Jaxon scent that barely lingered on his clothes at home, but here in person nearly overwhelmed her senses. She trailed her index finger along his tattoo. His biceps had grown stronger in their time apart. Her husband. Strong. Handsome. Capable.

Should she try cliff diving again? Try to say those three words and see if he would say them back now, when not distracted by tow trucks and highway noises? Surely, if he'd made love to her, he could say the words. He *would* say the words. She opened her mouth.

"Are you still on birth control?"

Jaxon's question screeched like a train in her mind. She blinked slowly several times. "Huh?"

"Just wondering, since we haven't been together in nearly a year. Thought maybe you'd stopped."

A sour feeling coated her stomach. She drew back an inch. "Hoped, you mean. You hoped I stopped."

Her body lifted with his shrug. "Maybe."

She sat up and pulled the sheet around herself. "Yes, I'm still taking birth control. Because that's the responsible thing to do."

"Responsible. Got it."

The disappointment in his tone tempted her heart to leap toward him in compassion. She rummaged through her mind for the reasons, the completely reasonable justifications as to why they shouldn't have children right now. A thought floated to the surface that her fear was keeping his dreams of a family at bay. She swatted the thought away like a pesky fly. Surely not. It couldn't be because of fear. It was because of his lack of job stability. Their finances. Crazy schedules. He was in a different state, for crying out loud. They couldn't raise children like this. Not now.

"It's easier to stay in the routine of taking the pills each morning, so yes, I've taken them like clockwork."

"Of course, you have. And you'll continue to." His eyes met hers, more gray now in this light. They held a weak plea, one with a single thread of hope.

She hated to snip it, but … "For now."

"We both know what that means." He rolled toward the side of the bed, sat up, and slipped a T-shirt over his head.

"You're getting dressed?"

The shifting of the bed as he stood was her only answer.

"Wait. You're leaving?"

He rubbed a tired-looking eye. "I'm going to head home."

She scrambled for her shirt. She couldn't cower in front of him naked while he stood above her in his shield of armor.

She fished under the covers. There. And there were her jeans. She wrestled them on. Stumbled to her feet beside the bed. Tilted up her chin. Squared her shoulders.

"If you leave now, it makes it feel like this was a one-night stand and not like we've been married for over a decade."

Jaxon rolled his eyes. Then he grabbed his wallet from the end table and stuffed it in his back pocket.

Her stomach sank down to her toes. How could she have been so naive? "Is that all this was to you? Was it only about physical desire? Nothing more?"

His eyes flickered. "Wow, Sahara. Really?"

She flung her arms out. "What else am I supposed to think?"

"Yeah, what else is there to think, huh? Other than I'm using you and I don't really love you. After everything, you insist on thinking the absolute worst about me." In three steps, he stalked out of the bedroom. In seven, he stood at the front door.

She followed at his heels and aimed a verbal dart at his retreating form. "You're making me feel cheap."

He turned. His voice came out in a haunting whisper, "I didn't make you feel cheap. You did that all by yourself." His eyes drooped heavy and sad.

She blinked.

He opened the door and stepped out into the night.

~

How utterly useless to try and sleep after that fight. She tossed and turned for a few minutes. The bed was warm from where Jaxon had been. She scooted to his side, buried her head in his pillow, and inhaled. And choked back a sob. Why did she ruin every good thing in her life? The perfect night. Ruined. Because she had to get defensive.

But did he have to leave because he wasn't getting his way? Pretty childish of him as well. Maybe it wasn't entirely her fault. Or his. Maybe they were too different to make this work.

She dug her nails into Jaxon's pillow. No, that couldn't be true. There had to be a way.

Myra was a night owl. She might be up. Sahara texted her. Her phone chirped a reply a minute later. Instead of texting back, Sahara called.

"He said I made myself feel used all by myself. What did he mean by that?"

"Context?"

Sahara filled her in, more or less.

"Maybe it's like Eleanor Roosevelt said, 'No one can make you feel inferior without your consent.'"

Sahara wrinkled her brow. "I let him make me feel used? Sounds like a cop-out to me."

"Or like … no one can make you feel anything. No one can make you angry. You choose anger. You choose your feelings."

"I chose to feel used?"

"Hey, I'm brainstorming here."

Sahara pinched the bridge of her nose. She needed a reader's guide to understand anything Jaxon said.

"Can we refocus here?" Myra sounded as if she stifled a yawn. "The more important question is if this is a hill you want to die on. The kids thing. Would you rather have children with Jaxon or live a childless existence without him?"

"What? I never said I wouldn't have children with Jaxon, I only said not right now."

"And you've been saying that for twelve years. The man's been more than patient."

"We're still not ready."

"You never will be, Sahara. Things will never be perfect enough for you. Do you want to have a family with Jaxon, or are you willing to let this marriage go over it?"

Blood whooshed in her ears. Let her marriage go? "Do you think he's giving me an ultimatum?"

"Maybe not yet, but it might come to that."

Her throat tightened. "I've got to go."

Myra spoke quick, as if afraid of being cut off. "I know you're scared, but I think you'd be a great mother. Nothing like your mom."

Tears choked out her "Thank you" as they dribbled down her cheeks and off her chin. She hung up the phone, confident her friend knew her appreciation.

What now?

You have the right to change your mind, to readjust your vision ... to build the life you want.

What did Jaxon want?

Children. A family.

What did Sahara want?

Him.

She could tear down the beams she'd erected to protect herself from motherhood, couldn't she? She'd been terrified of being saddled with the responsibility of another human being after decades of feeling responsible for the one who'd brought her into the world. Her mother's every failure hung on Sahara's shoulders. She thought she couldn't bear it. The burden of another life clinging to her own. The possibility of failing someone who depended on her like they depended on air. But maybe ...

If that's what Jaxon needed. If that's what it took.

After a quick Google search, she tumbled out of bed and marched to the kitchen. She grabbed the pill box from the cabinet and stepped outside to scoop a handful of dirt into a plastic bag. Taking a deep breath, she winced, popped open each day's pill, and dumped the contents into the bag with the dirt. She zipped the bag closed, shook the contents together, and pitched it into the trashcan.

There. She'd done it. Taken a huge leap of love. A leap into her husband's arms. Her arms shook and teeth chattered with nervous energy. She only needed to tell Jaxon of her change of heart. Shoot. She should have taken a video of her disposing of the pills. It would have made a moving text.

No. This wasn't news she could share over text.

Such a big announcement needed a giant grand gesture to go with it. Something large enough to encapsulate her heart. Like the book said, enough talking. It was time to show Jaxon she'd changed. Show him she was serious about becoming the person he needed her to be.

She pulled her laptop from the bedside table. Time to research.

~

Park City, Utah

Jaxon consulted his GPS. Only four minutes before he arrived at the Best Western for Sahara's secret request. What in the world was the woman up to now? He hadn't a clue, but he didn't trust it. She'd nearly begged him to come this morning, going all puppy dog on him with her big green eyes. He couldn't say no to her. Still, tension wove its way through his shoulder blades. Meeting in the parking lot of a hotel in Park City at seven on a Saturday morning? Beyond strange.

They'd gone back to awkward politeness on the job site, which made working there a blast. Thankfully, he had a good excuse to avoid that site altogether, as his days were often tied up with meetings about the new project. Pain pulsed when they were together. Regret, maybe. Was it what they'd said to each other or everything they'd never said? At any rate, it throbbed like a migraine. Better for both of them if he simply stocked the cooler with her tea, then ducked out for the day.

At the stoplight, he spotted Sahara in her hot-pink leopard-print V-neck that said *Exotic*, which he'd gotten her for her last birthday. The corner of his mouth lifted a fraction. She paced in the parking lot. So, she was as nervous as he was. Good to know. What was that in her hand?

He turned into the lot. Her face lit at the sight of him. Was she worried he wouldn't show? She was at his door before he cut his engine. He opened the door to her bright smile. Too bright. Something was majorly off.

"What's this about?" He scrutinized her face, searching for clues.

"It's a surprise."

"So you've said."

"Here. Bend down." He raised an eyebrow. A blindfold. She held a blindfold. Great. How was he supposed to detect what was off with this situation if he couldn't see anything? But he did as she requested.

She wrapped the blindfold around his eyes, then grabbed his elbow and led him across the parking lot. Her hand felt small and soft on his arm. He resisted the urge to weave the fingers of his other hand into hers. He couldn't get sucked in. He needed to keep a clear head. Figure out what she was up to.

"You're not even going to give me a hint?"

"You'll love it. That's your hint." They seemed to turn a corner, then they stopped. "Here we are."

"Great," a male voice said. "Let's get to … our location."

Their location? What on earth did that mean?

A pop and then the sliding of what had to be a van door. "Put your hand here." Sahara guided his fingers to a handle. "Then step up."

He did so while ducking. Where was the ceiling on this thing? She put her hands on his shoulders and nudged him until the back of his legs found the seat. He sat, and she buckled him in. Her nearness and perfume dredged up memories of the night they'd spent together. But then, she pulled away, like she always did. He drummed his fingers on the armrest.

"Don't worry," she whispered.

Did he look worried? Apparently, because she gave his hand a squeeze. Her hand felt a bit clammy. Perhaps he should reassure her.

The ride got bumpy. Where were they headed? Onto an uncharted dirt path in the middle of nowhere? Finally, the van slowed, then stopped. Sahara released a loud, slow exhale.

"Here we are." She sounded near giddy as she led him out. "Wait right there."

Okay? He'd just stand here, then. Wherever here was. Blindfolded.

"Sahara?" The breeze whipped her name from his lips.

Footsteps approached. Something clanked near his feet. Then, her body brushed into him, and her hands framed his face as she took off his blindfold.

He blinked against the sun. "What?" He whirled around in a circle. He stood in the middle of a grassy field with a massive red, yellow, and green-checkered hot-air balloon lying on its side. His breath hitched. A hot-air balloon? "Are you kidding?"

"No." Could her smile be any wider? "I wanted to make your dream come true."

He picked her up and spun her around. A laugh tumbled from her, light and airy. The grass swayed around their ankles as fire and air hissed.

She bent down and picked up a bottle of cider, fiddling to open it. She pulled off the foil from around the bottle's neck. Setting the bottle on the ground, she twisted the foil into a circle to make a ring. Her pulse throbbed at the base of her neck. His throat tightened at the gesture. Had she ever done something like this for him? Something so romantic and heartfelt?

"I want to have a family with you, children with you. Now—not sometime far in the future." A stray hair fell over her eyes. She brushed it away with the back of her hand. "I'll give you what you've always wanted. A child. A family." She held the foil ring out to him. "Jaxon, will you go on this grand adventure with me? Will you stay married to me?"

Was this really happening? His dream of a family with the woman he loved finally gifted to him? His eyes misted. She wanted to have children with him. Now. She wanted to … wait. Stay married to him? Did she think … Was this offer a last-ditch effort because she thought …

He shook his head, took a step back.

"I never said I wouldn't stay married. Did you think I wanted a divorce? Are you doing all this to try and keep us together?" His wide, wet gaze flashed to the bright balloon and back to her.

Her mouth parted. She didn't deny it.

The Lord knew he wanted a child, but not as a Band-Aid. Never as a Band-Aid to attempt to heal a gushing wound. If she was still going to push him away day in and day out … He couldn't accept a baby as a substitute to Sahara's entire heart. He had to have all his wife first and foremost. No walls. No barriers. And she wasn't there yet. He could tell by her posture, by the panicked look in her eyes.

"A baby won't fix us. This whole thing," he said and tossed a hand up as if flipping a coin through the air, "is beautiful and poignant, and all wrong. It's all wrong, Sahara. It's for the wrong reasons. I can't do this."

He turned and swished through the grass, heading for where? The side of the highway? Was he going to hitchhike back to his car? Guess so.

"Where are you going?"

Somewhere he could break down and cry.

"What part of 'you win' are you upset about now, Jaxon?" she yelled.

No, he hadn't won. Not at all.

~

Sahara floated above mountain peaks alone. Well, not completely. Greg, the pilot, stood only a foot away. He'd had the decency to wince when he informed her the exorbitantly priced flight was nonrefundable. He also had the decency not to mention her and Jaxon's little blowup. Good thing he didn't try to placate her with empty words. Silence would do nicely for a while. She had plenty of whirling thoughts to keep her company.

The mountains looked vastly different from several thousand feet above ground. No less majestic. Not even smaller, because she could see their vastness clearly from this vantage. Her respect for the impenetrable fortresses grew as she rose above them. How insignificant she was in the scheme of it all. How ridiculous for her to think she could move things that were stuck in their ways. And to think she'd planned on this balloon ride sealing their happy ending. She'd imagined him whisking her away in his arms and kissing her senseless. How naive.

Was she ready to admit it was time to give up?

Far below her, dots of color moved, cars drove, people went about their days, their lives. That was Jaxon before she'd arrived and crashed his party. He'd been happily going about his new, Saharaless life. His successful life. His fulfilling life. Then, she'd shown up and tried to rope him back into what he'd wrestled to get free from.

What was that old saying? If you love something, let it go?

She loved Jaxon. No doubt in her being she loved him. But she'd tried everything she could think of to be the person he wanted her to be, needed her to be. And it wasn't enough.

She wasn't enough.

A hiss and the balloon dipped a little lower.

She wasn't enough for him.

And if she loved him, shouldn't she free him to find what was enough for him? She needed to release him from his obligation to her. She wrapped her arms around herself to ward off the sudden chill, to hold herself together. This was what love meant. Letting go. The white flag of surrender. Putting someone else's happiness above your own.

"Did you say you were afraid of heights?" Will asked.

She sucked in a shaky breath and nodded.

"But you aren't afraid of this, are you?"

"No. I feel stable up here." The basket didn't shake or shift a bit. Only her heart. But perhaps she could see clearly for the first time.

"Safest form of aviation out there."

She found a smile for the man. "Can you take me all the way to South Carolina in one of these?" Because that was where she was headed next. Home.

He chuckled. "Now that'd be a mighty long distance to fly."

Yes, it was. A very long way to get back to where she'd started from.

Chapter 19

Bernie
November, 1862
Winchester, Virginia

Bernie paced in the room she shared with four ladies of ill repute. From the window of their makeshift cell inside the Frederick County Courthouse, Bernie could almost see the hospital door that sheltered Hermann. The blue gingham dress hung limply on her frame. It likely came from a rag bin and was three sizes too big. She knotted her hands in front of her.

"Sit, will you? You're making me nervous." Violet arched a brow in Bernie's direction.

Bernie sat on her cot and huffed. At Violet's pointed nod toward her bouncing knee, she stilled. "Sorry." For the hundredth time, she glanced out the window at the Confederate soldiers who patrolled the premises. They guarded the hundreds of Union prisoners in the yard outside the courthouse. They guarded her. "I can't believe I'm here."

Cherry rolled her eyes. "Not this again."

"I should be with my husband. He's right down the street." She flung her arm in the direction of the home turned hospital where Hermann rehabilitated. "I fought in this war to be with him." She dropped her head into her hands. Her voice came out in a strangled whisper, "I shouldn't be here."

"Aye, yes," Lynn said, her Irish brogue thick as her red hair. "We ought to call you Brave Bernie, for ya fought down giants to be with the one ya loved."

Cherry scoffed and brushed a lock of chestnut brown hair from her face. "Brave. Yes, indeed. Look at her." She inclined her chin in Bernie's direction. Scorn blazed in her eyes. "She's the most fearful brave soldier I've ever seen. She didn't go to war because she had courage. Bernie went to war because she was scared to death what would happen if things were out of her control. And look at her now. Pitiful."

Bernie scowled at the wretched woman. Who was this lady of the night to pass judgment on her? She didn't know a thing about her. She couldn't possibly. The whole idea was ludicrous. Bernie, fearful? She'd marched into battlefields that rained down bullets. What did these women know about fear?

"Hmm, that's interesting." Violet propped her chin on her hand. "Going to war because you're afraid of staying at home."

Bernie crossed her arms. "You don't know what you're talking about."

Cherry laughed. "Don't we? You're petrified of not being in control, aren't you?"

"No." Bernie resisted the urge to shift in her seat. That wasn't true, was it? Sure, she liked … directing her life. Didn't everyone? But she wasn't a controlling woman. She didn't manipulate to ensure everything turned out her way.

Lynn twirled a strand of hair around her finger and nodded at Bernie with encouragement. "If your husband recovers and returns to his regiment and they send you home, you'll be fine, right? Content with that lot?"

Bernie ground her jaw. They'd trapped her. There was no way she could say she'd be content to part with Hermann now.

But to deny it would add fuel to their fire. "I didn't come this far for nothing."

Cherry scooted directly across from her and looked into her eyes. "Then why did you come this far? Why'd you do it?"

Bernie didn't blink. "Because I love my husband."

"And?"

"Because I didn't want war to ruin him."

"And? What would happen if it did?"

"It'd ruin me." She wasn't prepared for the way her voice cracked at the confession. She dropped her gaze to the floor and spoke past her thick, hot throat, "The life Hermann and I built together is the ground beneath my feet. If it were to change—if he were to change—I wouldn't be able to stand." A warm tear leaked out and trailed down her right cheek.

Cherry's voice softened. "You were afraid, so you fought."

Bernie bit her lip and nodded.

"But were you ever really in control?"

No. No, she wasn't. Not when she took it upon herself to dress as a man. Not when she searched for Hermann's regiment. Certainly not in the heat of battle. And not now, confined in the courthouse turned jail. All her grasping for control ended up as futile as an attempt to clench the wind. She shook her head.

She was the most fearful brave soldier in the army.

Lynn sat next to Cherry, her face kind. "You said if war changed your husband, you wouldn't be able to stand."

Bernie managed a slight nod.

"That reminds me of a song my mum used to sing." Lynn lifted her voice in a soul-piercing melody.

"My hope is built on nothing less
      Than Jesus' blood and righteousness;
      I dare not trust the sweetest frame,
      But wholly lean on Jesus' name.
      On Christ, the solid rock, I stand;

All other ground is sinking sand,
All other ground is sinking sand."
"You have a beautiful voice, Lynn," Violet said.

Bernie offered a wobbly smile, but rising emotion had choked her too much to reply. Had she attempted to build her life's foundation apart from Christ? She'd always believed in the Good Lord. She said prayers to Him daily, went to Sunday services, and kept her Bible close at hand. But did she trust Him? Truly trust Him? Or had she built her life on what she could do in her own strength, asking for God's blessing along the way?

She thought back over her prayers. Weren't they mostly for God to help her get her way? When had she sought His will? Asked Him what was on His heart? An ache formed in her gut, something that opened up, yawned wide, yearned for more.

Why hadn't she asked Him for His will? His ways? The answer hit her with sudden clarity.

Because she didn't trust Him.

Why didn't she trust this God she'd always professed to believe in?

His whisper wrapped around her heart. *You don't apprehend My love for you.*

She sucked in a breath. Was it true? Did she not truly believe God loved her? Of course, she knew the words of the Good Book from John 3:16: "*For God so loved the world, that he gave his only begotten Son, that whosoever believeth in him should not perish, but have everlasting life.*" She'd memorized those words as a little girl. God loved the world. God loved everyone. But did she fully grasp that He extended the fullness of that love to Bernice Reisenfeld?

Because if He loved her the way a good father loves his precious child, He would take care of her, watch over her, and provide for her. And when hard times came, He would be right next to her, holding her hand, walking through it with her.

No, she didn't believe He loved her that way. Not deep down in her core. But she wanted to. She closed her eyes.

Lord, show me Your love for me. Help me to apprehend it.

And there, in the makeshift jailhouse, warmth and light filled Bernie from within. Hope surged within her as the Lord spoke His love to her heart. She was not overlooked. A perfectly good God saw her perfectly. He did not neglect one detail of her life, and she was safe in His hands.

~

A week later, a guard knocked on Bernie's door. "Follow me, ma'am. Your husband is downstairs. He means to fetch you."

Her hand flew to her mouth. Hermann was well enough to fetch her from jail?

It was all she could do not to step on the guard's heels as she followed him down the steps. There Hermann stood, leaning on a cane. A look of relief crested his face at the sight of her. Who was that older woman by his side? A nurse?

Bernie nearly flew into his arms, apologizing when he teetered off balance, and the nurse had to put a hand to his back to steady him. "Oh, Hermann. Am I glad to see you." She pressed a kiss to his cheek.

He pulled back and scanned her face. "Did they treat you okay in there?"

"Yes." She smiled her assurance. "I'm fine. Thankful to see you well."

"He isn't well." The nurse's pinched voice caused Bernie's head to snap in her direction. "Not well enough to be gallivanting all over town. He needs his rest. We best be getting back to the hospital." She zeroed her sour expression in on Bernie. "The doctor only cleared him for a short walk for fresh air. If I would have known this is what he had in mind—"

"Now, Dorris, everything's all right. We're heading back right now."

The guard nodded. "Your husband paid your bail, Mrs. Reisenfeld. You are free to go."

She bowed her head in gratitude. "Thank you."

The guard turned his attention to Hermann and lowered his voice, though not enough to prevent Bernie from overhearing. "Please keep an eye on your wife, Mr. Reisenfeld. That one may need a firm hand."

Hermann's sly smile spread into a grin. "You bet." As he turned away from the guard, he snuck her a wink.

Dorris gripped Hermann's elbow and guided him toward the door. "There we go. Easy does it."

Bernie filed in on his other side. Immense gratitude filled her as they stepped out onto the front porch and descended the stairs into the sunshine. She barely minded the November chill in the air, so thankful she was for a deep, clean breath.

When they'd skirted around the yard full of Union prisoners, Dorris guided Hermann to the other side of the street. "Best watch those filthy Yankees."

Bernie rolled her eyes. What could they possibly do when so heavily guarded? Her thoughts roamed to the Yankee on the picket line who'd traded them coffee and shared his hardtack. And his wisdom. *What are you fighting for?* Perhaps the entire time she thought she fought for her husband, she really fought for herself. But it was okay. No matter how she'd faltered, God was with her right in this moment. And He could turn all her fumbling around for good.

Hermann's gait slowed the longer they walked.

Dorris's frown deepened. "I told you he wasn't well enough to make this trek."

"I'm fine. We're almost there." Though his face showed signs of strain, his voice contained only gentleness. How she'd missed this man. Her heart felt lighter with him nearby. When at last they walked through the front door of the home turned hospital Herman had been staying at, perspiration beaded his forehead.

Dorris fussed over him like a mother hen and settled him back in bed, raising the blankets under his chin. Only after she'd made sure he had a drink and after he declined a bite to eat did she scurry away to attend to other patients.

Hermann chuckled as he watched her go. "She's worse than my mother."

"I'm glad you've been well cared for in my absence."

"I'm sorry it took so long for me to get to you. You wouldn't believe the hullaballoo in achieving leave to take a simple walk. I'm just glad they didn't send you to Richmond."

She shuddered. Yes, indeed. How would he have gotten to her if she were that far away? How long would it have taken? Her mouth twisted as she considered the man before her, one among dozens of patients in this hospital house in a city where every house had become a hospital.

"I've got to say, it's mighty nice to see you back in a pretty frock." His gaze drunk her in with tasteful appreciation.

So strange to no longer need to pretend. She twirled a hair peeking out of her bonnet at the nape of her neck, far longer than when McGrady had first cut it, yet far shorter than normal. Now that she could be herself openly with him, she could finally speak what she'd been holding inside ever since she'd found him. She wrapped her arms around her middle, as if that could protect her from the pain the memory produced.

After glancing around to ensure no eavesdroppers, she spilled forth her secret. Their child buried near a battlefield with hundreds of men. When his eyes filled, she lost herself in them for a moment. Did he blame her for risking the babe in order to pursue him? They cried together for a spell, their grief mingling.

When Hermann spoke, his words came out choked and broken. "I'm so sorry you had to go through that alone."

She couldn't tell him of Henrietta. Not here. If anyone overheard, it wouldn't bode well for her friend. So, she simply said, "I wasn't."

"That's true. The Good Lord is always with you."

She put a hand over her heart, closed her eyes, and let that truth sink in. He was. On the battlefield. In the woods. No matter who she pretended to be. He had never left her. She pulled a handkerchief from her pocket and dabbed at her eyes. Their conversation ventured into her other experiences since she'd enlisted. He chuckled when she told him of her medical examination and of her disgust the first time a soldier spit tobacco juice near her shoe.

She sat back with a contented sigh. "What now?"

His eyes twinkled back at her. He leaned closer and lowered his voice. "I have a plan."

~

Bernie took Hermann's arm and ushered him out of the hospital's front doors. His plan to feign injury substantial enough to be sent home and not back to the front lines proved trickier than they expected. He needed the doctor to dismiss him as able-bodied enough for travel back to South Carolina, but not so able-bodied they'd expect him to shoulder a rifle. It wasn't until just after the New Year that he achieved the doctor's release. Now in borrowed civilian clothes, with a ruddy complexion but a pronounced limp, he set out with Bernie at his side to procure passage home.

Home. It had been so long she could barely conjure up the image of the rolling hills. The sound of her babies calling out for her, speaking to each other. The way their soft wool felt between her fingers. All of it was such a distant memory it might as well have been a dream. Truly, she hadn't been away too many days. It wasn't even the miles that made what once loomed as close as her breath now stretch so distant. The experiences she'd walked through had aged her, changed her in a way that made her old life almost unrecognizable.

Everything she'd done was so that she could return to that place with the man she loved. She should be running to the train station. Why did her steps drag? Why did their farm, her safe place, not allure her as it once had?

Lord, are You trying to tell me something?

An unsettled feeling swirled in her gut. But why? This was what she wanted, wasn't it? It was what Hermann wanted as well, from what she could piece together. They hadn't been able to talk freely with listening ears around, but she gathered he did not support the Confederate cause and could no longer justify fighting for it.

Nor could she.

And here they were, headed home. They'd no longer be fighting to keep people in slavery. She should feel relieved. Her conscience should be able to take a deep, unburdened breath. Why did she feel like something wasn't right?

"What's going on?" The bustle of hundreds of soldiers swallowed Hermann's words. Bernie blinked. Stalled. Stared. Soldiers? Union soldiers. What indeed?

"Freedom to the slaves!" one man shouted, fist in the air.

Without thinking, she reached out and tugged one Yankee's sleeve. He turned to her with brows raised. "What's the meaning of this?"

"General Milroy has come to enforce President Lincoln's Emancipation Proclamation. Haven't you heard?" A grin spread across his stubbled face. "No more slavery. They're free now."

Elation crackled in her chest. "You don't say."

"Yes. The Union victory at Antietam made it possible. Now anyone who opposes the proclamation will be treated as a rebel in arms."

As the soldier turned to continue on his way, Bernie pressed her hands to her smiling cheeks.

Wait, Union victory? With the plethora of losses on both sides at Antietam, could either army claim a decisive victory? Her question fell away to the sound of the soldiers' jubilant shouts. Free! The slaves were free.

She caught Hermann's eye. His beaming face showed he was as overjoyed as she. Interesting. She never knew him to give much thought one way or another to the subject of slavery. Then again, neither had she. Had the war rearranged his convictions and priorities as it had hers?

Images of Bob and Abram drifted through her mind, followed by ones of Jimmy. Men she'd come to respect. Men who were now free to come and go as they pleased, no longer forced to bend to the will of a master.

She bit her lip. Wait. President Lincoln may have issued a proclamation of freedom. General Milroy may be in Winchester enforcing freedom for the slaves here. But a word issued from the mouth of a president Confederates didn't recognize would do nothing for those men far from Union-controlled territory. It wouldn't free Bob or Abram or Jimmy. Because this war wasn't over. The North hadn't won. Not yet.

Frazzled, Bernie grappled behind her for a bench and sat. Hermann lowered next to her, his eyes alight as he took in the energetic scene before them.

"Isn't it grand?" He patted her hand. "Look at these men, Bernie. Look at their faces. They're fighting for something they believe in, something bigger than themselves."

Yes, it was grand. The idea that one could fight for a cause without a shred of hesitation, without a smidgin of doubt about if they were doing the right thing. "I hate slavery." The words sneaked out before she could ascertain if they were safe to say or not, but as they slid from her tongue, they tasted truer than most anything she'd ever said.

"It's despicable." Hermann shook his head, a frown dimpling his chin.

Her mouth parted. What was that?

"Treating a human being as if he were an animal," Hermann continued. "It's incomprehensible."

"I didn't know you felt that way."

His gaze lowered to his hands for half a second, then rose to meet hers with piercing sincerity. "I didn't know I did either."

A burning sensation spread through her chest. Something like zeal. Passion? An idea sparked. She spoke tentatively. "If you could fight for the sake of emancipation, would you?"

His words fell fast from his lips. "In a heartbeat." He fumbled with his hands. "But of course, you are most important to me. After all you've done for me, I'll not leave you again."

"What if," she said as she leaned closer, the side of her mouth lifting, "you didn't have to."

"What do you mean?"

"Your leg is healed now, right? The limp is an act?"

"Yes. Bernie? What are you suggesting?"

She pulled off her bonnet and ran a hand through her short hair. "It's Bernard to you." She winked. Hermann's eyebrows shot up. When a man stopped and gawked, she stuffed the bonnet back on.

"You want to go back out there and fight again?" he whispered.

"Yes, Uncle Hermann. As long as we fight for a cause I can wholeheartedly stand behind."

"It's dangerous."

She sobered. "Yes."

"We'd fight against neighbors. Against friends."

She swallowed. She would pray she'd never have to face Henrietta or Freddy in battle. If it came to that, she'd never be able to pull the trigger. She'd die first.

"You could lose me." He ran his thumb down her cheek. "I could lose you."

"I know. Our original plan would be much safer."

"Then why do you want to risk it?"

Why indeed? Love bloomed in her heart for this man. Hermann had taken her from a rigid upbringing in which she could never quite fit, never take a full breath, and given her the wide-open space of his love. There, she'd been free to explore, free to discover who she truly was, free to express herself fully. He had become her safe place. And perhaps, in doing so, her idol. Because giving up all she'd gained in him had felt scarier than death itself. Yes, the Lord had given her Hermann as a precious gift, and yet, her husband was never meant to take the Lord's place in her life. He wasn't created to do that. He wasn't enough for that space. Her peace, her security, had to come from God alone.

Why would she risk losing everything that meant so much to her? "Because some things are more important than safety."

Hermann pressed his lips together. "Are you sure about this?"

She nodded.

"Then I'll need to secure men's clothing."

"And we'll need to find a regiment."

Hermann pressed a kiss to her forehead, then her cheek, then her lips. She closed her eyes and soaked in the feeling of his lips on her skin. How long would it be until they'd be able to show affection freely again? How long until the war ended? However long it took, she'd fight by her husband's side.

~

November 30, 1864
Honey Hill, South Carolina

Bernie and Hermann were in familiar territory, and yet, nothing felt familiar. Not since they disembarked from the transports yesterday afternoon into the dissipating fog. They were supposed to cut the railroad near Grahamville, and after getting turned around for a while, they'd finally been on their way when they encountered a Confederate force with a battery of seven guns blocking the road.

They'd fought ever since. Fought in tandem with companies of colored troops. Tried to hold the line, dislodge the Confederates despite the Union's inferior position. The Rebs fought from on top of a rocky hill about fifteen feet from the ground below. Their elevation gave them a coveted advantage. Already, hundreds of soldiers in blue lay wounded. Sure, they'd done some damage to the enemy's front lines, but it paled in comparison to the losses the Rebs had inflicted.

Bernie ducked into a trench by Hermann, a ditch behind a rice dike, as bullets flew over her head. Hermann peeked his head over the ridge, aimed, and fired. She did the same.

"We're not able to do a smidgen of good here," Hermann said. He let out a frustrated sigh.

Through the artillery smoke, she scanned the sparse pine forest in front of them. "We could make it there." She pointed. "To those two trees. You take the one on the left. I'll take the one on the right."

Hermann's brow furrowed. "It's risky."

"It's the only way we're going to make any headway."

Resolve settled over his features. "You're right. On the count of three. One." They both sprung into a crouched position. "Two." Bernie's gaze zeroed in on her target. "Three." The two soldiers sprinted to the protection of the pines. Hermann ducked behind his refuge and immediately looked to her. Almost there. She bounded for the final yard.

Searing pain sliced her calf. Fire. Her leg was on fire. She crumpled to the ground and emitted a feral groan. All air left her as her body pulsated with pain.

"Bernie!" In a second, Hermann appeared at her side. He hooked his hands under her arms and dragged her a few feet until they were both at least somewhat covered by the pine. His quick bursts of breath reminded her to breathe.

She gasped, then gritted her teeth to quell the cry that pressed against her chest.

"You're hit," he said as if in shock, as if he couldn't believe it was true. After all the battles she'd been in, after all the men she'd shot—she'd *killed*—it had finally happened to her. The agonizing bite of a bullet through her flesh.

In an instant, he'd ripped a strip off the sleeve of his Yankee uniform. Gently, he rolled up her pant leg and wrapped the piece of cloth around the wound. He smoothed her pant leg back down.

She glanced wildly around. Had anyone seen what had happened? With all the dead and wounded strewn about, surely no one would pay any attention to yet another bullet wound. She could not risk a doctor inspecting her.

"Come on." Hermann settled his arms underneath her and prepared to lift and carry her as if she were a baby. "Let's get you out of here."

"Out of here?" Her panicked gaze found the Confederate cannons on top of the earthworks above them. "Where?"

He brought his forehead to hers, drawing her attention back to his now steady, focused expression. "We're going home." Resoluteness seeped from his pores. This was as sure of himself as she'd ever seen him, and in that moment, her breath hitched, not because of pain or worry, but from the rightness of what she saw in the man in front of her.

The war had changed him, all right.

He lifted her as if she weighed nothing. Artillery and muskets sounded around them, but she'd never felt safer than she did right then in his arms. Her leg throbbed. Danger loomed. She wasn't oblivious to the fact either of them could die at any second. Yet, if they did—if he did, if she did—she'd be okay. She had found what she'd searched for.

Because it wasn't only Hermann's arms that carried her. It was the Lord's, and His arms were competent. It was clear now. So unmistakably clear how God had been able, this entire time, to take this ugly, wretched war and use it for good in her husband's life. In his heart. God was more than capable of using immense tragedy to shape something good in those who loved Him.

She ground out a smile for this man she loved more each day. "Well, don't just stand there. Let's go home."

He pressed a kiss to her forehead. Then he surveyed his surroundings and said, "Hold on."

He dashed from tree to tree to tree. She closed her eyes and rested her head against his chest. Eventually, the sounds of battle faded into the background. Then the song of birds filtered through. Rice stalks waved in the chilly breeze. The sun's rays kissed her face. Exhaustion gripped her. Her eyes fluttered open for a moment to see that Hermann walked upon a rice dike. Her heavy lids fell closed again.

"We're getting closer," he said as he kissed her temple.

Perhaps she slept, for it seemed like only a moment later when his voice startled her. "Just over the next hill."

The sting in her leg reminded her of where she was and what had happened. She pried her eyes open. The sun hung low on the horizon, bathing the fields in an orange glow. Her heart raced. Home! They were almost home. Home to her babies. She'd missed them so. Home to the place where their hard work had paid off. Their growing farm. The rewarding fruit of their labor. For the first time in over three years, she'd be able to work with her hands instead of destroying with them. Once she recovered, that is.

They crested the hill, and her heart leapt in expectation. But as her gaze searched the fields, unease soured her stomach. Where were the tufts of white dotting the green hillside? Where was the sound of bleating?

Hermann stilled for a second before he continued. "Looks like someone broke down our fence. Likely used it for firewood."

The fence was missing? She squinted but could only make out a few posts that remained. "Someone?" She swallowed.

His mouth twisted. "Don't know which army it was. Union or Confederate. Neither would hesitate to take what they needed."

Her mouth twisted. He was right. She'd been there. Witnessed it firsthand. "The sheep must have gotten out then. They must be lost." Her voice wavered as she grasped onto the thin thread of hope. Because she'd seen fellow soldiers slaughter cattle and hogs when they, bellies rumbling with hunger, came upon a farm. Lord help her, she'd even partaken of a slab of meat when offered some.

"I wish that were the case, but I fear …"

He didn't finish. He didn't have to. Bernie's throat pinched closed. No. Not her babies. Not Lillybell and Franny. Not Cecil. Her babies that she'd watched be born and nursed to health. She knew every nuance of their unique personalities. And some soldiers had killed them? For what? To satisfy their hunger for one more day? Yes, Tunis was a breed raised for both wool and meat. Just because they focused on wool production didn't mean she was ignorant of the fact that many raised the sheep for food. But to slaughter an entire fold without the owner's consent? How inhumane.

Desperately, she listened for mooing in the distance. Nothing. Her eyes filled. "Have we lost everything?" All that they'd worked relentlessly to build. Their livelihood.

Hermann's lips pressed together in a grim line. That and the cloud that descended in his eyes were her only answer.

He stumbled a bit as his feet transferred from the road to the field, dented with imprints of a thousand small hooves. The jostling jarred her leg and sent slices of pain trailing up her body. They met the ache that radiated from her heart and melded there in a heap that pressed down on her middle. It made it hard to breathe.

At the top of the hill, their house came into view. Except the pristine beacon of light she remembered with its white shutters and spindly porch railings was gone. In its place stood a bedraggled mess. As if hit by a twister, pieces of their beloved home were broken off, knocked down, or missing all together. No shutters. More than half the spindles gone. A porch step missing. Their door stood wide open like a mouth agape. What glinted in the fading sunlight there in the yard? Was that her silverware? She gasped.

Hermann carried her gingerly up the porch steps and into the house. Her heart pinched. Ransacked. All of it. Overturned chairs. Trails of flour, a spill of sugar. Their table with the legs sawed off. Curtains in a heap on the floor.

Hermann's voice hitched. "Good Lord."

Good Lord? Where was He now? How could He have allowed this to happen? He could have protected their farm. Their sheep. Their home. But He didn't.

Hermann set her on the mud-streaked settee and disappeared into the kitchen. He returned a moment later, hat in his hands.

"Is all the food gone?" She pushed the question past the lump in her throat.

"Yes."

Tears brimmed. "We *have* lost everything."

He came close and knelt before her, enveloping her hand in his. "No, we haven't. We have each other."

As she gazed into his eyes, no longer stormy but now a clear blue, the truth of his statement settled deep within her.

They had what mattered most.

They had enough.

The question of *"Where were You God?"* still pinged around in her chest, but softer now, less like an accusation and more like an inquiry. Because her heart still squeezed tight at the thought of her sweet sheep being sacrificed to satisfy a soldier's appetite. She may not have lost everything, but her losses hurt.

As did her leg. She winced.

Hermann blinked, then sprung into action. "I'll get McEvens. See if he has any brandy. Maybe he knows how to tend to a wound."

He took three steps toward the door before Bernie called out. "Wait!"

He turned.

"Look at you. You need to change. I have to change."

His eyes dropped to his blue uniform, and his chin dropped. "I suppose you're right. No one around these parts is liable to help a couple of traitors."

"Stash the uniforms under the bed."

He returned from the bedroom wearing civilian clothes and carrying a house dress for her, which he painstakingly helped her change into. Thank heavens the soldiers hadn't stolen their clothing. Once he'd settled her back down, he dashed out the door with the promise to return with half-blind McEvens.

~

No one had a lick of an idea what had become of McEvens. When Hermann had found McEvens's home empty, he ran to the next nearest neighbors, the Crossfoots. Mrs. Laura Crossfoot came at once, brandy and supplies in tow.

Upon seeing Bernie's bullet wound, bound in blue cloth soaked through with blood, she gasped. "How did this happen?"

The tips of Hermann's ears reddened as they always did when he was about to fib. "She was caught in the line of fire as she"—he hesitated only a second—"nursed the wounded."

Laura's forehead crinkled. "You're a nurse, Mrs. Reisenfeld? I heard you'd left, but I never could figure out where you went."

Best to keep her answer as honest as possible. "I tended to wounded soldiers during the war, yes."

"And you were hit while doing so?"

An image of the fiery cannon blasting into the barn sparked in her mind. She shuddered. "Yes."

"Oh, dear. I sent Sibley for the doctor. Who knows how long he'll be? Until then, I can at least clean and dress the wound."

She gave Bernie a bit of brandy for the pain and put Hermann to work fetching water. While she washed the area, she sucked in a breath. "Wait. There's an exit wound. The doctor won't need to remove a bullet after all."

Hermann escorted Laura back to her farm in the dark of night while crickets sung Bernie to sleep.

~

Relief had coursed through Bernie when the doctor announced she would not lose her leg. The bullet had missed the bone, and the doctor expected her to make a full, albeit slow, recovery, as long as she could steer clear of infection.

Now she set her empty bowl of potato soup on the bedside table. Hermann had managed to salvage a decent amount of root vegetables. He'd also found two of their chickens wandering in the woods. It wasn't much compared to what they'd lost, but they weren't starving.

She picked up the Bible from beside the empty soup bowl and fingered the gilded lettering on the leather cover. Her mother's Bible. Too precious to risk taking it with her to war, yet how hard it was to leave it behind.

Gingerly, she flipped open to her favorite passage, the Twenty-third Psalm. She didn't need to look at the words—they were written on her heart—yet a prompting inside her wooed her to do so. To take in the text afresh. Her eyes dipped down to the page—and widened.

Someone had nestled a note inside the pages of her Bible, right there in the place of Psalm 23. Who? Her hands shook as she opened the missive.

Dear Bernie,

I needed to leave you word somewhere I knew you would find it but no one else would. I hope you will soon read your favorite passage of Scripture. I want you to know I'm taking four of your sheep and hiding away in the woods and in some back pastureland. I hope to keep far away from any army's approach. Soldiers on both sides have destroyed folds all over the South, and I fear there will be no sheep left if it continues. They decimated my stock and most of yours, but I have Cecil, Franny, Judy, and Mary Sue. I'll do my best to keep them safe and bring them back to you after the war.

Your friend,

Russell

Hot tears pooled as she read the letter again and again. Four of her babies were safe. Russell McEvens was safe. Her blurry gaze dipped to the words of the Psalm.

The LORD is my shepherd; I shall not want.

He was, indeed, the shepherd of her soul. And a shepherd cared for the sheep.

The question that had reverberated within her as she first surveyed their ravaged home bubbled up now with a spark of recognition. *Where were you, God?*

Where was He? He'd been with Russell, prompting him to secret away a ram and three ewes to safety. He'd been with those four sheep, hiding them from the soldiers' eyes so McEvens had a chance to sneak them away before the soldiers could eat them. God had been right there on their farmland, breathing on the potatoes and carrots in their absence so that they'd grow, sending rain from heaven to water the soil. God had been there saying, "Hitherto shalt thou come, but no further," not allowing the men to pillage their clothing or furniture.

And God was right there with her, next to her every second. He'd never left her alone. Not even when she'd been foolish. Not when she'd tried to be her husband's savior. Nor when she'd tried to be her own. Even when she'd failed Him, He hadn't failed her. Not once. Not for a moment. He had fought for her heart because to Him, she was worth every battle.

~

One year later
Shulerville, South Carolina

Bernie dragged her hand through Franny's soft, thick wool. "Yes, baby. You look especially lovely today."

Franny bleated her agreement.

Bernie chuckled. "Ready to be a mother again?" She rubbed under Franny's chin until the animal nearly smiled.

Breeding season had come again, and with it, the chance to expand their fold. The ewes birthed the last four lambs in the spring, on the very day the Civil War officially ended. Bernie had named the rams Lincoln and Grant after the late president and the general. She named the ewes Mary and Clara after the first lady and Clara Barton, the heroic nurse. And now? How many lambs would they welcome this spring?

She straightened and fingered the letter in her apron pocket. Henrietta's letter. Gratitude coursed over her at the news that her friend was safe and well. The war had taken much. Her gaze settled on the small shrub gracing their front lawn in memory of the babe they'd lost on the battlefield. Much indeed. Yet despite all that heartache, new beginnings called to them.

"Bernie, dear." Hermann emerged from the house and bounded down the porch steps. "Someone wants to see you."

She craned her ear. Oh yes. Past the bleating of her sheep and melody of her wind chimes, the sound drifted out. Whimpering. She had about a minute and a half before it turned into a full-blown wail.

Just enough time to greet her husband with a kiss. She encircled his waist as he wrapped his arms around her back. She raised her mouth to his. He met her with a soft kiss that drew her in and curled her toes.

He trailed a finger across her upper lip. "Good morning, sunshine."

"Morning." She beamed at him. Perhaps one more—

A cry sounded. She took a step back. Maybe later.

She tossed her husband a wry smile. "I'll go tend to the baby. You go ahead and milk your cows." They only had two cows for now, but it was enough. They had everything they needed.

"You'd better keep an eye on your girl in there." He twirled a finger in the direction of the front door, then winked. "She's got pluck."

Bernie's laugh erupted forth. "Remind you of anyone?"

"Sure does. Reminds me of the most courageous woman I know. Her mother."

Lifting her skirts, she took the steps two at a time and flung open the door, then stopped. "Courageous, huh?"

"That's right."

"I like that. It's similar to brave, but …" But what?

Hermann rocked back on his heels. "But courage comes from the Lord."

She quoted from Ephesians 6:10. "'Be strong in the Lord, and in the power of His might.'" The power of *His* might. Not her own. Yes, she liked it. Courageous Bernie might not have the same ring as Brave Bernie, but it suited her. "Very wise of you, Hermann." She cast a glance toward the door. "Now your courageous wife must tend to your plucky daughter before we have another war on our hands."

Chapter 20

"SINCE THERE'S NO HELP" BY MICHAEL DRAYTON

Sahara
Present Day
Provo, Utah

She hadn't said a word to Jaxon in a week and a half. Not one word, not one text. He hadn't spoken to her either. Avoidance was now a two-way street between them. A dance they'd perfected. She had to give the lawyer time to draw up the paperwork. In the meantime, she'd used her evenings to catch up on accounts instead of pouring over marriage books. And she'd packed.

She'd flown to Utah, but she planned to drive her Mercedes back. If Jaxon agreed, of course. And maybe he wouldn't. Maybe he'd take the car back from her when he realized she was taking her vows back from him. But not likely. He'd given the car to her as a gift. She would give the divorce papers to him as a gift as well. Their parting would be amiable, wouldn't it? She couldn't stand the thought of remaining enemies forever.

When everyone left for the day, she'd approach him. Give him the papers. Release him. Watch his shoulders relax in relief. Then she'd turn in her apartment keys and drive away. Drive home. To start a new life, whatever that looked like. She'd give him anything he wanted as far as splitting their possessions went. If she couldn't keep her dream Georgetown house, then so be it. She'd find a new place to make a new start. She was done fighting Jaxon. She should have been done years ago.

She had nailed a beam into place when, out of the corner of her eye, she saw Jaxon head for his Jeep. No. Wait. Where did he think he was going? She needed to have a conversation with him later when everyone else left for the day. He couldn't walk out now.

She set down her nail gun and jogged toward him. Picked up the pace as he reached his vehicle. "Jaxon, wait!"

He glanced over his shoulder and frowned.

"Where are you going?" She stopped a few feet from him and planted her hands on her knees as she struggled to catch her breath.

"To the other site."

"Will you be back?"

"Not today."

"I need to talk to you. Today."

He crossed his arms and leaned against the blue door. "Talk."

She held up a finger. "Hold on a sec." Pressing a hand to the stich in her side, she rushed to her car and grabbed the manilla envelope. She returned to him checking his watch in an exaggerated fashion. Okay, she got it. He was a busy man with important things to do. If he'd just give her a minute of his precious time, she wouldn't bother him again.

She handed him the envelope.

His brow furrowed as he took it. "What's this?"

She dropped her gaze. Studied her boots. Suddenly, shame cascaded over her as the flap of the envelope and rustle of papers told her he was answering his own question.

"Sahara, what's this?" His voice fell like lead.

She bit her lip and chanced a glance at him. Why did he look … pained? Panicked, even. Maybe he didn't understand. "I release you from your obligation to me."

"What?" He spat out the question.

It hit her like a punch. She couldn't get a full breath. "You can be free to live the life you want."

He shook his head. His breaths came in short, heavy bursts. He opened his mouth, but all that came out was a grunt. Then he held up the papers and ripped them in two.

"Jaxon! What in the world?"

"This isn't what I want."

"Of course, it is. It has to be. I can't figure out any way I can possibly change to fit what you need. You said it yourself. I will never be enough for you. You need something more."

"You're infuriating." He thrust the ripped papers at Sahara.

Oh, yes. She was the infuriating one. She pinched the bridge of her nose, ignoring his outstretched, paper-strewn arms. "I'm starting the drive home tonight. That is, if you say it's okay that I keep the Mercedes. If not, it's fine. I'll book a flight."

"You can't leave." He dropped the papers. They fluttered to the gravel.

She stomped on them, securing them under her boot to keep them from blowing away, then blinked back at Jaxon. "Excuse me?"

"You have a contract."

She rolled her eyes. "I think you'll manage to get this mansion done just fine without my help."

He scrubbed his beard. Looked up at the sky as if it held answers. "We're supposed to go skiing. You promised you'd ski with me."

She pressed her lips together. Yeah, that would have been nice. "You also promised to love me forever, yet here we are."

He took a step back as if she'd slapped him. Stumbled against the car. Oh no. Oh, heavens. She'd hurt him again. His eyes flashed, then misted. See! This was why she needed to stay far, far away from this man.

His voice came out broken as he recited. Haunting.
"Far in the pillared dark

> Thrush music went—
> Almost like a call to come in
> To the dark and lament.
> But no, I was out for stars:
> I would not come in.
> I meant not even if asked,
> And I hadn't been."

She'd heard that one before. "Frost?"

He nodded.

"Isn't that poem about a forest?" Why couldn't the man talk plain English?

"Don't you see, Sahara? I've loved you from the beginning, and I never stopped. Not once did I want a different version of you. I only wanted you to let me love the version of you I've always loved. To stop pushing me away."

"Pushing you away?" When had she done that?

"Constantly." He sniffed. "It's exhausting to keep loving someone who will never quite accept your love for them." He looked down at his hands. "I got tired. But I never stopped."

Thoughts swarmed her mind like bees. "But you won't even say the words. Won't even say 'I love you.'"

"Haven't I shown you?"

She swallowed. How could a look make her heart feel as if it shattered? And yet, his broken heart was breaking hers. Shards of it lay in the gravel between them.

He pressed the heels of his palms against his eyes. "Now I have to go to this meeting with the owner and I can't even think straight." He took a deep breath.

"I'm sorry."

"We'll talk later. Just don't leave. You're not"—he twirled a finger in the air—"released."

He slid into the car and drove off before she could collect a single comeback. She couldn't leave? Wasn't released? Who was he to boss her around like that? The corner of her mouth twitched. Well, he was her boss. And she had signed a work contract. And—his words hit her then, penetrating the confusion—he loved her. He wanted her to stay. He wanted to be her husband.

A whoosh of air escaped from her lungs. He wanted to stay married to her! He didn't want a divorce, didn't want her to let him go. She bent and picked up the ripped papers from under her foot. A dirty shoe print and dust marred them, but they were beautiful to her. Pretty enough to frame.

She let out a whoop as she spun around. Where had she put her nail gun? She had a house to build. She wasn't going anywhere.

~

A package sat on her doorstep when she arrived at her apartment that evening. Strange. She hadn't ordered anything else from Amazon. She picked up the small box and studied the return label. Aunt Trish. Must be the Bible her aunt had promised. Took her long enough.

Once inside, Sahara opened the box to find a leather-bound Bible with her name engraved on the cover. Trish had tucked a note inside.

Dawn,

> *Sorry this took so long to get to you. I had it engraved at the Christian bookstore. I pray you'll find love between the pages.*
> *Affectionately,*
> *Trish*

Love between the pages. Right. Sahara dropped onto the couch and called her aunt, who answered on the second ring.

"Did you get my package?"

"Yes. Thank you."

"You're welcome. I'm delighted you've taken an interest—"

Okay. Stop right there. "I did read the passage you told me about, but I haven't opened the Bible app since."

"Oh?"

"I appreciate the help. But I can't be like that. Like it says in First Corinthians. Patient, kind, not envious, not boastful … whatever else it said. I can't do it. I always end up fumbling up."

A chuckle from her aunt grew into an outright laugh.

"What's so funny?"

"You read that passage as if it was a to-do list?"

"Yes." What other way was there?

"Oh, no, sweetheart. That's not a list of how you are supposed to try to love. It's a list of how God already loves you."

What now? "Hold on." She flipped her new Bible open, searched the index for First Corinthians, and found the right page number. She read it again. "This is about God's love."

"Yes. There's no way we can love that way in our own strength."

Huh. Interesting.

"How are you and Jaxon doing?"

She rubbed her temples. What a question. "I have no clue. I'm so confused. I was all set to divorce him, had the papers drawn up and everything."

A tiny gasp sounded from Trish's end. "Go on."

"He tore the papers up. Said he's always loved me, but I've pushed him away."

"Sounds about right."

"What do you mean by that?"

"You do it to everyone. You're afraid. I get it."

No. She wasn't the problem here. "I asked why he wouldn't say the words 'I love you,' and he said, 'Haven't I shown you?'"

"Well, hasn't he? What kind things has he done for you? That's Jaxon's way of showing his love."

She sank back deeper into the recesses of the couch. "A lot, actually."

"The best way you can love Jaxon is to receive Jaxon's love for you. It's like he's giving you a present every time he does something for you, but you won't even open it because you want it to come in different packaging. Open the gifts, child. Let him love you."

A niggle of worry remained. "But why won't he tell me he loves me?"

"You know Jaxon. He doesn't always have the words. It's why he uses other people's poems to try and get his point across. Stop demanding something from him that he doesn't have to give and instead receive the love he's freely offering you."

Receive Jaxon's love.

"How different would your relationship be if you lived like you were fully loved?"

The question burst through her, echoing in her mind, her heart. That flicker of hurt in Jaxon's eyes every time she questioned his love for her. Was that the chisel that had been etching away at their marriage?

"Thanks, Aunt Trish." She ran a finger over the silky-thin paper of the passage in her Bible.

"Anytime. And I know you might not want to hear it, but God loves you too. So much more and better than Jaxon does. He's giving you presents of love each day too. Why don't you try opening a few instead of chucking them?"

Receive God's love.

That was something else entirely. Unless … Had God been trying to love her all along, and she'd been pushing Him away too, like she'd done to Jaxon?

She shook the thought from her head. One thing at a time. And she knew what she needed to do next.

~

Sahara waved both hands over her head, but Myra didn't seem to see her amidst the myriad of passengers jetting this way and that. She put two fingers in her mouth and let out a short, shrill whistle. That did the trick. Myra's gaze shot straight toward her.

Her friend dashed to her as fast as her rolling carry-on would allow. Sahara met her halfway and wrapped her in a bear hug.

"I missed you so much." Sahara's voice came out muffled against Myra's hair.

Myra squeezed tighter. "Missed you more."

"Thank you for coming."

"Of course. I couldn't miss this. It's going to be epic."

Sahara chuckled. Epic. She would have thought the hot-air balloon ride fit more in that category than this meager plan. Of course, she could have done it on her own. But when she spilled her new revelation to her best friend, Myra squealed, then said she *had* to be a part of it. And there she was with her fancy pants camera in tow.

They grabbed Myra's luggage and headed to the parking garage. "Too bad I couldn't pack the frames."

Sahara shrugged. "We'll get new ones." She'd dropped over a grand on a balloon ride for one. What was a couple hundred for new picture frames?

When Sahara hit the unlock button on her key fob, Myra gasped. "That's it? That's your car?"

Sahara grinned and popped the trunk. "Yes."

"She's beautiful. What'd you name her?"

"I haven't yet. Can't decide."

"What about Moonbeam?" Myra hoisted her bags inside.

Sahara grabbed her friend's arm. "You're a genius. Moonbeam. That's from a poem."

"Really? I was only thinking about the color."

Flickers of words flittered through her memory. "Something about moonbeams flashing. Oh! 'While moonbeams flash and fly so fast we scarce can say they smiled.'" She pulled her phone from her back pocket and googled the phrase as they slid into the car. "Here it is. 'Come Walk with Me' by Emily Bronte." She took a breath and let the words flow.

> "Come, walk with me,
> There's only thee
> To bless my spirit now –
> We used to love on winter nights
> To wander through the snow;
> Can we not woo back old delights?
> The clouds rush dark and wild
> They fleck with shade our mountain heights
> The same as long ago
> And on the horizon rest at last
> In looming masses piled;
> While moonbeams flash and fly so fast
> We scarce can say they smiled."

Myra raised an eyebrow. "What does it mean?"

"I have no idea. It sounds sad, doesn't it? But also, kind of like Jaxon and me." She chewed on her lip. "'Can we not woo back old delights?'"

"Yes, you can, baby. Yes, you can." Myra buckled her seat belt. "Now, let's see how Moonbeam handles the road."

On the way to her apartment, Sahara and Myra discussed the plan.

"We're getting a picture of the car, right?" Myra asked.

"Oh yeah. Definitely. I want twelve pictures, one for each year we've been married. Help me think."

"You mentioned the galvanized nails and the tea. What else?"

They tossed ideas back and forth on the drive and throughout the night. In the morning, they set out to capture in pictures all the ways that Jaxon had showered her with love all along.

~

They arrived back at the apartment laden with picture frames, prints, and Chinese takeout.

Sahara set down a bag of twinkle lights on the dining room chair and splayed the pictures on the table. "I can't wait to get started."

Myra slouched on the couch. "Slow down, lady. Put your feet up for a few. We'll get to it."

"Sorry. I'm excited. But you're right. We should probably eat." She dug into another bag and fished out their containers of sweet and sour chicken and egg rolls, then brought them to the coffee table. When she set down the fare, Myra was thumbing through her Bible. "Aunt Trish sent that to me." Why did she feel the need to explain?

"I have one that looks exactly like this. Same version and everything."

Sahara stilled. Myra had a Bible? "Seriously?"

Myra flashed a half smile. "Just because I don't push my faith on you doesn't mean I don't have one."

Sahara lowered onto the couch next to her friend. "I don't know what to think of it all."

"I know." She continued to leaf through the pages. "Hey, what's this?" She pulled out a worn piece of paper.

Sahara leaned closer. No. Not a piece of paper. A picture. She took it from Myra's hand and held it closer. It was grainy and old and …

"It's Bernie." Her great-grandmother looked back at her. Same angular jaw, same shape of the eyes and mouth, but something struck her as vastly different from the picture on her mantle. Sahara's focus shifted to the man who stood beside Bernie in the picture. Her great-grandfather Hermann? Both were dressed as men in uniform, only the uniforms were different from the other picture.

"I thought Bernie fought for the Confederates." Myra's voice came as a whisper beside her.

"She did."

"That's her, right?" Myra pointed. "In the Union uniform?"

Confusion swirled. "Yeah. That's her. And maybe her husband? I don't know what's going on. Were they spies? Or did they switch sides?"

Myra took her hand and placed her cellphone inside. "Call Trish. She must have put the picture inside. She'll know the story."

Sahara stood and paced as she dialed Trish's number and waited for her to pick up. Myra sat, hands clasped in her lap, watching.

"Dawn. Nice of you to call."

"Hey, Trish. I found a picture in the Bible you sent and I—"

"Oh, my goodness. I forgot I snuck that in there."

"What's the story? What happened to Bernie?"

Sahara perched on the edge of the sofa and put the phone on speaker as Trish relayed Bernie's journey from a Confederate soldier, desperate to find her husband at any cost, to a Union soldier fighting side by side with her husband against a common enemy. "So, yes, she changed course. She found out what she'd fought for wasn't what she thought it was, and she and Hermann ended up fighting together on a side they could both believe in. They banded together. Became inseparable."

Sahara spoke through a sheen of tears. "I never knew that part of the story."

"Throughout the years, some of the family felt divided about it. Hermann and Bernie deserted the Southern cause. It was seen as a disgrace. Something best kept hidden."

Myra flinched ever so slightly, as if trying to contain herself.

"I'm glad you shared it with me."

"Of course. It's your heritage."

Her heritage. Her legacy. She swallowed and thanked her aunt, then hung up. She met Myra's watery gaze with her own. "Well, there's that."

Myra managed a smile. "You come from good stock, Sahara Dawn."

That she did. She'd always been told stubbornness ran in the family, and she'd bought into that. Dug her roots deep into her right to never give up, never change her mind, and never look back. And yes, some of that was good. One needed perseverance for most any reward. But what if one held on too tightly to the wrong things? Was there wisdom in learning what was worth clinging to and what was worth letting go?

Jaxon's words echoed through her mind.

"You are allowed to change your mind. You're allowed to readjust your vision. You're allowed to examine if what you thought you wanted is what you truly want. That's all part of building the life you want."

Bernie did that. She readjusted her vision and built the life she wanted with the man she wanted to build it with.

Sahara sighed, grabbed the lukewarm containers of Chinese, and slid them into the microwave. As they turned round and round her mind spun with the years of reaching for the dream of her historic Georgetown house. History. Grounding. The smell of old wood. The feel of ancient metal. Sleeping within walls that she knew wouldn't go anywhere because they'd weathered year upon year upon year. She'd searched for security in her fairy-tale neighborhood, and she loved every inch of her house. Except that it was *her* house, not *their* home. She could dig in her heels and insist her roots intertwine with those of the ancient live oaks in Georgetown soil. Or she could … readjust.

The microwave pinged. She slid the cardboard containers out and returned them to the coffee table. She moistened her lips. Lowered onto the couch. Laced her fingers together and spoke. "I'm not going back to South Carolina."

Myra's attention flicked from the container of egg rolls to Sahara's face. Her friend's mouth spread in a knowing smile. "I hoped you'd say that." She put a hand on Sahara's knee. "Not that I won't miss you like crazy, mind you. But it's good and right for you to be here."

Sahara leaned over and rested her head on Myra's shoulder, her throat tight and hot. "You loved me when you didn't know I came from good stock."

Her gaze drifted to Bernie's picture on the mantle. The one Myra had enlarged for her. What a sacrifice for the beautiful woman who sat next to her. What love.

"I always knew what you were made of, Sahara. I've only been waiting for you to figure it out."

"Waiting?"

"And praying."

Praying? Myra prayed? For her?

"You are dearly loved." Myra wrapped an arm around her shoulder and gave a gentle squeeze. The words inflated Sahara like a balloon. Her chest filled with warmth and light.

"I am, aren't I?" By Jaxon and Myra and Trish. Three people who had loved her all along, never asking her to change, never expecting her to be anything other than who God created her to be. Wait, God? Had He also been loving her this way all along?

"Yes. Now, can we eat already before this food gets cold again?"

Sahara chuckled. "Of course." Though she didn't know how she could be any fuller.

~

When the doorbell rang the next night, Sahara's pulse skittered. It was a different kind of nervous than when she'd planned the balloon extravaganza, a different kind than when she'd asked him out to dinner. Her heart now thrummed with expectation and promise instead of fear. Still like jumping off a cliff, but this time, confidence bloomed that her parachute would catch her. After all, her apartment walls were covered with proof of the chute catching the wind and breaking her fall.

She swung open the door to see Jaxon, handsome as ever in a gray V-necked tee and khaki shorts, his beard neatly trimmed. His confident stance belied his nervous smile.

She took both his hands in hers and drew him inside. "Welcome."

"Okay, Sahara. What are you up to now?"

She chuckled. Fair question. She had kept him guessing the past couple of months. Might as well cut the chitchat and get to the reason she'd asked him over. "I finally figured something out, and I had to tell you."

"What?" Suspicion shone through his narrowed eyes.

She beamed up at him. "You love me."

He angled his head. Stared.

"You love me," she repeated as she squeezed his hands. A statement of trust. Of belief. Not a question.

"Yes." Power and purpose filled that one word. Twelve years of history and heartache. Twelve years of hanging on. Twelve years of trying again. Twelve years of *yes*.

"Want to know how I know?" She could feel her eyes twinkle as his sparked back at her.

He nodded. She dropped one of his hands but kept her grasp on his other one as she led him around the apartment to peruse the pictures on display. First was a photo of the galvanized nails Jaxon had special ordered for her to use on the construction site, with the mountain mansion blurred in the background. She watched his mouth tip upward as he viewed the picture. Though she'd planned out words to say, they were sand falling through her fingers now. Lost to her. Just as well. He didn't seem to need her to say a thing.

With a slight tug, she led him on a few steps to the picture of a glass bottle of iced tea with three sugar packets taped to it. Jaxon's daily offering of love. He met her gaze then and winked. She felt it all the way to her toes. His grip on her hand tightened as she nudged him another step down the hall to the picture of her sun hat with the tag cut off. Another two steps and there was the picture of them by the limber pine at Bear Lake. He'd shown her an abundance of love when he took her to his favorite place in Utah. Next to that picture hung one of Moonbeam. Then one of a chicken salad Subway sandwich. Okay, that one was a bit corny, but she'd never forget his tender care for her the day her car died on the side of the road. He didn't have to get her dinner. He did it because he loved her.

His thumb caressed hers. That light touch of affection shot a tingle up her spine. Her eyes searched his. Oh my. She'd forgotten the intensity there. How overwhelming it could be to have all that affection focused on her. She'd gotten used to dodging it. Blocking it with distractions and excuses. But right here and now, she didn't look away. She soaked it in. He trailed a finger along her jawline. She swallowed. But she didn't break his gaze, didn't close her eyes until his lips were upon hers, soft, warm, and oh so welcome. His kiss lingered like their phone conversations had when they'd first started dating, neither one wanting to hang up and say goodbye.

He pressed his forehead to hers. "I love you, Sahara Dawn."

"I know."

He breathed a laugh. "Is there more?"

More? Oh, more pictures. "Yes."

On the other side of the apartment were the photos she'd uploaded from her computer. One of the Georgetown house, his special gift for her. That was one picture she'd treasure forever, even though she'd talked to a realtor last night. Then a few old pictures of the two of them. One where she'd worn her paper engagement ring. He'd been so in love with her, he couldn't wait to ask her to be his wife. Then one of them playing paintball. He always loved to spend time with her and bring her into his adventures. What love. Then a picture of the two of them at the sheep farm, surrounded by her babies. Jaxon bent low petting … wait, that was Iyla! The same sheep that faced off with the coyote. She sucked in a breath. How serendipitous.

At the end of the hall by the bedroom was not a picture but the dirty, torn divorce papers in a frame. If she ever again doubted Jaxon's love for her, she needed to look no further.

"There's twelve. One for every year we've been married."

The corner of his mouth tipped. "Not one shoe picture?"

"Not one." She nodded toward the bedroom. "Come on. I want to show you something else."

Mischief lit his eyes. "Ah. Exactly the direction I want to go to show you how much I love you." He nuzzled her neck.

Her laugh bubbled forth. She spun around. "Hold on. Now I want to show you how much I love you."

He turned serious. "No evidence needed." He took her hand and brought it to his lips. "You came to me."

"Just … look." She took a couple steps backward into the dim bedroom where twinkle lights surrounded the window. Next to the window, she'd hung the framed poem "Tree at My Window" by Robert Frost.

He ran a finger over the title. "Oh, Sahara."

"I thought this place might make a good home for us. For now, I mean. Once we start having children, we'll have to move into someplace bigger, of course, but that'll take at least nine months, so—"

He pivoted to face her. "What are you saying?"

"I mean, I haven't even seen your place, so if you prefer it, that's fine. But this one does have the tree out the window. That's a definite plus."

He placed both hands on her shoulders and dipped down to her eye level. "Speak clearly, woman."

She laughed at that, then sobered at the confusion in his expression. "I want to stay here with you. Indefinitely."

"But your dream house..."

She shook her head. "That wasn't the dream. You were. I thought the house is what I wanted, but I really wanted deep roots. The house has history, yes, but now we do too. And we're building more. I'm readjusting my vision."

His brow furrowed. "Are you sure?"

"One hundred percent."

"I'm so sorry I've handled things poorly. You being out here. I've been a giant klutz. A jerk, really. I didn't mean to be. I didn't know how—"

She brought a finger to his lips. "It's okay."

He took both her hands in his and implored her with his eyes. "Will you receive my apology? I am deeply sorry for hurting you."

Receive his apology? Was that like receiving his love? The Lord had healed her heart, and she didn't feel she needed anything from her husband, but best not to brush him off. He had put his heart on the line for her again. Oh, to treat it like the gift it was.

"I appreciate your apology, Jaxon. I receive it, and I forgive you." She brushed her lips to his knuckles.

He enveloped her in his arms. She inhaled deeply, taking in his woodsy scent, the solid feel of him, and his warmth. She was home.

Epilogue

Sahara
One year later
Provo, Utah

Sahara grinned as Moonbeam crested the hill.

Jaxon glanced at Sahara and winked. "Are you ready?"

"I can't wait."

Two more turns and Jaxon pulled onto the lane that would soon grace their mail, checkbooks, and driver's licenses. Their new address. At the end stood the house Jaxon had designed and built for them, now nearly complete. By the end of the month, they'd settle into this four-bedroom ranch with a stunning mountain view. And a tree outside the bedroom window.

She'd hung up her hard hat for good—turns out construction wasn't her life's passion—but bouncing ideas back and forth on this beauty with Jaxon had been quite a wild ride. She exited the car, and in a moment, Jaxon stood beside her, his hand on the small of her back.

"Doing okay? You look uncomfortable."

"I'm seven months pregnant. I *am* uncomfortable," she teased. "But yes, I'm okay. Mountain Man must be practicing snowboarding because he's all over the place."

Jaxon chuckled and placed a gentle hand on her belly. "That's my boy. He's excited to see his new room."

Well, he couldn't *see* it, but she didn't need to point out that minuscule detail. She took Jaxon's hand in her own. "Let's go, then."

281

He led her up the shrub-lined path and unlocked and opened the door. He bowed with a flourish. "After you, my lady."

The scent of fresh paint emanated. Shining floors. Everything shouted of newness. Of fresh possibilities. Her flats clunked on the hardwood in an entirely different way than they had creaked on the aged floors of her historic Georgetown house. A new sound for a new life. It reverberated through her, and gratitude swelled. God had been so very good to her, to them.

They walked into the kitchen where the window over the fireclay kitchen sink gave a breathtaking view of a field of wildflowers in the forefront and mountains in the distance. Giant holes stood in the places where stainless steel appliances would soon occupy. She pictured the granite island covered in spilled milk and Cheerios and a table covered in crayons, paper, and glue. They'd fill this home with life. Messy, chaotic, beautiful life.

"It's how you wanted it, right?" Jaxon's brow quirked.

"Yes. Absolutely."

"Good." He squeezed her hand and led her to the living room with a stone fireplace as the focal point.

"I can't wait to host home group here." Their small band of friends was developing into a solid support system. She missed Myra daily. Thank heavens for frequent flyer miles.

She ran a finger across the mantle. The two pictures of Bernie they'd display here would likely be a conversation piece. The Confederate and Union soldier, side by side. The same woman who fought for different things in different seasons of her life. Interesting how some people in her family thought it best to hide one part of the story. It was the side Sahara most wanted to flaunt. Honestly, she'd rather hide the other picture. But it was all part of Bernie's story. Some parts were as hard to look at as an untreated wound, but hiding such things would only fester the ugly. Perhaps no one's story was pristine from beginning to end. If examined, they all contained cringe-worthy elements. And yet, this is what it is to be human. To grow. To learn. To love.

It's what they'd been dealing with in counseling. How to be vulnerable. Mankind's greatest fear. But to love is to risk, and so as Sahara's heart was healing, she was learning how to not hide. How to come forward into the light. That's why they would put *both* of Bernie's pictures on the mantle.

"On to Mountain Man's room." Jaxon led the way. They explored the baby's room, the family room, then their bedroom, and finally, the other two rooms they hoped to fill with children in the coming years.

Their tour finished, Jaxon turned to her and rubbed her shoulders, his gaze caressing hers. "Does it meet with your approval?"

"Oh, Jaxon, I love it. It's a perfect gift. You have loved me so well."

He wrapped her in an embrace and kissed the top of her head. "I'm glad. Thank you for letting me build you a house."

She lifted her chin. Her lips sought his. Their first kiss in this new space that they'd woven together. Tender and sweet, he cradled the back of her head and met her with all the fresh promises that this home boasted.

"Now, to the sheep farm?"

She beamed up at him. "To the sheep farm."

The biggest kiss to her heart—a sheep farm stood a mile down the road. Not Shetlands, of course, but Navajo-Churro sheep. Sahara had already made friends with the owners and was on her way to getting to know the inhabitants. She could raise her child with at least a peripheral knowledge of this life she'd become attached to growing up.

Cindy and George, the owners, had invited Jaxon and Sahara over for lunch, which meant they'd forgo their usual Sunday excursion to the Peruvian restaurant Sahara had grown to adore. No matter. There'd be plenty of opportunities for Jaxon's playful teasing about octopus in the future.

For now, Sahara opened Moonbeam's door and slid in. As she did, a glance in the back seat revealed her Bible nestled next to Jaxon's. The two of them, side by side, underlined, highlighted, and dog-eared. Her heart brimmed with the love poured out for her by this God who declared that, above everything, her heart was worth fighting for.

Author's Note

Writing a book about marriage turned out to be nearly as hard as marriage itself. I'm exaggerating, as nothing compares to the unique challenge of the refinement of matrimony. This book, however, was the most difficult one to write thus far. I'd been mulling over the characters of Sahara and Jaxon for years, but when I sat down to flesh out their story, they wouldn't cooperate. They couldn't seem to communicate well. They got frustrated. I got all up in my feelings. What a mess! But we sat down and worked it out. I believed their story was worth that. It was worth muddling through the mess to get to the other side. Isn't that what their story is about?

I'm thankful to an amazing group of writer friends—Kristine Delano, Sherry Shindelar, and Jamie Ogle—for challenging me and making me better. I'm also thankful to my husband for fighting for my heart these eighteen years and counting and for listening to me whine about misbehaving fictional characters. Thank you for not pressuring me to eat octopus.

Now for an interesting historical note: soldiers on both sides of the Civil War nearly destroyed all Southern stock of Tunis sheep. Although Russell McEvens is a figment of my imagination, historians do credit a man from South Carolina for saving the breed from extinction. We can thank Maynard Spigener for hiding the last flock of Tunis on his land by the Congoree River near Columbia, South Carolina.

Many thanks to Don and Peggy McCallie of Wild Flower Farm in Dittmer, Missouri, for welcoming me to their sheep farm and teaching me about Shetlands. I based much of

Sahara's experience of Aunt Trish's farm (minus its broken-down state—that was strictly for the purpose of the story) on Wild Flower, including the story of the coyote. After meeting them myself, I have to agree: Shetlands are special.

Thank you, reader, for spending your time with my story. I hope it's encouraged you today. Please keep in touch. I'd love to hear from you.

Sarah Hanks

www.sarah-hanks.com

@authorsarahhanks on Facebook and Instagram

www.ingramcontent.com/pod-product-compliance
Lightning Source LLC
Chambersburg PA
CBHW061227310726

48971CB00007B/1971